BEHIND THE SCENES

A Project Artemis Novel

K.M. SCOTT

ANINA COLLINS

Behind the Scenes

Alexis Marchand is one of the biggest movie stars in the world, loved by millions of fans around the globe. Her meteoric rise to fame has come with its fair share of heartache, but she's remained strong, thanks to those closest to her and their unfailing support. Life as a movie star is good.

Until one day a simple letter arrives and turns her world upside down. Now she lives in terror, afraid of that one fan who has taken it too far.

Hunter McKary knows something of movie stars because of his time as a LAPD detective. He thought he left those days behind him, but when he's sent to find out who's stalking the beautiful blond actress the world adores, he grudgingly goes to New York, expecting to find a typical spoiled diva like those he met so many times before back in LA.

The woman he finds isn't anything like he expected, and a job he dreaded becomes something else entirely. But someone out there has different plans for Alexis.

CHAPTER ONE

"LET ME GO!"

Alexis Marchand sat bolt upright in her bed and looked down at her arms where the man had held her tightly as she desperately tried to pull away. It had been a nightmare like the one the night before, but it felt more real this time. Like she should see red marks where his fingers pressed hard into the flesh.

But there was nothing there. It had all been in her mind.

She took a deep breath and closed her eyes. He wasn't going to do this. He wasn't going to ruin her life. She'd worked too damn hard to let some stranger take it all away from her.

Thankfully, none of her staff had heard her scream. She didn't need them frantically rushing in and hovering over her like some broken bird.

She had screamed, right? Or had that been a part of the nightmare too? Jesus, she didn't know what was real and what wasn't anymore.

Slowly, she lowered herself back down onto

the bed. "I won't let you take my life away from me. You aren't going to win," she whispered defiantly into the darkness of her room to the stranger who'd upended her world with one simple letter.

Closing her eyes, she silently swore he wouldn't succeed.

✧　✧　✧

ALEXIS STORMED FROM one room to the next in her Hollywood Hills mansion as everyone around her packed up every last thing she owned. That she had to leave the house of her dreams broke her heart and enraged her. One minute she wanted to curl up into a ball and cry, and then the next she wanted to throw pointy things at people's heads.

This whole thing made her feel stabby. And when Alexis got in that mood, heaven help everyone around her. They didn't call her a diva in the gossip rags for nothing.

Not that anything those hacks said was true in any real way. Yes, she had, on occasion, had what could be technically called temper tantrums. And yes, they had occurred in public once or twice. Or maybe a few times more.

And yes, she had been drunk a few times when those incidents occurred. But that didn't make what they said about her right.

But that's not who she really was. At least, it

wasn't who she wanted to be.

At the moment, though, what she really didn't want to be was a woman forced to move from a home she loved to a new apartment in a city that felt foreign to her. She'd fallen in love with this house the moment she stepped foot inside the front door for the first time. The grand two-story foyer with the wrought-iron railed staircase that curved down from the second floor like something straight out of the movies had charmed her instantly, and she knew right then and there she wanted to own this gorgeous home. The fact that the rest of the property impressed everyone else in her entourage didn't matter as much as the emotions that entrance made bubble up inside her.

And now because of some asshole, she had to abandon her dream home for something much smaller, she was sure, in a city she had no interest in even visiting.

New York.

Everyone could tell her how wonderful that city was until they were blue in the face. It didn't matter. She had no desire to go live in any place called the Big Apple. Sure it had Broadway and there would be parties like there always had been in LA, but it wouldn't be the same. She wouldn't be near the beach, and half the year she'd be stuck under grey skies. And she'd have to get used to a real winter again!

Winter. Godforsaken winter.

Leaving the home she loved was bad enough, but moving to a place that had winter like she'd gone through growing up in Minnesota made her shoulders sag as depression set in once again. She already felt beaten down by all that had happened in the past couple months, and now this would be the final blow.

One of the moving men shuffled by her as she stood lost in her misery in the hallway. In his left hand, he swung a vase like he was carrying a baseball glove that had no worth at all.

Horrified, Alexis screamed, "Watch that vase! What the hell are you swinging it like that for?"

The man stopped dead and looked at her in shock that she'd yelled at him. What did he expect acting like that?

"That vase is priceless to me. No swinging. Carefully walk it into that room and ask the woman in there named Carla to make sure it gets packed with everything else from my bedroom. Got it?"

He nodded but said nothing, and Alexis didn't know if he listened to a word she said. She'd never met him before that morning when he showed up with a dozen other men to pack up all her belongings. She hadn't bothered to ask their names or even tried to differentiate between one or another of them.

She didn't need to make friends with them. She just needed every one of them to not break the things that meant the world to her. The last thing Alexis needed was to move to New York and find boxes of broken valuables when she started unpacking there.

The mere thought of relocating made her think she might just not unpack at all. All she needed to do was stay there until they found the guy who'd been terrorizing her and then she could move back here to sunny California.

Problem solved. So no need to unpack. Assuming they found the son of a bitch who'd been sending her threatening letters. As long as he was out there walking around, she'd have to stay in New York.

Her assistant Carla walked out of the bedroom with the glass and crystal music box Alexis received for her last birthday from her father. He'd given her that gift right before he died.

And now Carla had gotten her fingerprints all over the top of the box, making Alexis furious.

Swiveling her head, she looked for something pointy to throw but found nothing but packing boxes and bubble wrap. At this rate, she'd need a full roll of that stuff just to calm her nerves by the time this day was over.

"I swear if that music box isn't cleaned off of all your fingerprints by the time it's carefully placed into the box, I'm going to have someone's head!"

Carla nodded and gave Alexis her best apologetic eyes. "I'm sorry. I won't let it happen again. I know how much this means to you, Alexis. I took care of the vase that man brought me too. I swear I don't know where Paul found these guys."

Knowing her assistant well enough, she recognized her sucking up for what it was, along with her attempt to divert her attention to the unknown moving men so her anger would be directed at them instead of Carla. Everyone thought Alexis wasn't clever enough to figure out when they were playing her, but she knew.

Even if she didn't bother to show it.

"Just take care of the music box and get those smudgy fingerprints off it," she said as she walked away toward her bedroom to see how the packing had progressed so far in that room. "And get me a drink!"

The fact that it was barely afternoon was beside the point. Some days, it didn't matter what time it was.

It was five o'clock somewhere anyway.

Two steps into her bedroom, Alexis saw the woman packing up her clothes bunch a dress into a ball of fabric—very expensive fabric—and nearly lost her mind right there. Running up to her, she tore the dress from her hold.

"Treat these dresses with care. They're worth more than your life!"

The woman stammered out an apology, but it fell on deaf ears. Alexis carefully laid the dress out on the bed and pointed at it. "Do you see that? This isn't goddamned Wal-Mart. We do not ball up clothes here. Use a hanger for every one of my dresses and put them in garment bags, for God's sake!"

Frustrated, she stormed out and marched downstairs to her office to find some solitude. Maybe if she could get her head in the right space, she could handle this day.

Lauren, her closest friend since childhood and the assistant she depended on more than any other, sat at her desk packing up scripts. Just seeing them being stuffed into boxes made leaving so much more real than she could face at that moment.

She collapsed onto the white chaise lounge she'd just picked out for her favorite room in the house and sighed. "Be careful with those. I may never get another one. I'm going to want something to remember this life."

"Oh, Alexis, don't say that," Lauren said with sadness in her voice. "Your fans love you. It won't matter where you live. You're one of the hottest actresses in this town. You could live on Mars and it wouldn't matter."

Throwing her arm over her eyes, Alexis wished Lauren could be right. She knew better, though. Out of sight meant out of mind. In the movie business, if you weren't seen around town, you were viewed as a missing person.

And very few actors could withstand being tagged as that. Unless you were one of those famous stars who appeared in a film every few years and had the luck of being seen as one of the greats, being out of the circuit of parties and events in Hollywood meant people forgot about you.

"In this town. Those are the operative words, aren't they?" she mumbled, turning toward the wall.

As always, Lauren tried to cheer her up with supportive words that Alexis believed she really meant. Of all the people who surrounded her, she had never let her down. Lauren could be depended on when everyone else abandoned her. At least she had that to look forward to.

Kneeling beside the chaise lounge, she touched Alexis on the shoulder. "Please don't worry, Alexis. Everything will work out. I know it. Do you believe me?"

She wanted to. She just couldn't.

Alexis rolled over and looked at her dearest friend in the world. In her blue eyes, she saw the sympathy she knew Lauren truly felt for her and what she was going through. Of all the people she'd met in the business, none could replace the friend she'd met in grade school back in Minnesota.

Looking around the all-white room she'd had redecorated when she moved in, she sighed. "I'm going to miss this house so much. The new place is going to be like a shoebox, and don't even get me started on how much I'm going to miss being able to look outside and see trees. Whatever anyone else thinks, this was paradise for me. Now, it's all being taken away."

Lauren smiled and squeezed her hand in support. "It's nearly three thousand square feet and a penthouse overlooking the city. Plus, I have to believe New York City has trees. It must. I've seen pictures and there were trees in them."

"Not like here," Alexis sulked.

"Maybe not, but once you choose some new furnishings and get the place exactly the way you like it, I think you're going to love it as much as you love this house."

"It won't be the same. I hate the city. It's grey. That's all I think of when I think of New York. Grey."

"Los Angeles is a city, you know," she said

with a smile.

"Not like New York."

"Then you can get a place in the mountains that reminds you of Minnesota in the summer," Lauren suggested.

Nothing she said helped. Alexis jumped up and stormed across the room. "Why do I have to move at all? I love my home! I belong here."

Her assistant followed her and stopped in front of her as she began to pace. "We need to do whatever we can to keep you safe. Paul thinks this is best. Just give it a chance. Your safety is the only concern, Alexis."

Just because her manager thought moving from the place she loved to somewhere she had no interest in even flying over didn't mean she should do that. He didn't necessarily know best.

But Alexis knew if she didn't do as he suggested and if something happened to her, she'd never hear the end of it from him. "He better be right."

Lauren's blue eyes filled with concern. "The police think that you moving might be a good idea too."

The police? Talk about people who didn't give a damn.

Yanking her hands away, Alexis marched over to sit behind her nearly empty desk. "What the hell do the police know? It's been months since I started getting these damn letters from that maniac, and all they can say is it's an obsessed fan and to increase my security. I've hired twice as many bodyguards and still those damn letters keep coming!"

Ever the optimist, Lauren said, "But there hasn't been an attack, which is more important than anything else."

"How could there be? I rarely go out anymore because of him."

"Or her," her assistant said, correcting Alexis. "The police aren't sure of the sex of the person doing this."

Out of the corner of her eye, she saw on the end of the desk the picture of her and Jackson in the gold frame. They'd looked so happy then. The two of them had just spent all day on the beach in Mexico on the first day of their honeymoon, and they'd asked the bartender at the hotel to take their picture.

Alexis sighed as she remembered that day. Jackson had been her knight in shining armor from the moment she met him. The director on her first picture, she fell in love with his talent before she fell in love with him as a man, but it didn't matter. From the very moment they set eyes on each other, it felt like fate took over. It was only a matter of time before they were a couple, and less than a year later, they were married and frolicking on the beach like they didn't have a care in the world. His career was taking off, and Alexis became Hollywood's It Girl everyone wanted in their film.

But as with every time she saw that picture, her mind traveled to another day. The day she found out he was cheating on her with another actress who was barely twenty years old. Twenty-four at the time, Alexis had married him three years earlier and foolishly believed she'd found the man she'd spend forever with.

Closing her eyes, she remembered that reporter asking her if she knew her husband was with another woman as she began to walk the red carpet for the Golden Globes. All night she had to pretend to be happy as her world crumbled around her.

And for what?

Because her thirty-five year old husband was too much of a coward to tell her the truth before some goddamned reporter got to her. Nothing like finding out in front of the entire world that your husband's on-location shoot for his latest movie wasn't the only thing he'd been enjoying in New Zealand.

Disgusted by the memory, she rolled her eyes. "No, it's a man. I'm sure of that. No woman in the history of the world has ever been such a coward. Only a man would do this kind of thing to someone."

Three of her security detail walked past the office, and then she heard a box crash to the floor. Furious, she barked, "Does no one know how to be careful with anything in this house?"

As she marched out to see how much damage they'd done, she snapped at Lauren, "Don't bother with that picture of Jackson and me. It's not coming with us to the new place."

Three muscular men stared down at a singular box tipped over on the hardwood floor in the hallway. In front of them lay broken pieces of snow globes Alexis had collected from every place she visited since she began modeling at fifteen years old. Liquid ran along the wood planks and around the shards of glass from the collectables, including the blue water from the globe she'd bought in Fiji on her very first modeling job.

"All you had to do was carry the damn boxes and you couldn't even do that!" she screamed, struggling to hold back tears as she stared down at the shattered remnants of her cherished memories.

Lauren came up behind her and wrapped her arms around Alexis's shoulders as she sobbed, "He's taking everything I love away from me. Even my snow globes."

"Don't worry. I'll take care of this. You go relax," her assistant said in her ear.

True to her word, she began ordering the men

around. Pointing at all of them, she said, "Clean up this mess and pack up the remaining globes more carefully. Then make sure you're careful, for God's sake."

As Alexis began to walk away, one of the bodyguards apologized for their mistake, but she just nodded, too upset to say anything in response. No matter how many times they said I'm sorry, it wouldn't bring back those trinkets she loved.

She walked upstairs to her room and found Carla finishing up with packing up the bedroom. The maid stood by waiting to strip the bed, but Alexis waved them away and pointed toward the door.

"Leave me alone."

They hurried out without saying a word as she collapsed onto her bed and began sobbing into her pillow. Forget the drink. All she wanted to do was fade away into unconsciousness.

THE DOOR TO her New York penthouse apartment opened in front of her to reveal what resembled a cavernous, sunless space. Alexis walked in and looked around at the dark and heavy decorative moldings where the ceilings and walls met and immediately felt oppressed.

Lauren squeezed her arm. "It's a beautiful home, isn't it?"

She scanned the space filled with dark woods that made the place feel like it was closing in around her and missed her spacious home back in California. "No green trees and I feel like this place is going to smother me. For the amount I paid for this place, I should at least be able to feel like my home wasn't swallowing me whole."

"The designer will be here next Monday at eleven. You'll see. She'll make this place into a home you'll love even more than LA," Lauren said, trying to be supportive.

Alexis couldn't help but smile. Hugging her assistant, she said, "You're not going to let me wallow in my misery and hate for this place, are you?"

"I've known you since we were nine years old. You couldn't hate if you tried. I know this is hard, but you can handle this. I know you can."

A sense of shame washed over Alexis. They grew up two poor kids in rural Minnesota in families that often didn't have enough money for new shoes more than once a year. That was hard. Getting used to a six million dollar penthouse wasn't hard.

She took her assistant's hand and walked with her toward the kitchen. "I guess I better check out my new kitchen because I'm starving."

"I made sure everyone involved in the move put every fork and dish and pan just where it should be before you got here. It's situated just like it was back in the old house."

Alexis chuckled. "I never once cooked back in the LA house, so there's no reason to believe I'm going to start here, Lauren."

One foot into the kitchen and Alexis knew this room looked nothing like the one at the old house. Instead of having an open feeling, this one had walls on all sides that felt like they were closing in on her.

And cabinets. So many cabinets. How many dishes and glasses did the person who built this place have? As she stared up at the dark wood cabinets that seemed to go up forever, she thought to herself that they could house every glass she'd ever drank out of in her entire life and still have room for more.

"Let's hope no one here ever needs to get something down from one of those cabinets on the top," she said craning her neck to look at the highest cabinet next to the ceiling.

"It can all be changed. That's what the designer is for. No worries," Lauren said with far more assurance than Alexis felt.

Her assistant motioned for her to sit down at the table at the end of the room while she headed toward the refrigerator. "I think this calls for some champagne. We need to christen this new house, don't you think?"

"Sounds good to me," Alexis said as she sat down at the old wooden table that had come with the place and looked out the window at the darkness outside.

Definitely not like LA.

Lauren poured them both a glass champagne and raised her glass to make a toast. "To your wonderful new home."

Clinking her glass against Lauren's, Alexis took a sip of champagne and sighed. "To my new home."

She knew her assistant wanted her to be happy, but so far, all that made her happy in this place was knowing she had her oldest and dearest friend by her side. Everything else about her new place felt foreign and just reminded her of all she'd been forced to leave behind.

Carla appeared in the doorway a moment later with a box in her hands. "The doorman brought this up. He said it was just delivered by courier."

Alexis smiled and waved her over toward the table, eager to see what gift she'd been sent. "It's probably a housewarming gift from Paul. How much do you want to bet?"

"Probably," Lauren said before taking another sip of champagne. "He can be a pain, but he never forgets the little things."

The three women stood around the table, and Alexis set the cardboard box down in the center of it. Ripping open the top, she looked inside and saw a snow globe with the Empire State Building inside it. Charmed by the gift, she lifted it out and handed it to Lauren as she reached in to grab the card sent with it. Paul always knew how to say just the right thing to make Alexis smile.

"This is gorgeous," Lauren cooed as Carla nodded in agreement.

Opening the envelope, Alexis slid a folded piece of paper out and opened it up. Her eyes opened wide in horror as she saw cut out letters just like her stalker always used that said, "Welcome to New York! I'll be seeing you."

"It's from him!" she screamed and then threw the card away onto the table. "He knows exactly where I am!"

"Who?" Lauren asked as she set the snow globe down to walk around table to comfort Alexis as she began to cry.

As she sobbed into her hands, she said the words that had taken over her life. "Him. My stalker. He knows just where I am. I left my home for nothing!"

Chapter Two

H UNTER LIFTED HIS legs to rest his feet on the coffee table in front of him while Gideon and Xavier argued over which team would go all the way to the Super Bowl this year. He didn't mind hanging out in the game room with them like others on the estate did, but their insistence on having this same damn fight over and over was beginning to get under his skin.

"Are you fucking kidding me with the Rams? No way, Xavier," Gideon said as he threw a basketball he'd been holding straight at his best friend's head.

It ricocheted off the foosball table and rolled over toward the dart board near where Hunter sat.

"They'll get to the playoffs maybe, but forget about them going any further. Maybe in a few years, but this year? No way."

As always, Xavier took that as his cue to stand up full of indignation, righteous or not, and respond with his usual attack he knew would bother Gideon, a lifelong Washington fan. "At least they'll make it to the playoffs. Not like your Redskins, who can't find their ass with both hands. You guys got the shaft when you got the wrong Gruden brother, dude."

And on and on it would go until the game came on and they glued their eyes to the big screen TV on the wall in front of them. Thankfully, that wouldn't be too long from now because the last thing Hunter wanted was to get pulled into their football argument. His team hadn't seen the playoffs in so long he wondered why he still stayed true to them, and he didn't need to defend them against Gideon and Xavier, who would definitely turn their attacks against him once they heard the name Chargers.

Nope. Better to just let them fight it out while he relaxed and pretended not to hear their argument.

His phone began to ring in his pocket, stopping the conversation occurring nearby. He pulled it out and saw Tess's name on the screen. Persephone's assistant, she probably wanted to talk to him about a case.

"Tess, let me guess. You couldn't do without seeing me today, even though it's Sunday," he said with a smile, instinctively flirting with her as he had from the moment he met her.

Gorgeous and single, Tess Andrews had no business being around so many men and looking so incredibly hot all the time. She had a sexy librarian thing going on with the way she sometimes wore her hair in a bun and glasses that made her look studious. One look down her body, though, made anyone with an ounce of testosterone in his body think those long legs and perfect ass would look much better without those skirts she wore, even though they often barely came to the middle of her thighs and only highlighted how hot she was.

"You know we don't work regular hours around here, Hunter," she said sweetly with a lilt in her voice that told him she was flirting with him too.

"True. Then I'm guessing you just wanted to talk to me then?"

"Sorry, no. Persephone would like you to come to the office."

Their banter over, he accepted that he'd likely have to work that day. Not until after the game, though. A man had to have some time to himself. After the last few weeks, he deserved at least a few hours of relaxation.

"Sure. Tell her I'll be up right after the game."

His answer was met with a few moments of silence and then Persephone's voice came through loud and clear into his ear. "Now, please, Hunter. There's a situation that requires our special brand of help."

There went his day off. He knew they didn't work like that in Project Artemis, but for Christ's sake, he couldn't be the only one of them who could take this case, whatever it was. Looking over at the two men in front of him who rarely seemed to be anywhere but right there in the game room, he resented having to go to work once more.

Resigned to how this day would go, he answered, "Sure. I'll be right there."

Standing from the leather recliner he'd planned to spend the afternoon in, he stuffed his phone into his pocket as Gideon and Xavier began to bust his ass. Smug fucks.

"Hunter is Persephone's lapdog," Xavier joked in a singsong tone.

Gideon, who always tended to be less juvenile, teased, "Yeah, man. What is it with you? Did you get on her bad side? You've gone on three assignments in the past few weeks. She's working you like a dog. You need to bite back, bro. Show her you're a man who doesn't take shit from anyone."

He knew if Nick was anywhere in earshot, these two wouldn't be so mouthy about the woman who ran Project Artemis. Intensely protective of her, Nick would lay them both out for shit like that.

"Oh, yeah, Gideon? Why don't you do that first and see how it goes when Nick fucks you up six ways to Sunday?" Hunter asked as he picked up the basketball and hurled it in their direction.

That got the both of them to back off, and Gideon put his hands up as if to surrender while Xavier caught the ball. "Okay, okay. I was just busting balls. I didn't mean anything by that. It's just that she does seem to always turn to you lately when there's a case. Xavier and I haven't been out on one in over a month."

At that, Xavier piped up and said, "Not that we have any problem with that, so don't go blowing our gig. Better you than us, man."

"You have a real all-for-one-and-one-for-all thing going there, X," Hunter said as he turned to leave. "I'll make sure to mention it to the boss when I talk to her."

As he walked out of the game room, he heard the two of them return to busting his ass about being Persephone's lapdog. He wished he didn't feel exactly like that lately. If she sent him out today, this would be the third assignment in a row given to him. Granted, he knew what he signed up for, but why did he have to be the one she looked to all the time lately?

He made his way down the hallway toward the other side of the house as he thought about the fact that Nick's being gone for the past few weeks likely coincided with how much she'd relied on him to go out on cases. Nick had probably told her to stick with the tried and true, and since Marius and Dax were busy on their own cases and Roman had moved to the admin side of things since meeting Kate, that left him, the two frat boys, and Julian since they hadn't gotten anyone to replace Roman yet.

No wonder she kept picking him.

Crossing through the living room, he caught sight of Tess waiting for him at the end of the hallway that led to her office and her boss's. As he walked toward her, he regretted the part in his contract that stipulated there was to be no fraternizing between any employees of Project Artemis.

Not that Tess had ever given him any clear sign she wanted more than flirting, but a guy could always dream, right?

She wore her warm brown hair in a bun today, and as he let his gaze slide down her body, he saw the usual grey business suit of a skirt and blazer over a pink silk blouse. Miles of legs ended with stiletto heels that made him wish that stupid line in the contract never existed. He never tired of seeing Tess, even though it always meant he'd be leaving for work right afterward.

"No glasses? You're ruining my whole sexy librarian fantasy, Tess," he said and winked when he stopped in front of her.

"They're back at my desk. You know, if Nick

or Persephone hear you talking like that, they won't be happy. I also think I can bring you up on sexual harassment charges for that crack, by the way."

She smiled as she said that to let him know she didn't mean it. Or if she did, she had no plans to get him in trouble. Hunter knew better than to cross the line, even if he pushed right up against it.

"But for now, Persephone wants to see you so we need to get to her office," Tess said as she began walking down the dimly lit hallway.

For a moment, he watched her hips sway beautifully, appreciating just how gorgeous his boss's assistant really was. He might never get to lay a hand on her, but that didn't mean he couldn't notice the obvious beauty she possessed.

"Stop staring at my ass, Hunter, and let's go," Tess called back without turning around.

Gorgeous and sharp-tongued. Exactly how he loved his women.

He caught up to her just as she sat down at her desk. "Thanks, Tess. See you on the flip side."

She put her hand up to stop him before he could go into Persephone's office. "Not yet. She's tied up right now. Give her a minute."

"I guess that means I get to spend time with you then. There are worse ways to kill a few minutes," he said with a smile as he let his eyes roam where he wished his hands could.

Giving him a knowing smile, she said, "You know the rules, Hunter. No fraternizing between you guys and us. It's against Persephone's rules."

He sat down on the edge of her desk and leaned over toward her. "We weren't supposed to be able to stay on here if we became involved, but Roman's still here. Rules were made to be broken."

Just then, Persephone appeared in his peripheral vision and cleared her throat. "Not this rule, Hunter."

Tess quickly stood up and backed away. "I didn't realize you'd finished your phone call."

"Thank you, Tess. Hunter, please come in. Let's see if we can get your mind back on why you're part of Project Artemis."

Caught in the act, he had little choice but to do as she said. Standing, he looked over at Tess and saw worry etched into her face. He gave her a wink to let her know he'd be sure to smooth things over with Persephone so she knew he'd been the instigator and not her assistant.

By the time he closed the office door behind him, Persephone had already sat down at her desk. As he walked toward the chair in front of it to take his seat, he had to admit his boss looked right at home behind that expensive old desk she'd supposedly had imported from Italy right after she dropped a couple million on the house. Persephone oozed money and power.

And like Tess, she had a look about her that made it hard to turn away. Long dark hair hung far past her shoulders in soft waves over her green turtleneck sweater, giving her a girl-next-door look. Her face only added to that almost sweet feel she gave off, especially when she smiled.

Nothing less than stunning, she only revealed herself to be anything other than a pretty face when she opened her mouth. Then you knew you were dealing with a far shrewder person than the outside gave any hint of.

Hunter appreciated that, though. While she tended to be more serious than he preferred women to be, she had a great mind and her passion for what they did there made her even more beautiful to anyone who didn't find a committed woman intimidating. Since he didn't, he admired her.

How she felt about him he couldn't say. Since she employed his talents quite often recently, he thought she admired him. His behavior with Tess had probably put a dent in that impression, though, so he quickly worked to clean up any mess he may have created with his completely innocent flirting.

"I was only joking with Tess out there. She wasn't doing anything to encourage me. Honest," he said, hoping to save his flirting partner from a lecture from her boss.

Persephone leveled her gaze on him and gave him a tiny smile that barely lifted the corners of her mouth. "I'm sure. And I'm sure if I ask her about it, she'll say the same thing, so I'm not worried. I know who's who around here."

That didn't sound like anything he'd hoped she'd say. He was looking for her to give him a reprimand so Tess could be in the clear. But that last line—I know who's who around here—made him think she might have pegged her assistant for something she hadn't done.

"Really. She's never anything other than professional. I'm completely to blame," he continued in an attempt to smooth things over more.

Persephone's gaze never wavered, and she nodded as he finished. "I know. I'm not blaming Tess. That would be like blaming a beautiful woman who wears beautiful clothes for men noticing her. Can we get to what I wanted to see you about or would you like to dig that hole you're in a little deeper?"

Like Tess, her boss had a sharp tongue to her too, but he didn't dare try any verbal sparring with her. "Sure. I'm here to serve. What can I do for you?"

"I have an assignment for you, Hunter."

He nodded, not needing a statement of the obvious. "I'm just wondering why I seem to be the main blip on your radar lately. X hasn't gone out on an assignment in so long I think it was another sport's season the last time he left that game room."

Instead of discussing his comment, Persephone ignored it and began to read from a file in front of her on her desk. "I got a call earlier tonight about a principal who needs your special kind of help."

"My special kind of help?" he asked, wondering exactly what part of him she considered special.

"Do you know who Alexis Marchand is?" she asked, answering his question with one of her own.

Hunter thought for a moment. Had he ever heard that name? Nothing rang any bells about it. Shaking his head, he said, "No. Should I?"

"That's why I chose you for this assignment. Something told me you aren't like those two Peter Pans. I'd bet they both know who she is."

Sure that meant she had something to do with sports, Hunter focused his mind on female athletes and tried to remember Xavier or Gideon ever mentioning that name. Alexis Marchand. Sounded like she might play tennis.

As he ran through the many conversations

he'd had with them, Persephone began to explain who the woman actually was. "Alexis Marchand is one of the biggest actresses in Hollywood today. She might even be called America's Sweetheart. She has legions of devoted fans who adore her, which is where the current problem comes in."

"Let me guess. Constant adoration is now considered a problem. Oh to be America's Sweetheart," he said, not trying to hide his irritation at how too many people bitched and complained about every last thing in their lives.

Persephone's face twisted into a scowl, cluing him in to how his comment hadn't been received well even before she snapped, "Don't be a smartass, Hunter. Your BFFs downstairs might find the insensitive ass act appealing, but I don't. Miss Marchand's problem isn't that her fans adore her. It's that one fan in particular is stalking her and making her life a living hell for the past few months. Her manager tells me she's moved across the country to get away from him and still he found her. This is where you come in."

He held his tongue and waited for her to explain what that meant, wondering what special talent he possessed that could help some Hollywood starlet. He'd met more than his fair share as a detective out in LA and had happily left that world behind him, so she may have chosen wrong this time when she picked him for this assignment.

"You're going to join her security team and while you're protecting her, you're going to figure out who's stalking this woman."

"A bodyguard for some diva actress? You're kidding, right? She's famous, for Christ's sake. I'm sure the police wherever she's living now will be bending over backwards to help her. Trust me. I worked in the LAPD. I know we worked overtime for celebrities. I'm sure nothing's changed in that area."

His complaining earned him a nasty look. "You'll join her security team in New York City tomorrow. Tess will give you all the details. See her on your way back to your seat in the game room."

Hunter saw that she'd made her mind up and there would be no getting out of this, so he stood to leave and asked, "Any chance I'll get some time off after this assignment?"

She looked up at him and nodded as she gave him a rare smile. "I promise after this one you'll get some much-deserved time off. You will have earned it."

Well, at least he could look forward to a vacation after this case. Not that he wanted anything to do with babysitting some celebrity while at the same time trying to figure out which pathetic soul was out there trying to get close to her.

Tess sat at her desk with a packet ready to hand to him as he exited her boss's office. Handing it to him, she smiled. "For you."

He took it and sat down on the edge of her desk again. "Will you miss me?"

"Of course. I get more exercise when you're around, Hunter. All that chasing you do."

"It's the least I can do. See you when I get back."

A look of concern suddenly filled her eyes. "Stay safe, Hunter."

Brushing off her worry, he stood and began to walk back to the game room. "Don't fret about me on this one, Tess. This might be the easiest assignment I've ever gotten since I started working here."

He returned to the empty leather recliner across from the frat brothers who sat watching the football game and flopped down in the chair. At least he didn't have to leave that afternoon, so he'd get to see a game or two.

"So what did she want? You going out again?" Xavier asked before muting the TV to hear his answer.

"Yeah. Some actress who needs to be watched. Like I'm some fucking babysitter. I get to play bodyguard because some sicko is stalking her."

Gideon threw his head back and laughed.

"Bodyguard? Man, you must have pissed off the boss. Who are you guarding?"

"Some actress named Alexis Marchand, whoever the hell that is. Persephone seemed to think you two would know who she was, which is why I got stuck taking this assignment. Maybe if I start acting like you overgrown juvenile delinquents I could get out of work too," Hunter grumbled.

Xavier whistled. "Damn. Alexis Marchand. She's hot."

Turning in his chair, Gideon agreed with him. "Dude, she's smokin' hot. I'd take that case in a heartbeat."

Maybe this would be better than he thought.

His interest piqued, Hunter asked, "Oh, yeah? Like how hot?"

"She was a model before she became an actress. And not one of those stick figure models either. She's got a body on her that doesn't quit. Fuck. Wait until you see," Xavier said, clearly impressed with Hunter's new assignment.

"Yeah, he's right," Gideon said. "It sucks that you can't seem to get any time off, but at least you'll have her to look at while you're on the job. Trust me, man. Persephone might not hate you as much as I thought giving you this case."

Pretending to be fine with it all, Hunter shrugged. "I lived in LA for years. I've seen gorgeous women. Trust me. If she was that incredible, I would have heard about her before now."

Gideon shook his head. "You'll see. It might be work, but it will be work with a smokin' hot woman."

The two of them turned back to focus their attention on the football game as Hunter hoped this assignment would be as good as they thought. Having a beautiful woman to look at certainly didn't make it the worst thing in the world. He just hoped it was over quick. No matter how good looking Alexis Marchand was, she was still an actress and his experience from his time back in LA told him some spoiled diva would more likely than not be a pain in the ass.

And hot or not, that kind of woman was definitely not what he wanted to spend his time with.

All he had to do was protect her and find out who was stalking her and he'd be free to finally get some much-needed vacation time under his belt. If he could focus on that, maybe this assignment wouldn't be too bad after all.

CHAPTER THREE

FOR THE THIRD time in less than five minutes, Alexis paced across the floor of her bedroom. Two days into living in her new home, she already felt like a caged animal. Wringing her hands, she cursed Paul and everyone else who told her she had to move to be safe from the person stalking her.

A lot of good that had done. She hadn't been in this new place not even an hour before that son of a bitch made sure she knew he had seen she moved and he'd followed her.

She'd traveled three thousand miles to feel the same way she'd felt in the home she loved. At least in California she could go out in her backyard and feel the sun on her face. Now she had none of that.

Trapped. That's what he'd done to her. He'd trapped her in her own home.

God, why did she listen to everyone instead of following her own gut? She never wanted to leave her home, and now she knew why.

Her fingers ached from her tugging on them, a nervous habit she'd had since she was a child. Looking down at her hands, she cringed at the sight of her fingertips red from what she'd done to them.

"Alexis, please come sit down. You're going to make a path in the carpet if you keep pacing," Lauren said on one of her passes near where she sat in a chair at the end of the room.

"I can't. I feel like I want to run away and never look back, but I can't because that bastard has me trapped here. Again. Nothing's changed, Lauren. Nothing at all, except now I'm stuck here in this damn city instead of being back in LA. At least if I was there, I'd be happy in my own home."

She reached out to grab a hold of Alexis as she spun on her heels to march off toward the other side of the room. "I know, but it does no good to get yourself all tied up in knots about it. Paul is coming over and he'll know what you should do."

Alexis stopped and threw her a nasty glare. "Paul? He's the reason I'm stuck here in this godforsaken apartment!"

A sound in the hallway outside her room startled her, and she froze on the spot as she waited to see who had made the noise. Eyes wide, she held her breath as the bedroom door slowly began to open, her heart slamming into her chest as she waited in terror.

Her manager appeared a few seconds later grinning like a fool. "Lexi, honey! What do you think of this place? Gorgeous, huh? I knew you'd love it."

It felt like all the blood ran out of her body as she realized it was only Paul. Dressed in his usual three-piece suit, he looked tanned and relaxed like he'd just spent a week in the Caribbean. Probably on the exorbitant salary she paid him.

His blond hair looked like it was two weeks late for a trim and hung in his eyes until he pushed it off his forehead in a casual movement that gave him a surfer guy look that only served to remind Alexis how much she missed LA.

"I hate this place. I want to go home."

"Lexi, you fit into New York like you were born here. You're a natural," he said with a huge smile as he closed her bedroom door behind him.

All his chipper talk made her more miserable. "Don't try to bullshit me, Paul. I'm like a fish out of water here. It's crowded, noisy, and I haven't seen the sun since I got here. And this penthouse looks like it hasn't been updated since before the war. I just can't decide if it's the First World War or the Second."

He walked over to the doorway and ran his hand down the dark woodwork. "This craftsmanship is classic, Lexi. People pay handsomely for this."

Alexis looked over toward the doorframe in disgust. "I know. This place cost me a pretty penny. As far as prisons go, it was very expensive. But starting whenever that designer gets here, all the walls other than a few in the bedrooms are going. Living in a house full of tiny boxes isn't my idea of six million spent wisely. I need open spaces in my prison."

Completely ignoring how unhappy she was about this new place, he said, "Speaking of open spaces, did you hear from Melanie about that part? If you get it, you'll have open spaces, all right. There's not much more open than Canada."

All his gushing about that part she hadn't heard about yet only served to irritate Alexis even more. The thought of Canada usually disgusted her, but even that would have been better than being stuck in the Upper West Side of Manhattan.

"No, she hasn't called me yet," Alexis said as she threw herself down onto the chair. "I'm not even sure I want that part."

She waited for him to rush over and talk her down from that claim, but instead he sat down and quietly said, "I think I found someone who can solve your letter writer problem."

God, did he ever say anything straightforward? Always double-talk from him.

"You mean my stalker, Paul. At least call him by the proper term. He's a stalker, not some pen pal from some far off land who has great handwriting."

Scowling at her insistence that he speak plainly, he rolled his eyes. "Fine. Your stalker problem. I called a friend who has experience handling this type of thing and she's sending someone today."

Alexis felt her chest tighten at the thought of someone new coming into her world, someone she'd never spoken to or seen before. "How well do you know this person? I'm supposed to trust some stranger I've never even met? They could be the person stalking me."

Now Paul hurried over to her side and patted her arm, like she was some frightened child or some confused elderly woman who'd lost her way. "It's okay. I promise. I've never met the person she's sending, but I trust Persephone completely. She's good people. Her father is Marshall Gilmore, the media mogul, and she's using her wealth to help people who need precisely the kind of assistance you need now."

His explanation sounded like more double-talk. Narrowing her eyes in suspicion that he'd done something she wouldn't like, she asked, "What do you mean precisely the kind of assistance I need?"

"She runs a company that specializes in protecting women. Her guys are former military, police, and even FBI. I trust her, Lexi. I know whoever she's sending will get to the bottom of who's doing this to you."

Alexis pulled her arm away from his continued patting and began to pace again. "You make it sound like I'm some damsel in distress, Paul."

He shook his head. "No. You're a good person who can use some help. That's all."

Still not convinced this new person could do anything more than the police had for months, she asked, "How much is this help costing me? I already pay all those guys I have to guard me."

Paul shook his head again and smiled. "Not a dime. Persephone's organization takes nothing in return for what they do. If her guy helps out and you want to give her something and pay it forward so she can help someone else, then so be it. But she's not in it for money."

None of this sounded even remotely believable. Who in this world didn't work for money? "Sounds like something out of a film script, Paul. How come I've never heard of this group of hers before? What's the name of this organization?"

"Project Artemis, and she's one of the

wealthiest women in the world. She doesn't need money."

"Nobody works for free," she grumbled as she paced past him.

"This reminds me of Mr. Thompson from when we were kids. Remember how he used to give free cab rides to anyone who got too drunk at the bar?" Lauren said, reminding Alexis of that sweet man from back home in Biwabik.

Thinking of their childhood in Minnesota made her smile. "He was a nice man. He used to say he did it because it was worth losing a few bucks to save a family from losing a father or mother."

Lauren nodded. "I know many nights he brought my father home from the bar. Who knows what would have happened if he had gotten into his car drunk."

As Alexis reminisced about the old days and how kind everyone was back home, Paul tried to steer the conversation back to what he wanted to discuss. "See? So it's settled. The guy will be here this afternoon and he'll join your security team."

Nothing about this seemed settled to her, but if someone could find this person who'd been terrorizing her, then she'd give him a chance because if he couldn't, at least she wouldn't be any worse off.

And that fact alone showed how bad things

had gotten.

AFTER PACING UNTIL her legs felt like they'd give out, Alexis closed the door behind her and settled into the most comfortable spot in the house—her new office chair. Plush and comfy, it practically swallowed her up in its softness, just what she needed to feel safe again. She still felt trapped in her own home, but at least in that dark blue chair, she could pretend that her life hadn't become a series of tiny rooms connected by dark hallways.

She began reading a script her agent Melanie had told her about weeks ago and had finally been delivered to her the day before she left LA. Titled Haunted By Love, it told the story of a woman who was being haunted by her dead husband, who everyone believed she killed. Alexis had only gotten a third of the way into the story, but she already hated it with a white hot passion.

All the parts she got offered were the same. All the characters felt delicate and frail, like at any moment in the film someone could come up behind them and say boo and they'd crumble into a thousand terrified pieces.

She wanted to play strong women. Kickass women. Characters who could stand on their own and brave whatever the big, bad world threw at them. Instead, the woman she sat reading sounded far too much like herself lately.

Terrorized and afraid to leave her house.

Pitching the script onto the floor, she brought her knees up to her chest and closed her eyes. This was how she'd spend the rest of the day. Curled up in a ball and pretending the world outside didn't exist.

A knock on her office door ruined that plan not five minutes later, though. Why couldn't they just leave her alone?

She leaned back on the arm of the chair and yelled in the direction of the door, "I'm busy. Whatever it is, talk to Lauren!"

As she watched in horror, the door opened against her explicit instructions and Paul walked in with a man Alexis had never seen before. Smiling, her manager showed the man off like he'd just created him in a lab or something.

"Alexis, this is Hunter McKary. He's the man we talked about earlier today. He just arrived, so I wanted to introduce the two of you."

Her gaze traveled from Paul to this Hunter person and then down the full length of his body, from head to toe. Her first impression was he looked like a cop. Or someone who could play a cop in the movies. He had short brown hair a little too much like that ex of hers, but his face had a rugged look she liked in men. This Hunter certainly didn't have a pretty boy appearance so many of her co-stars had lately.

He didn't smile, which unnerved her. There he stood in her home and he couldn't even crack a tiny smile on their introduction? That seemed rude. He was probably one of those stereotypical overly serious bodyguard types she'd never liked.

She did like how that rugged look made him appear tough, so maybe she could tolerate the sour puss thing he had going on. For once, though, she wished the men who came into her life didn't look like stone cut outs of real men.

As that drifted through her mind, her gaze slid down to his body again. He looked hard there too, like he could protect someone. Well, if his job was going to be doing just that for her, he fit the bill.

"Alexis, did you hear me?" Paul asked, tearing her out of her thoughts about Hunter.

She stood up and extended her hand to shake his hand. "It's nice to meet you, Hunter. How long have you been a bodyguard?"

He shook her hand for a moment and then pulled his away abruptly. "I'm not a bodyguard. I spent time as an LAPD detective, and now I work for Project Artemis as a specialist helping people who need protection. A bodyguard is what the world will think I am, but trust me. I'm far more than just a mere bodyguard."

She stood shocked at how terse he'd been. Unnecessarily terse considering she'd been more than polite with him.

Cocky men were top on her list of things she didn't want to deal with in life, so she needed him to understand she wouldn't be treated rudely like that, no matter how much Paul thought of his boss.

"Well, if you're anything like the cops in LA now, I don't see what you could possibly do for me. They haven't been able to find out the identity of my stalker for months, and I've had to move clear across the country because they couldn't do their jobs."

Hunter remained stone-faced as she spoke, and when she finished, he said nothing to her. Not a single word. Instead, he turned toward Paul and said, "I need to know the layout of this whole place. Anywhere someone can get in, I want to know about it."

Then he walked out, leaving her standing there feeling insulted and wondering what made this guy think he could pull that cocky shit on her. How dare he ignore her like that! He worked for her. Who did he think he was?

Paul remained behind, smiling as if things had gone swimmingly. God, did he ever not think everything was just fine?

Pointing at the door Hunter had just walked through when he left so rudely, she asked, "And you think that person is going to be the one who helps me get my life back?"

He looked away and nodded. "Well, he isn't exactly the chattiest guy in the world, but I trust Persephone. If she thinks he can help, I say give him a chance."

"Says the man who promised me that moving cross country to this awful place would solve my problems. I'm guessing this Persephone finds his Cro-Magnon routine perfectly acceptable, but I don't. If you think I'm going to take being treated like that in my own home by some for-hire security guard, you can forget it. Tell him to go find a job at the mall because I'm not having it!"

Alexis sat back down on her comfy chair and folded her arms across her chest as steam practically shot out the top of her head she was so furious at Paul for bringing that man to her home. She wouldn't be treated like some insignificant thing who didn't even deserve an answer by any man, least of all some stranger in her own home.

"Lexi, just listen to me. Give him a chance. I promise you Persephone wouldn't have sent him if she didn't think he could help. Just give him a week. If you don't like him by that time, then he's gone. Promise me you'll give him at least that long, though?"

The look on Paul's face told her he was worried, and he had good reason to be. She'd had enough of men pushing her around for an entire lifetime. She wouldn't be taking this Hunter guy's shit not one more time.

"The problem isn't with me, so you're wasting your breath talking to me, Paul. The problem is with him. He's rude to the person he's supposed to be helping and in her own house, no less. If he can't change his attitude, then he'll have to leave and not after a week. Now. So you have a choice. You can continue to stand here and stare at me with that terrified look in your eyes, or you can go find your friend's guy and explain to him how things go here at Casa Alexis. Whatever you do, shut the door on your way out and tell Lauren I want to see her."

He scurried away, knowing full well she meant every word she'd said. She didn't make hollow threats. Not to men who cheated on her and then thought she'd merely stand idly by when they stepped out with other women, and certainly not about a man she'd just met and already didn't like enough to want him thrown out into the street on his ear.

Reaching down, she picked up the script for Haunted By Love off the floor and flipped to the last page she'd read. After only a few lines, it became apparent trying to focus on anything would be a complete waste of time, so she threw the script across the room in frustration. It knocked over a lamp, which crashed to the floor and smashed into a million pieces.

This day just got better and better.

Her head began to pound from a stress headache as a result of Hunter McKary and his rudeness. She didn't want to play a victim in any more films or in her own life either anymore. Even more, she didn't want to be someone the Hunters of the world thought they could ignore so easily and never pay a price.

She heard a light tap on the door she recognized as Lauren's signature knock and called out, "Come in!"

Her best friend and assistant peeked her head around the door and smiled. "Paul said you wanted to see me?"

Alexis nodded and waved her in. "Yes. I need to see a friendly face after meeting that odious man."

Lauren closed the door and came over to sit down on the floor in front of her. With her usual sweetness, she touched her hand and smiled. "It didn't go so well? He looked very handsome, at least."

Handsome didn't matter if the man had the manners of a pig.

"Nothing special, if you ask me. I've dated much better looking men, so whatever he thinks he's got going on, it isn't much."

"What made him so odious?" Lauren asked

innocently.

Alexis opened her mouth to explain what happened, but nothing came out. She was so furious. The man had actually made her speechless.

Finally, she said, "I don't want to talk about it now. Just take my word for it. He won't be here long if he doesn't realize who's the boss here."

"It's your home, Alexis. Paul needs to understand that if you don't want someone in it, they need to go. I think he's forgotten that lately."

She smiled down at Lauren. "Thank you for reminding me. This is why you're irreplaceable, you know that? Everyone else could go away, but as long as I have you to rely on, I know I'll be okay."

"You can rely on me. Always. Never forget that."

Alexis closed her eyes and took a deep breath in. At least she had one person she could trust in the world.

CHAPTER FOUR

HUNTER CAREFULLY EXAMINED every square inch of Alexis Marchand's penthouse apartment, and after two hours of checking each window and door, he felt satisfied that at the very least that part of protecting her wouldn't be a problem. The fact that her home took up one-fourth of the top floor of the building had given him concern, but after checking out all the entrances, he didn't worry as much.

A single elevator as the only means of reaching the apartment meant anyone trying to get in would have to get by security on the main floor. Hunter immediately decided at least one of Alexis's security detail would have to be stationed near the front door of the building at all times. To trust her safety to the single security guard who manned the entire main floor wouldn't be wise.

He found Paul waiting for him in the dining room next to the kitchen. The manager sat alone at a long table that seated ten, so he pulled out a chair and sat down next to him.

"I've done my preliminary examination of the penthouse. The location on the top floor makes creating a security plan much easier since there's only one way into the apartment, unless your stalker plans on scaling the side of the building."

Paul laughed. "You have no idea how dedicated some of her fans are. I wouldn't be a bit surprised if one tried it sometime."

"I'll keep that in mind. Other than that, I think at least one, if not two, of her security guys should be stationed in the lobby of the building at all times round the clock."

"Okay," Paul said, nodding in agreement. "That won't be a problem."

"Good. I don't think we should rely on the building's security when it comes to things like a stalker. Other than that, all packages need to be inspected by me before anyone does anything with them."

That made Paul grimace, and he stopped nodding. "On that, we might have an issue."

"Oh?" Hunter asked, wondering why something so simple would cause a problem.

Hesitating, Paul took a deep breath in and blew it out slowly before he answered. "Lexi isn't going to be happy about that. She's going to see it as an invasion of her privacy."

"Well, she can get over it or she go through what you described happened the other night again. Which do you think she'd find less of a hassle?" Hunter asked, already getting irritated at how this place worked.

If Alexis Marchand wanted to be protected, she'd have to accept the fact that it might mean some things needed to change. If she couldn't, he'd never be able to help her or find out who was stalking her.

Paul drew his eyebrows in toward his nose in an expression of worry. "I'll just have to explain it to her. I'm sure if I do that she'll understand."

The two men sat silently for a long moment before Hunter asked a question he needed answered. "Why did you call Persephone for help with this? Did Alexis ask you to?"

"Oh no," he answered, shaking his head quickly. "She'd never ask for help like this. It's not in her nature. She might not know how to solve this problem, but she's stubborn. She would have kept going like she has been for months if I hadn't contacted you guys."

"I think maybe this might have worked better if she actually wanted the kind of help I can offer. As it is now, she's not very receptive to it."

"You just have to understand Lexi. She's strong, and I mean that in any number of ways. She doesn't want to be considered helpless, but that's exactly what this guy has done to her. If you knew her before all this began, you wouldn't recognize her now."

Curious as to why Paul kept referring to the stalker as a male, Hunter said, "You keep saying he and him when you talk about her stalker. Do you have an idea of who it might be that makes you think it's a man? An ex-boyfriend, for example?"

"No, not really. I think I keep saying it's a man because Alexis is sure the stalker is a guy."

"Why?"

Paul shrugged. "It might be that she's suspicious of men more than women. After her divorce, she didn't trust men much anymore. Even with me, something changed, and I'm her manager. I always want the best for her, but she doesn't trust like she used to. Unless you're Lauren. They've known each other since they were kids growing up in Minnesota, so Lexi trusts her with her life. The rest of us? Not so much, and even less lately. I'm actually surprised she took my advice and moved here to New York. I would have put money on her fighting me tooth and nail."

Hunter didn't know what to say to him. He looked sad about Alexis not trusting him, but he couldn't help him with that. All he could do was keep her safe and hopefully find out who was behind the threatening letters and gifts quickly so she could get back to living her life.

"I better get going. Do you need me for anything else?" Paul asked as he stood from the table.

"Nope. I'm going to start talking to her staff to see if I can get any ideas from what they might know. I have free reign here, right? I can't do my job without it."

A slight smile brightened up Paul's face. "As far as I'm concerned, sure. I think I should warn you, though. Lexi was pretty offended by the way you were earlier. You should probably find a different way to deal with her."

Just the suggestion that he'd have to kiss the diva's ring or whatever she expected him to do rankled Hunter. Shaking his head, he tried to make Paul understand he wasn't there to make his client feel good. He was there to protect her. Period.

"I'm not sure what you all think this is, but I'm not worried about if she likes me or not. I've got a job to do. That's it. She doesn't have to like me for me to do it."

Paul's face contorted in a wince. "Actually, she does. Let's put it this way. She's already told me if you're like you were before one more time, she's calling this all off. I don't want to see her hurt, and I want you to get to the bottom of what's going on here. All I'm asking is that you remember she's feeling very vulnerable these days and running roughshod over her feelings isn't going to help her stay safe. I know Lexi. She'll rebel, and if she doesn't simply kick you out, she'll lash out in other ways."

Hunter already hated this job, and now this guy was basically telling him he had to pamper some Hollywood diva to be able to do his job? Fuck. Persephone was going to owe him weeks of vacation time at this rate.

"Fine. I'll try to stay as far away from her as possible, and when I do have to deal with her, I promise to be civil. How's that?"

His offer brought a big smile back to Paul's face. "She's actually a great person. Give her a chance. You might find out you like her. But civil will probably be enough."

As Paul walked into the kitchen, Hunter mumbled to himself, "Civil it is. That can't be too hard."

Before he had a chance to talk himself out of being civil to Alexis when all he wanted to do was his job, a woman appeared in front of him and sat down on the other side of the table. Pretty, with dark blonde hair and blue eyes, she paled in comparison to her employer. For what it was worth, though, she had a sweeter look to her that he liked at that moment.

"Mr. McKary, I'm Lauren Henderson. I'm Alexis's personal assistant. I hope you'll be able to solve this so whoever is torturing her will finally stop. She's so giving to her fans. I can't imagine who would do this to her."

In her eyes, Hunter saw real concern and sadness over what had happened to her boss. "How long have you known Alexis?" he asked, curious if there could be even the hint of bad blood between the two women.

He had no reason to suspect Lauren of being behind the stalking, but as he always had since his first day on the job as a cop, he had to keep an open mind about everyone involved in the case. As far as he was concerned, any one of them could be guilty and everyone was still innocent.

With a big smile, she explained how long she'd been friends with Alexis Marchand, sounding almost like a fan herself. "We met the first day of school in first grade. I had just moved to Minnesota from Ohio, and I didn't know a soul. Alexis walked right up to me before school and with a big smile said, 'Hi, I'm Alexis!' From that moment on, we've been thick as thieves."

Hunter quickly did the math in his head and guessed Lauren and Alexis had been friends for nearly twenty years. If anyone knew the star, it was the woman in front of him. Sensing that, he wanted to get as much information about her as he could from Lauren.

"Have you always been her assistant once she

began acting?" he asked.

"Even before that," Lauren said, beaming with pride. "When she hit it big in modeling less than a year after she was discovered, she asked me to be her assistant. Of course, I said yes, so I put off college and I've been working with her ever since."

"How was she discovered?" Hunter asked, suddenly curious about that part of Alexis Marchand's history.

Lauren clapped her hands together in excitement, like she adored telling this story. "It's almost unbelievable. She was at the mall and the owner of Ketton Modeling Agency had gotten lost driving to St. Paul. He ran into Alexis walking into the food court and knocked her tray of food out of her hands. The food and her soda crashed to the floor, and as he was apologizing for his clumsiness, he says he realized he'd just run into his next superstar. He gave her his card and told her to call him if she wanted to be a model. I remember she came to my house on her way home and asked me if she should do it. I told her of course she should. Just look at her. She's a born model. She called him the next day, and as they say, the rest is history."

"So she began to model in high school?"

"Yeah. And by the time we graduated, she was a star and I was her assistant."

"You two have been together for a long time. Have you ever fought, or has it always been best friends between the two of you?"

He watched for any change in her expression, especially looking for a hint of any problem in the past as she said, "Just once. We were in seventh grade and both of us liked the same boy. He liked Alexis and they went out for a few weeks before it ended. The whole time, we didn't talk, but I think she missed me as much as I missed her. After that, we made a pledge never to let a guy come between us again. We've never really fought since."

"Never really?" Hunter asked, seizing on the way she phrased that.

Lauren looked around to make sure no one else was within earshot and said in a low voice, "Alexis is under tremendous pressure. You don't know what it's like to be a star like her. Everyone seems to put their needs on her. They expect her to be beautiful and charming and a great businesswoman at the same time. She's expected to be perfect. If she says one wrong word, the press will jump on her like a pack of hyenas."

"Is it really that bad?"

She nodded and looked at him with sadness in her eyes. "No one remembers the charities she's given so much to or how incredible an actress she is or even how gracious she was when she found out right before the Golden Globes that her husband was cheating on her with a woman even younger than her and wasn't even trying to be secretive about it. Nope. All of those things disappear if she makes one mistake. So when she's alone with those of us who are closest to her, she has to let off some steam. Everyone deserves a release, and I'm happy to give Alexis that from time to time when she needs it."

Clearly, Lauren loved her friend. Hunter didn't know if he could completely rule her out as the person behind the letters Alexis had been getting, but he had a gut feeling she was just what she seemed to be.

A good friend.

"Lauren, can you think of anyone who would want to do this to Alexis?"

She shook her head sadly. "No. No one I know would do this to her. Carla and I love her, and although she isn't close to any of her bodyguards, they are devoted to her."

"What about her ex-husband? He did cheat on her."

After thinking about his question, she shook her head. "No way. Jackson is an ass, but he's moved on. He never held anything against Alexis, even when she took him to the cleaners."

"Okay. I just wanted to ask. And the bodyguards are all fans of hers, in your opinion?"

he asked, still unsure what he thought of her security detail, even after meeting with them briefly earlier.

Paul had told him how much Alexis Marchand paid her bodyguards, so even if they hated the very sight of her, they'd be devoted to their salary. He was curious, though, if she'd ever slept with any of them. Love always changed things.

And lust definitely could.

"Like with us, Alexis can be difficult with them, but I don't think any would want to hurt her."

"Have any of her bodyguards become more at any time?"

For a moment, Lauren seemed confused as to what he meant by that, opening her mouth to answer but saying nothing. Then, as if a lightbulb turned on in her head, she smiled.

"Oh, you mean that. Just one but that was last year when her divorce was finalized."

"Who?"

"Kyle. Kyle Murdoch."

"How long were they together?"

"Only once. She got drunk out of her mind and Kyle was there. I'm not even sure they..." Lauren hesitated to finish her thought for a moment and then continued, "...I mean...you know...slept together. I'm not sure Alexis was in any condition to do that," she said, blushing.

As charming as Lauren looked all embarrassed by the discussion of sex, Hunter still needed to know about Kyle and what he may have felt after that rendezvous with Alexis. "And nothing more ever happened between the two of them?"

She shook her head. "Nothing. It's as if that night never happened."

"What about for Kyle? Have you ever had any sense that he wanted something more to come of that night?"

Lauren looked away and thought for a moment before shaking her head again. "No, I don't think so. Kyle doesn't say much, so it wouldn't be like he'd talk to me about it. But I've never seen him looking longingly at her, if that's what you mean."

Hunter smiled at the way she said that. "Not exactly what I meant, but I get the picture. Would he talk to anyone else if he had feelings for Alexis?"

"I'm not sure. I'm not really close to the bodyguards. They always live separately from those of us who lived in the main house. I'm not even sure where they'll be living here in New York."

Surprised to hear Alexis didn't have her security team close by at all times, Hunter said, "Well, that's going to change. No wonder someone thinks they can get to her."

He'd already sat down with her head of security, Malcolm Batish, but he hadn't mentioned the living arrangements back in LA or there in New York. He'd have to make it clear to him that situation would end right now.

From the other side of the apartment, Alexis yelled, "Lauren, I need you!"

Lauren jumped up from her seat and bolted toward her boss's office. Then after only a few steps, she stopped and turned around to look at Hunter, who stared in amazement that merely by yelling for someone, Alexis Marchand could get people up and running.

"Please don't mention to her that I told you all of this. I don't know if she'd want you to know."

"I can't find out who's behind the threats and letters if I don't ask questions like that and even more personal ones. If they embarrass her, better that than her being hurt or killed."

Alexis yelled again, this time with impatience lacing every word. "Lauren, where are you? I need you now!"

Her assistant hurried away toward her boss, so Hunter went to find Paul. He stood near the counter eating a bagel with cream cheese and smiled when Hunter walked into the room.

"How are things coming?" he asked as he

quickly wiped food from his mouth.

"Did you know that her bodyguards aren't usually anywhere near her when she's at home? For God's sake, they're in another residence, if I'm understanding the set up in LA correctly."

Paul nodded and then shrugged, like all of this sounded normal to him. "Yeah. Lexi doesn't like having them hanging around."

"Well, they need to be close by. They aren't just giant sized paper weights. Where did she plan on having them live now that she's here in New York?"

"Hmmm, I don't know. Now that you bring it up, I have no idea. They can't stay here since there are only four bedrooms and she's using one of them for an office."

"Well, she's going to have to make some decisions on that and quick because they need to be nearby until we get to the bottom of who's stalking her."

A look of worry came over Paul's face. Frowning, he said, "She's not going to like that."

Hunter slapped him on the arm and smiled. "I'll tell you what. Let me tell her and you'll avoid being the one in the line of fire when she blows up. Sound good?"

That brought a smile to the manager's face. "I like that. Anything to avoid the wrath of Lexi."

"For that, I need you to get me the names of

every assistant, bodyguard, and anyone else who's been paid by Alexis in the past year."

"Okay. I can get on that today. I'll get you everything I can tonight or latest tomorrow."

Slapping him on the arm again, Hunter smiled. "Great! Now I need to go speak to the woman herself."

As he walked out of the kitchen, he heard Paul say, "Good luck."

He didn't need luck. This was a job, and she was a client. Simple as that. It's not like he planned to make her do much anyway. All he needed her to do was answer a few questions.

Making his way to her office, he stopped in front of it and listened for a moment. He heard nothing, so he knocked on the door.

She responded by barking, "Go away!"

Hunter had already had enough of this shit. If he was ever going to find out who was stalking this woman, he needed cooperation.

Her cooperation. And right now.

Throwing the door open, he walked in and stared her down as Lauren looked on with terror in her eyes. "I'm not going to be able to do my job if you don't work with me, Miss Marchand. If you want to ever be free of whoever is stalking you, I suggest you help me."

He watched as rage filled her brown eyes, and she said to her assistant through gritted teeth,

"Lauren, leave us alone."

She did just that, hurrying past him and shutting the door behind her. Now maybe he'd get some answers that could help him. He'd dealt with feisty women before. He actually preferred women to have some spunk.

Too bad Alexis Marchand had a bit too much of it. Not to worry. He'd handled women like that too. All it took was a firm hand and letting them know who was in charge.

And he would have no problem making her understand the person in charge of this job was him.

Chapter Five

RAGE BUBBLED UP inside Alexis. How dare he barge in there without being asked! The nerve of this man! Did his rudeness have no end? First, he ignored her when she tried to be nice and strike up a conversation, and now he thought he could just march into her private office and demand to speak to her.

Nobody demanded anything of Alexis Marchand, especially some man she didn't even much like. If he thought she was going to simply let this pass, he was sadly confused.

Standing from her comfy chair, she walked over to where he stood looking like some conquering Alpha male and stopped directly in front of him. Only a few inches taller than her five foot ten, she looked him in the eye and let him know whatever he thought he'd accomplish by walking in on her, he'd only succeeded in angering her even more.

"Mr. McKary, I'm not a fan of being told what to do, especially by men. Strangers who have shown me nothing but disrespect don't get to tell me what to do either."

She didn't see surprise in his eyes so much as something that resembled disappointment. Had he expected her to act like some helpless damsel in distress? If so, this job of his was going to be nothing but disappointment because she would never be that.

Better he started understanding who he was dealing with right now. She had no intention of being a spectator to her own life, no matter how good or bad it got.

"It seems you've been laboring under the false impression that I'm just some pathetic creature who needs your help. Well, let me disabuse you of that right now. Paul called your boss, not me. He's the one who thinks you can help. As far as I can tell from how you've acted so far, you don't seem any more capable of solving this case than the cops in the city where you used to work."

Hunter stepped toward her, decreasing the space between them so much that she had to tilt her head back to keep staring him in the eye. Was this supposed to be some kind of intimidation tactic to get her to submit to his power?

If it was, he had grossly underestimated her.

He didn't say anything for a long moment, and as Alexis stood her ground, she couldn't help but notice how beautiful his eyes were. The darkest green she'd ever seen, they stared down at her with an intensity that made her feel like she was getting lost in their forest green color.

When he finally spoke, she felt like she'd been put under some kind of magical spell that made her want to listen to his deep voice.

"You're going to find that my methods work best when the client doesn't get in my way, Miss Marchand."

Unlike when he'd spoken to her before, this time he didn't sound rude or disrespectful. Hearing a hint of kindness in his tone, she responded with a question she wasn't sure he could answer.

"Do you even know my first name?"

For a second, he said nothing. Just as she'd suspected. He didn't even bother to note her name when he came barging into her world, thinking he could come in and take over and she'd be thrilled to let him mistreat her like that.

She made a move to turn away, to leave him standing there alone, but he grabbed her arm and spun her around to face him. Stunned, she couldn't even bring herself to tell him off like she wanted to.

"Alexis."

His voice washed over her, making her head swim. She'd never heard her name sound like that. Strong. Powerful. Confident. It made her want to hear him speak it again.

His intense stare unnerved her now, and she looked down at where his hand sat on her forearm. It should have enraged her, but strangely, it didn't. His hand didn't squeeze her so much as gently but insistently hold her right where he wanted her to remain. That alone should have infuriated her, but as she looked at his strong hands touching her skin, she didn't feel angry at all.

Alexis looked up at him and tried to speak, but at first, nothing came out. Words became impossible as her mind whirled from his touch.

Finally, she gathered her thoughts and cleared her throat to speak. "Mr. McKary…Hunter, I work best when I'm an active participant in my life. You may be used to timid women, but I'm not one of them. I'm not tied to the railroad tracks. I respect your expertise. Please respect my desire to help in my own defense."

When she finished, he said nothing and simply stared into her eyes as she looked up at him. It felt almost as if he didn't know what to say either. And yet, Alexis had never felt so at ease with anyone this close to her since Jackson.

Hunter nodded and gave her a smile. "I can respect that, Alexis. Maybe we got off on the wrong foot before. Let's start over again. Nice to meet you. I'm Hunter. I'm going to do everything

I can to make sure this person stalking you is stopped."

"Thank you, Hunter. It's nice to meet you too."

He smiled again, and this time Alexis noticed how sexy he looked when he wasn't scowling. She liked that and hoped she'd get to see that side of him more.

"I think it would be a good idea if we talked about your staff. I need to know all about them, and you're the best person to tell me about them. But first, I noticed that Paul calls you Lexi. Would you prefer me to call you that, or is that name reserved only for him?"

The sweetness she'd felt a second earlier instantly evaporated at hearing Paul's pet name for her coming out of Hunter's mouth. "No, I'd prefer Alexis, thank you."

"Okay, Alexis. Now about your staff."

"Just tell me what you need to know," she said as she walked back to her favorite chair.

Hunter took a seat on the tan loveseat across from her, not in the chair further away near the desk. Alexis watched as he leaned back against the cushion and spread his arm across the top of it. Hunter looked like a man comfortable in his own skin, something she saw far too little of in all the men she'd ever met. She liked that kind of confidence. It looked good on him.

Even more interesting, he seemed comfortable with her now. No one but Lauren acted like that with her, and she'd known her since they were children.

He took out a pen and notepad from his shirt and began writing. "I need to know how long each person has been with you and if you've ever had any problem with any one of them."

"Paul can give you all the details on that. He handles all the employees' and their pay."

Hunter looked up from his notes. "I need to know your point of view about these people. I'm trying to figure out who is stalking you, so hearing what you think of the people around you is important. If one of them has an ax to grind with you, knowing how you interact with them might help me figure out who's behind it all."

As much as she believed what she thought was important, Alexis had never had anyone ask her about how she felt in all of this. Everyone had always been worried about her, but no one investigating had wanted to know her opinions. They'd just always listened to her story about the most recent letter and then assured her they'd find out who did it, but never had they asked what she believed about any of it.

She'd always just been a victim in their eyes. A woman who needed their help to survive in the world.

One by one she listed her bodyguards first, starting with her head of security. "Malcolm has been with me the longest of all my guards. Paul hired him right after my first film four years ago."

"Any problems between the two of you?" Hunter asked as he jotted down notes on what she said.

She shook her head and answered without giving the question a second thought. "No. He's always been a wonderful man to have protecting me. I sort of feel bad for him, actually. I think he feels like this whole thing is a reflection on him, but I don't think that at all."

Hunter lifted his head and squinted his eyes. "What makes you think that? Has he ever said anything to you about it?"

"No, no, nothing like that. I just get a sense that he feels bad for me and worries I might fire him if this continues. That's probably more because I tend to have a short fuse and yell at people more than him feeling anything like guilt."

Once again, Hunter smiled in that way that made him look very sexy. "Yeah. I can see that."

She wanted to explain herself, to make him see that she wasn't just some raving lunatic with too much money and too much fame. Pulling her legs up to her chest, she wrapped her arms around her knees and hugged them to her.

"I'm not some Hollywood diva, Hunter. I'm

really not. I admit I have been known to yell and scream sometimes, but everyone who knows me knows that's just my way. I don't mean any harm. I just need a release from the pressure of the world outside my home, but I care about all these people who work for me. I'd be lost without them, especially Lauren."

"She cares a lot about you. I can tell just from talking to her."

Alexis smiled, happy to hear him say that. "I love her. She's the sister I never had. I don't know what I'd do without her."

"Okay, back to your bodyguards. Who's next?"

She explained how long each man had worked for her, and after each name, Hunter asked, "Any reason he would want to hurt you personally or professionally?"

Every time she answered the same way. "No."

When she gave that answer about Kyle Murdoch, Hunter stared at her, clearly wanting more information. Confused, she wondered why he'd singled out that one bodyguard until she remembered the night she'd spent with Kyle when her divorce became final.

Oh, God. She didn't want to talk about *that* with him.

Looking away, she quietly said, "Whatever you heard, it wasn't anything."

"Are you sure he felt the same way? Maybe he thought it was more something than nothing."

She turned back to face him and nodded. "Trust me. He didn't think it was anything, just like I said."

Hunter smiled. "Alexis, you're a beautiful and successful woman millions of men love from afar. It's not ridiculous to think Kyle would want to be with you for more than just one night. Maybe he wanted more and didn't get it, so he became resentful. The male ego can be a very fragile thing."

Rolling her eyes, she laughed at his comment about millions of men loving her. For someone who was supposed to be such an object of affection for so many, she spent every night alone or with her best friend from childhood. That didn't sound like anyone loved her.

At least not the way she wished a man would.

"I don't know about millions of men, but trust me, Kyle didn't want anything from me."

She hoped that would make him drop the subject, but he continued asking questions about that one stupid night. "Did anything change between the two of you after your time together?"

"No. Believe me. You're barking up the wrong tree, Hunter."

The wrongest of trees, but she didn't want to explain to him how the man she turned to in a moment of drunken need couldn't get it up.

But still he kept focusing on Kyle and that night. "Has he ever mentioned it or shown any problem with you since? Have you ever gotten the feeling he wanted to talk about it, even if you didn't?"

Looking away, she desperately wished he would just drop the subject. "No, he's never said anything about it, and he never wanted to. Kyle has been a loyal employee and nothing more, except for that one night and it meant nothing to either of us."

Hunter said nothing for nearly a minute, and Alexis hoped that would be the end of it and he'd just move on. When he began to ask about the other staff, she breathed a sigh of relief.

"I had a cook named France who was with me for two years. She didn't come with me to New York, though. She's still back in LA taking care of the house, along with a maid named Pam."

"Any issues with either one of them?"

"No, none that I can think of. I loved France's cooking. I'm going to miss it, in fact."

"Did she know how much you loved her food?"

Alexis chuckled. "Yes. I used to tell her all the time, and she used to tell me how she made everything low calorie while still making it taste good. The woman was a magician in the kitchen."

"Ever yell at either one of them? Ever chastise them in front of others?" Hunter asked with a knowing look.

"You've been here less than a day and I know you've heard me yell already, Hunter. Let's assume I did, but I really don't think my staff cares about that kind of stuff. I pay them handsomely, so there is that."

He didn't respond to her attempt at defending her behavior, and for one of the first times since she became famous, she didn't like hearing herself say she yelled and screamed at people. True, she meant it when she said she needed a release from the rest of the world when she was in her own home, but his silence felt like judgment about the way she acted.

She didn't like it at all.

As he wrote his notes, she said, "I know you probably think I'm some kind of spoiled prima donna because I've gotten excited a few times and let my emotions get the best of me. My staff understands I don't mean anything by it, though. They know me well enough to know I don't mean anything by it."

"Uh-huh. I'm going to need to contact both of those women in LA," he said without looking up from his notebook.

He said nothing more and just continued to jot down notes. Alexis didn't like how his continued silence made her feel. She never meant to hurt anyone. Is that what had happened? Had she inadvertently hurt someone's feelings and now that person wanted to hurt her back?

Finally, Hunter lifted his head and asked, "Two years ago means you had a different cook before? Who did she replace?"

"Shari Thompson. She left when she became pregnant."

"What about employees when you and your husband were together?"

The mention of Jackson made her feel vulnerable and exposed, so she looked away and answered, "I'll have to think about that and get you a list."

As she prayed to God he wouldn't continue to ask about that time in her life, he said, "Okay. That leaves how many other employees?"

"Just Carla and Lauren. Carla's been with me for four years. She came on right before I got married. And Lauren's been like my sister since first grade. Neither one of them would want to hurt me for the world."

"So no problems with either of them?"

Alexis dropped her legs off the chair and sat up straight. "Absolutely not. They're like family. They were there when I found out my husband was cheating on me. They were there when my husband and his girlfriend began showing up in the tabloids making me feel like a fool. They were there when less than a month after our divorce was final my husband married his girlfriend he'd been cheating with, a woman three years younger than me."

Her emotions began to get the best of her, so she stopped talking and looked down at her hands in her lap. The last thing she wanted to do was let Hunter see how talking about what Jackson did upset her. She never talked about it anymore, but it still hurt to even say the words. If she could, she'd never say them again.

"Paul told me the first letter arrived three months ago, and since then, you've gotten one every week. Other than the package the other night, have there been any other packages in addition to the letters?" Hunter asked, thankfully moving on from the subject of her ex-husband and what he did to her.

"No. Just that one."

Out of the corner of her eye, she saw Hunter stand to leave. "I'm assuming you handed the letters over to the police. Do you have copies of them, by any chance?"

Looking up at him, she shook her head. "No. We gave the police everything."

Her head began to throb from the stress of thinking of all the people who might want to hurt her. Having her life put under a microscope yet again just brought into focus how unsafe she truly was, even in her own home.

It frightened her more than she wanted to admit.

"I'll get them on my own then. Don't worry. We'll find out who's doing this, Alexis."

She smiled up at him and realized he'd used we instead of I, including her just as she'd asked him to earlier. Not one of the officers back in LA had ever made her feel like anything more than a passive target, a woman who could do nothing more than just wait until the next letter came and upended her life once again.

"Thank you."

"Oh, I forgot to mention one thing. Your bodyguards can't be so far away from you anymore. Paul told me they used to stay in another house back in LA, but here they need to be much closer."

"Closer? As in the same house? Because that's not going to work. There aren't enough rooms in this place. As it is, we're practically falling over one another the place is so small."

Alexis knew how ridiculous it sounded for someone to say a three thousand foot penthouse apartment was too small, but if the four security guards joined her, Lauren, and Carla, that would be seven people living there. Just the thought made her cringe. They'd be packed in like sardines.

"Well, you have a choice. You can find them a place to stay in this building and I can stay with them, or you can have me living here and they can go somewhere nearby. But not more than a block or two. In addition, I want one or two of them stationed downstairs at all times to make sure no one gets up here who isn't supposed to."

She didn't have to think long about the choice he offered. Alexis hated the idea of her security being so close. It's why she made sure when she bought her house in LA that it had a second place on the property for them to stay. She didn't want to be reminded every moment of her life that she needed protection. It made her feel helpless, and that was the last thing she wanted to be.

"Fine. I take you living here, and for the rest of the guys, I'll have Paul find somewhere nearby. I promise it won't be further than two blocks away. Sound good?"

"Perfect," he said with that smile she'd already grown to like seeing.

"I'm going to have to figure out how to fit all of us here, though," she said, more thinking out loud than continuing the conversation.

"It's okay. No need to displace either of your assistants. I can sleep on the couch," he said as he opened the door and walked out.

Alexis hadn't lived with a man since leaving

Jackson three years before. She'd sworn if she ever let another man back into her home, he'd know who the boss was. Now that Hunter would be living under the same roof as her, she strangely didn't care so much to be in control.

Even though her stalker was still out there somewhere, likely preparing for the next time he would send her something and throw her life into chaos, she felt safer for the first time in months. She didn't like the new apartment and she didn't want to spend any more time in New York as the chill of fall settled in, but somehow knowing Hunter would be close by made her hate all of it just a little less.

Chapter Six

After talking to Paul and finding out the bodyguards would be put up in a hotel a few blocks away until he could find a place with enough bedrooms Alexis would approve, Hunter spent some time in the living room watching as people hurried all around him every time she yelled their names. He had to give it to her. She sure did know how to command an audience.

He'd seen another side to her too, though, and it was only because he believed she was more than just the diva she showed the rest of the household that he had to admit he finally was beginning to understand why men around the world fell in love with her. Behind the gorgeous outside and past the demanding Hollywood star routine existed a strong woman who wanted to control her own destiny.

For Hunter, that alone made him think that the gossip magazines got it all wrong when they talked about Alexis Marchand. Then again, showing her to be strong and independent wouldn't sell as much as discussing the finer points of her personal life, which they seemed to relish, no matter who they trashed.

The few he'd read before arriving in New York speculated on her having a secret love affair with one of her married co-stars from her last film, a long-lost relative that she allowed to live in squalor in a rundown trailer somewhere in the Midwest, and a penchant for spending thousands of dollars a day on special food to keep her thin and beautiful that she imported from some monastery in Finland.

That last one had been a head-scratcher for Hunter. He had a hard time imagining monks spending their days specially preparing food for a movie star halfway around the world.

A little basic investigative work showed him that the love affair with her co-star Jake Howard never happened. In fact, he was actually cheating on his wife with a man. Hunter had to admit he'd been surprised at that piece of gossip and even more shocked that the tabloids didn't run with that story instead of the lie about Alexis and Jake.

As for the destitute relative she supposedly refused to help despite having millions, she didn't exist. Some woman in Kansas City claimed she and Alexis's mother were related, but that proved false too.

And the fancy food from Finland that

possessed secret powers to make her thin and beautiful? Other than the bagels and cream cheese Paul had brought with him, all Hunter had found in the house was food any other person in America ate. Alexis certainly didn't seem to be a sugar junkie since he hadn't seen any sweets in any of the cabinets, but there did seem to be a large amount of vegetables.

Not that anyone had cooked the entire time he'd been there. As far as he could tell, Alexis and her assistants hadn't eaten a meal all day.

So much for what the gossip magazines called The Glamorous Life of Alexis Marchand. It seemed more ordinary than extraordinary.

Hunter smiled as he thought to himself that Gideon and Xavier would be disappointed to find out Alexis was like any other woman in the world. Well, except for being stunning and wealthy.

By nearly midnight, the apartment had settled down. Lauren and Carla had gone to the room they'd share until someone put furniture in the fourth bedroom, and Alexis remained in her room with the door closed. Hunter hoped the place remained quiet so he could get at least a few hours of sleep before he had to wake up and start working on finding out just who the hell was stalking her and why.

He closed his eyes and began to drift off to sleep as thoughts of suspects preoccupied his mind.

"Hunter? Are you asleep?"

The sound of a voice that felt sort of familiar roused him from a deep sleep, and he sat bolt upright, startled to be awake in what seemed to still be the middle of the night, if the darkness around him was any indication.

Scrubbing the sleep from his face, he quickly sized up the situation around him. His gun sat on the floor next to the couch, easily within reach if he needed it. Alexis stood next to the couch staring down at him, but other than her, no one else was around. No lights were on in the living room, but in the dim light from the hallway he saw she wore a pair of jean shorts that showed off her great legs and a red tank top with no bra.

All of this raced through his brain as he woke up in a matter of seconds. When he finally had a sense of where he was, he looked up at her and asked, "Is something wrong?"

She didn't answer him and instead asked him her own question. "What are you doing sleeping on the couch? Why didn't you go with the rest of the bodyguards?"

After she finished speaking, she turned on the table light and sat down in a chair opposite the couch, casually folding her long, tan legs underneath her.

Had she woke him up to ask him why he was

sleeping?

"I need to be close to you if I'm going to protect you and find out who's stalking you, Alexis."

He watched as a confused look came over her. "But you can't sleep here on the couch."

"I told you that's what I was going to do when we talked earlier."

"I know, but I figured you'd go with the others until we got things straightened out here."

"I'm fine. I don't require much more than a place to lay my head for a few hours each night."

Alexis leaned forward, clearly interested in what he'd just said. "You don't sleep much?"

He shook his head. "Haven't for a long time. Goes back to my time on the force."

"Me neither," she said, frowning. "Some nights I'm lucky to get two or three hours of sleep."

Hunter studied her face and wondered how she could look so beautiful getting so little sleep. Maybe she did something with makeup to make her look that way, but she seemed so natural and unmade up. Then again, he knew nothing of how women made themselves look the way they did. He just appreciated the final outcome.

"Is that because of the letters you've been getting?" he asked.

"No. I haven't been able to sleep much ever

since my modeling days. Everyone tells me I should take something to help me get to sleep, but I won't."

"Why not?" he asked, curious why she'd choose to not go to sleep.

"That's a road to ruin," she said, shaking her head. "I don't want to become addicted to anything. Not sleeping pills or anything like that."

Her strength came through loud and clear, impressing him. It would have been nothing for her to have doctors giving her whatever she wanted for anything that ailed her. That she didn't showed Hunter he'd been wrong about her. She wasn't the person he thought she was when he first got this assignment.

"That's smart. Lots of stars have gotten trapped in that world. They don't come back from it sometimes."

She smiled. "I bet you're surprised to say that about me. That I'm smart."

Hunter shook his head, knowing his denial was at least a half-lie. "Why would you say that?"

"Because you probably thought I would be just another Hollywood diva and not very smart. I mean, I never went to college, but I'm no dummy, Hunter."

He didn't know what to say to that. He'd never judged her to be stupid. He hadn't even thought of her intelligence, in fact. The truth of the matter was like with many other beautiful women, he'd never considered her in any other way than what he saw of her looks in the tabloids and what he heard from Gideon and Xavier before he met her, and that had colored his view of her from the very beginning. Then when he saw her acting spoiled, that seemed to just reinforce what he'd already thought of her.

She fidgeted in her chair and began to look uncomfortable. A few seconds later, she stood and said, "I guess I'll go to bed now. Have a good night."

He watched her hurry away toward her room before he lay back down on the couch, unsure what to think of Alexis Marchand. He'd been prepared for a spoiled diva, but her strength and confidence surprised him. Staring up at the ceiling, he thought to himself that Gideon and Xavier had no idea of who Alexis really was.

A FLURRY OF activity woke him up a second time, but now at least he'd gotten a few more hours of sleep. Lauren and Carla rushed through the living room with arms full of office supplies, but Hunter's eyes weren't focused enough to ask why or really even care. Alexis sure had a way of keeping those women busy.

Whatever they were doing, he had to get a shower if he ever expected to wake up. And coffee.

But first, a shower. He grabbed his gun from the floor and stuffed it into his bag behind the couch before slinging it over his shoulder and heading toward the bathroom furthest away from the bedrooms.

As he passed by the office, he saw every piece of furniture had been moved out. Mumbling to himself, he said, "That explains why those two were running around with notepads and whiteboard markers."

Curious where everything had gone to, he backtracked down the hall and found Alexis's entire office stacked up in the dining room. Slowly waking up, he looked around and wondered why.

And where the hell was Alexis?

He'd find out soon enough, he felt pretty sure. Making his way back to the bathroom, he ran into Carla. "Where is Alexis?"

She stopped short and a box of pens fell to the floor. Crouching down, she scrambled to pick them up as she explained, "She and Lauren are downstairs waiting for a delivery. But don't worry. She had the guys here early to help her, so they're not alone."

"Help her with what?" he asked, happy at least that she'd listened to him about having her bodyguards around whenever she left the apartment.

Carla stood up to her full height and smiled. "Alexis decided she wanted new furniture. It's due here this morning, so she got the guys up early to help move it all in."

She hurried down the hall and ducked into the kitchen out of sight, leaving Hunter standing there in the hallway feeling disgusted. Last night, he thought he'd seen a different side to Alexis, but he'd been wrong. She was exactly what he expected when he got this assignment.

A spoiled diva who thought waking up an entire group of men to move her furniture because she wanted to redo her office was anything close to okay.

Spoiled and bored.

He wanted nothing to do with that shit. Closing the bathroom door behind him, he stripped and let himself enjoy a hot shower as he tried to put all he'd thought about Alexis hours before out of his mind. He should have known better than to let himself think she could be more than a shallow movie star.

People were what they were. They couldn't be blamed for that, even if Hunter felt disappointed that Alexis had turned out to be merely what the rest of the world thought she was.

Well, maybe not that bad since he had no evidence of her sleeping with a married man or refusing to help a poor relative. It didn't matter who Alexis Marchand was anyway. He had a job to do, so he'd do it. He didn't have to like or respect her.

After the longest shower he'd gotten to enjoy in months, Hunter headed toward the kitchen and the smell of coffee brewing. On his way, he saw the bodyguards moving furniture into the room that had been Alexis's office.

But what they carried in wasn't a new desk or anything else for an office. He still hadn't seen Alexis yet that morning, so he asked one of them, "Who's with Alexis?"

The man whose name he didn't remember at the moment wiped the sweat from his brow and pointed down the hall. "No one. She's in her room."

At least he didn't have to worry about that or chasing her down somewhere. The whole furniture thing still disgusted him, so he walked to the kitchen for a much-needed cup of coffee. It probably wouldn't put him in a better mood about everything, but at least it would help him shake the last bit of sleep from his head.

Thankfully, everyone else in the house seemed preoccupied doing Alexis's busy work, so he could drink his coffee alone. Staring out the window in the living room, he watched as the people of the Upper West Side headed off toward work or school or wherever they may have been going. He doubted many of them had the luxury of living in a penthouse apartment like Alexis and her assistants, and yet he suspected those people appreciated what they had more than she did.

"The sooner I find out who's stalking her and finish this assignment, the better."

When he finished his coffee and the last trace of sleep had left him, he walked back toward the kitchen to start his day. He needed to get copies of those letters from the LAPD first. A call to his old partner would do the trick. Mike never had a problem helping him on cases when he could, and Hunter doubted this time would be any different. If anything, he suspected the LAPD would be happy for the help to get this case off their desks since the longer it remained unsolved, the worse it looked for them.

While he stood at the sink reminiscing about his days back in LA, Alexis joined him in the kitchen. She tapped him on the shoulder, and he turned to see her all smiles for him.

"Good morning, Hunter. Come and see what just arrived!" she said excitedly.

But he had no interest in seeing anything. He didn't want to have to stand around staring at her purchases and complimenting her on the early morning shopping haul.

"I'm good. I'm sure if you've seen one room, you've seen them all," he said, dismissing her as he washed his coffee cup.

Unfortunately, that answer didn't dissuade her. She grabbed his arm as he turned to leave, and he looked down with surprise at where her hand sat. She may have been used to everyone around her fawning all over her expensive things, but he had no interest in joining her this morning.

Smiling up at him, she said, "I really want you to see it. I insist!"

There was no point in fighting her, and if he ever wanted to get to work, he figured it would be easier to just go along with her on this. He'd pretend to like whatever she showed him, and then he'd be free to get on with his day.

Alexis tugged his arm to lead him to the room, stopping in front of the door. Turning to face him, she beamed, "I can't wait to show you this."

Forcing a smile, he nodded. "Okay. I'm here, so let's see it."

She opened the door and there in front of him he saw a brand new bedroom set, ready for whoever would stay there. Lauren hurried around the bed finishing up as she straightened the tan and white bedspread.

"Well, what do you think?" Alexis asked, her eyes wide and hopeful.

"It's nice," Hunter said, not really caring

about her furniture buying spree.

She walked into the room and spread her right arm out like those models on game shows did when they showed off the prizes contestants could win. With a huge smile, she said, "It's yours."

Hunter could honestly say he'd been rendered speechless very few times in his life, and most of those times involved something horrible and grisly on the job. Now, as he stood there in the doorway to the room she'd made for him, no words came.

She'd left him speechless.

And no woman had ever done that to him.

Chapter Seven

Lauren looked at Alexis and mouthed, "Why isn't he saying anything?"

She didn't have an answer for her assistant. She thought giving up her office so he could have somewhere of his own in the apartment would make him happy. When she saw him sleeping on her couch like some uninvited visitor, she instantly knew she wanted to change that.

Didn't he like that what she'd done?

Alexis looked over at him as he stood as still as statue in the doorway, no expression on his face at all. But in those beautiful dark green eyes she saw surprise registered in them.

After waiting for so long that it became uncomfortable to just stand there, she asked, "Do you like it? I thought since you don't plan to leave me alone while you're working on this case that you should at least have a proper bedroom. So I moved my office out so you could have this room all to yourself."

Hunter opened his mouth to speak, but no

words came out. She waited for him to say something, but he remained silent. As the seconds ticked by, she began to wonder if she should have even bothered trying to be nice if this was how he reacted to kindness.

Every moment he didn't say anything made her defensiveness ratchet up another notch. Finally, she said, "Well, say something. It's got to be better than sleeping on the couch, right?"

He avoided looking at her as he said, "You didn't have to do this."

She waited all that time for him to say something, and that's what he chose to tell her?

"I don't have to do anything. I wanted to do this."

When he didn't respond, she looked over at Lauren to at least see a friendly face. "I thought you'd like this, Hunter."

Again, he didn't look at her when he said, "I appreciate it. Thanks."

The way he said that without a hint of kindness or emotion hurt her feelings. She wanted to lash out, to tell him how his callous reaction to her effort made her feel, but she didn't want to give him the satisfaction of knowing he'd had that effect on her.

So she just barked at Lauren, "Let's go. We have things to do."

Her assistant rushed out of the room, and

Alexis followed her, steering them toward her bedroom. Closing the door behind them, she flopped down on her bed, disappointed at how her surprise had gone over.

"I want to get away from all these people and do something fun," she said as she threw her arm over her eyes.

Lauren sat down on the bed next to her and sighed. "Would you like me to get a driver so you can go shopping on Fifth Avenue today? You mentioned when we were back in LA that you'd want to do that when we got to New York."

"I don't want to go shopping. I don't want to buy anything else."

"What do you want to do then?"

Alexis lifted her arm and looked up at Lauren. "I want to see Atlantic City. I've never been there. I want to see the Boardwalk and walk on the beach. I miss the feel of sand between my toes."

"Atlantic City? I've never been there. I bet not many of the guys have either."

Sitting up, Alexis shook her head. "No, I just want it to be the two of us. We can see the sights, gamble, go to the beach. We have to do this!"

Lauren's eyes opened wide in surprise, and she shook her head like she couldn't believe what she'd just heard. "We can't go alone, Alexis. What if someone recognizes you? You'll only have me to protect you. What if that awful person who's stalking you finds us? I don't know what I'd do if you got hurt. I'd never forgive myself."

"I'm tired of constantly being watched like I'm some kind of China doll. I've been hidden away because of that bastard for way too long. I want to have fun with my best friend. Say you'll keep this secret. Say you'll do it!"

Always the more fearful of the two, Lauren shook her head as worry settled into her expression. "Alexis, you just got Hunter to help you. Shouldn't we at least tell him?"

The last thing she wanted to do was tell Hunter about this. Let him hang around here and do whatever he had to. She craved freedom from him and everyone else who wanted to hem her in.

"No! It's just going to be us girls. We'll wear wigs and sunglasses so nobody recognizes us. You get a driver and a car. I want to leave by nine."

Lauren still worried about the details. Frowning, she asked, "What are we going to tell everyone? We can't just leave without someone noticing."

Alexis had a plan to handle all of these issues. "Leave that up to me. Just make sure no one knows about the car. And get Carla to come in here. I need to talk to her."

Taking hold of her hands, Lauren looked into her eyes like she always did when she worried Alexis was about to make a huge mistake. "Are you sure we should do this?"

"Yes. We deserve to have some fun. Real fun and not that supervised bullshit like we're children. Don't worry. We're competent women. All we're doing is going to the beach. No big deal. You'll see. It'll be great fun."

But Lauren wasn't convinced. "I don't want to see you get hurt. Promise me if we get into any trouble that we'll call Hunter. If you promise me that, I'll do whatever you want."

Although Alexis had no intention of calling him about anything, she faked a smile and nodded her agreement to Lauren's terms. "I promise. But we won't need to because nothing's going to happen. We're just going to enjoy a day at the beach like two friends."

"Okay, but it's fall, Alexis. This place isn't like LA. Isn't it going to be too cold to go to the beach?"

She had a point. October in New York City had been a little cooler than they were used to, and the weather at Atlantic City probably wouldn't be any warmer. It didn't matter, though. They didn't need to go in the water. She just wanted to enjoy being near the ocean again and out of the house and away from under the watchful eye of everyone.

"We'll be fine. Just bring a sweater. Now go get Carla for me and find us a driver. But remember, don't let anyone know what we're doing. Got it?"

Lauren hesitated for a moment, but Alexis knew she'd agree to whatever she wanted. She never had told her no before. She wasn't going to start today. Not on something so small.

"Okay. I'll do it. I just hope we don't get into trouble."

As she trotted out into the hallway to find Carla, Alexis thought about how much she hated that she thought they would get into trouble. She was a grown adult, a successful woman with enough money to do anything she wanted in the world. Why should she have to ask anyone for permission to do any damn thing she wanted to do?

A minute later, Carla opened the door a crack and poked her head in. "Lauren said you wanted to see me?"

"Yes! Come in. I want to talk to you," Alexis said, enthusiastically waving her in.

She stopped at the foot of the bed and meekly smiled. "Is everything okay, Alexis? Did I do something wrong?"

"No, no! Come! Sit down with me. I need your help with something important."

"Really?" she asked as she sat down on the bed next to her boss.

"I have a very important job for you, Carla. I

need you to do exactly as I say, okay?"

Carla's dark eyes opened wide as she nodded eagerly. "Okay. What do I have to do?"

Alexis took hold of her trembling hands. Giving them a gentle squeeze, she said, "I need you to distract Hunter for me. I want you to find him and keep him busy for as long as you can near your room. He can't know I'm leaving the house."

"You're leaving?" she asked in a voice full of fear.

"It's okay. I'll be fine. I'll have Lauren with me. Now I need you to distract Hunter until at least nine-fifteen and then pretend like I've locked myself in my room and won't come out. Stand outside the door begging me to talk and stuff like that. Make it believable. I'm counting on you, Carla."

"What if he finds out you're not really in your room?"

Alexis believed Carla could be trusted, even if she worried about her acting not being good enough to fool Hunter. Reassuring her, she said, "Don't worry. I just need you to keep him busy and away from this side of the house. After that, it won't be difficult to convince him I'm in my room. It's not like he'll actually check. Got it?"

Carla nodded, although it was obvious she didn't have any faith in her acting abilities. "Got it."

"Good. I knew I could count on you. Now remember, go keep him distracted and away from this side of the apartment until at least nine-fifteen."

"I will. I promise."

She stood up to leave, but Alexis grabbed her by the wrist. "No matter what, no one is to know I'm gone."

"Okay. I'll do my best. Where are you guys going?"

Smiling, Alexis lay back on her pillows. "Atlantic City. I hear they have delicious salt water taffy. I'll bring you some back."

"Thank you, Alexis. I won't let you down. Hunter won't know a thing."

"Good. I know you'll do great."

Carla left, so Alexis sprang into action, stuffing a bag with the brunette wig she used whenever she went out and didn't want to be recognized and an extra dark wig, two pair of big sunglasses, and a grey sweater for her and a black one for Lauren. She couldn't wait to be back at the beach again and smell the salty air. It had been too long since she filled her lungs with that delicious scent.

At just before nine, Lauren knocked on the bedroom door and stuck her worried face in. "The car is going to be here in just a minute. I told them to wait outside and not come into the building."

Slinging the bag over her shoulder, Alexis beamed at Lauren's sneakiness. "Perfect! I knew you'd take care of it. You ready for a day at the beach?"

"I just hope we don't get caught."

"Caught doing what? Having a good time? Doing things two single adult women should be able to do whenever they damn well please?"

She'd had enough of being held prisoner by people who wanted to protect her and some guy who thought he could upend her life every time he felt the urge to send her a letter. To hell with them. She was going to go to the beach, and she was going to enjoy every minute of it.

"How are we going to make it down the hall and to the car, Alexis? The bodyguards are already here."

Leaning in, she whispered in Lauren's ear, "I've got a plan. Just watch."

Before she closed her bedroom door, she locked it from the inside. Then they crept quietly down the hallway toward the elevator, listening to Carla talking to Hunter on the other side of the house.

The plan was working!

Just then as they reached the elevator to go downstairs, one of her bodyguards who rarely ever spoke to her came up behind them. She turned around to see Kevin standing there looking confused.

"Excuse me, Alexis, but we got all the office furniture moved into the new room."

She hadn't planned on this part, so she had to improvise as well as any actress could. In barely more than a whisper, she told him, "I made a mistake. I need the office furniture put in the hallway for now because I'm going downstairs to accept delivery of more bedroom furniture. I need you guys to hurry, so no taking a break before all the office furniture is put out into the hallway. Got it?"

He looked even more confused than before, but that didn't matter. He and his fellow bodyguards would create such chaos for the next half hour or so as they moved her office furniture from the bedroom to the hallway, and she and Lauren would be able to get away in the mess.

"Okay. We'll get on it right now."

When he and all the other bodyguards filed down the hall toward the dining room, she tugged on Lauren's arm to get her into the elevator. As the doors closed, Alexis heard Carla still droning on about something with Hunter and keeping him occupied just as she'd told her to.

"I'm going to get that girl the biggest box of salt water taffy the world has ever seen," she said, squeezing Lauren's hand in excitement. They were so close to freedom!

The seconds ticked by as they dropped slowly down to the main floor of the building. Alexis stared at the buttons, terrified at any moment she'd see the penthouse button light up.

But it never did. Carla had succeeded in keeping Hunter a captive audience, and the bodyguards were too busy moving more furniture to notice she and Lauren had escaped.

As if fate had decided to be on their side, the doorman and security guard were preoccupied in some argument about some game the night before, so the two women walked right out the front door without anyone asking a single question. They rushed out onto the sidewalk and saw the driver standing by the black Town Car waiting for them.

"Oh, my God, Alexis! We did it!" Lauren squealed as they ran toward the car.

"Of course we did. We're two clever women!"

Out of the corner of her eye, Alexis saw a man rush up toward them. She turned in fear and saw one of the paparazzi next to her snapping a picture. Covering her face with her hand, she had a feeling of relief that it was only a photographer and not her stalker.

"Alexis! Alexis! Where are you going? How do you like New York City? How long will you be here?"

The driver opened the back passenger door for them as more paparazzi began to show up to pepper her with questions. As they crowded her and snapped their pictures, Alexis and Lauren climbed into the backseat. Seconds later, the car sped away as they giggled about how exciting the whole thing had been.

"Atlantic City, here we come!" Alexis said as she flopped back onto the seat, happy to once again be free.

CHAPTER EIGHT

FOR THE FOURTH time, Carla explained how her aunt had a dream that Alexis might be in danger from someone six months ago. The woman seemed to think her relative had some kind of prophetic powers or something that helped her predict events. Her claim sounded like a pretty general one that could be made about virtually anyone, especially an actress as famous as Alexis.

Hunter watched as her dark eyes darted back and forth between him and the direction of Alexis's room. He suspected she worried at any moment her boss might bellow and she'd have to go running.

"And then when she began getting the letters, my aunt told me that I should be careful too. She said one night she woke up in a cold sweat because she had seen me instead of Alexis as the victim in the dream. I swear, she sounded like she'd seen a ghost when she called me that morning," Carla said, flailing her hands as she spoke.

"I don't think you have to worry, Carla. I'm not going to let anyone get hurt. I promise you that."

"But you're only here to protect Alexis. I know that. She's the star. I'm just some girl who works for her. What if someone came after me or Lauren? I worry that we'd be vulnerable and no one would want to help us."

What had gotten her so excited about this? Had another letter come?

The thought of that made him pay attention suddenly. "Carla, did Alexis get another letter or package from the stalker?"

She shook her head quickly so her long black hair swung around her head. "No, no. She's fine. She didn't get anything since that snow globe. No, I'm just worried that my aunt is right."

"Well, I swear to you there's nothing to worry about. I promise that I plan to find this stalker and stop him. You don't have to worry, and if anything happens to you or Lauren, I won't stand idly by. I'm not going to let any of you get hurt."

He turned to leave, but Carla's hand clamped down on his forearm. Looking back at her, he saw real fear in her eyes.

"Wait! I want to show you something."

Hunter's suspicious mind began to wonder if Carla had something to do with the stalker. She seemed far too nervous and frightened, but about what?

"What's wrong?"

Tugging on his arm to pull him toward her bedroom, she said, "In my room. The windows."

He let her take him into the room as she explained, "I want you to look at them. To make sure no one can break in."

"Break in? Into a penthouse? We're nineteen floors up. Who's breaking in? Spiderman? Some other superhero?" he asked, only slightly kidding with the superhero crack.

She ignored his joke and walked him over to the window on the far wall. Opening it toward her, she shook it frantically. "I don't think there's even a lock on it. Is that safe?"

As much as he didn't think a window this high up would be an issue, he humored her and pretended to examine it. After a few seconds, he smiled. "I think it's safe. No need to worry."

Carla looked at her cell phone and then back at him. "Okay. I just wanted to be sure. I better go check to see if Alexis has anything she wants me to do this morning. She's been very busy so far, so I'm sure she does."

Just as she wanted him so badly to check out the window in her room, now she practically pushed him out into the hallway. Then without saying another word, she ran away down the hall, leaving him confused about the whole thing.

Had all that really been necessary?

Hunter thought about it and wondered if she'd been trying to flirt with him. At least that made some sense. Worrying about someone scaling a New York City high rise apartment building to break in through a bedroom window hundreds of feet up didn't.

As all of that rambled around his brain, he headed to the kitchen to get another cup of coffee. Maybe more caffeine would help him understand these people. He stood at the counter and listened to Carla talking to Alexis through her bedroom door and decided he was surrounded by crazy people. One minute Alexis was buying an entire bedroom set and moving all her office furniture out so he could have a room to stay in, and the next minute she was hiding out in her room and forcing her assistant to talk to her through a door.

"Must be a Hollywood thing," he said, knowing all too well how bizarre movie stars could be.

He did have to admit that what she did for him with the bedroom after seeing him sleeping on the couch last night had been a really nice gesture.

"Alexis, talk to me. What's wrong?" Carla asked.

Hunter listened but heard no response.

Was she having a temper tantrum?

"Honey, is Lauren in there with you?"

At that moment, Hunter wished Gideon or Xavier had been the one chosen for this assignment. He didn't work well in a nuthouse. If only he was back at the estate and one of them had to deal with this nonsense.

"Just tell me what you need. Tell me and I'll do whatever you want," Carla said, pleading with her employer.

Hunter had listened to enough of this. He needed to find some peace and quiet. Thankfully, he had a room now he could escape to.

One step out of the kitchen told him it wouldn't be easy getting to that room, however, since the bodyguards had been acting like moving men again and had piled up Alexis's entire office in the hallway. They stood in front of all the furniture talking, as if the scene in front of them seemed normal.

"We got all the furniture out of the other bedroom. Alexis was in a big hurry, so I want to tell her we got it done."

Looking over the desk and chair stacked up against the wall, Hunter wondered why Carla didn't tell her they'd finished or ask Alexis why she wanted everything out in the hallway. The bodyguards began walking toward the elevator, squeezing past Hunter as he stood in the doorway to the kitchen.

Curious why Kyle didn't stop at Alexis's room, he said, "You're going the wrong way. She's in her room."

The bodyguard looked confused. "Oh yeah? I guess she's done with the furniture downstairs then. Where'd they put it?"

Hunter pointed in the direction of his room. "Right in there."

Kyle looked around and then shook his head. "No, I know about that furniture. We moved that in early this morning. She told Kevin she had another delivery coming, so after having us move everything in her office out of that room and into one of the bedrooms, she decided she wanted it all out of there and into the hallway instead. She said she was in a big hurry too."

Damn, she liked to abuse these poor men. Hunter was thankful he wasn't one of her lapdogs.

"Sounds like a lot of work," he mumbled as he started to make his way toward his room.

The bodyguard headed toward the elevator but returned a few seconds later to ask Carla, "She's in there now? Where's the furniture that was supposed to be delivered?"

Hunter listened for Carla's answer, curious why there was so much confusion about a simple thing like a furniture delivery, but she didn't say a thing. He made his way down toward Alexis's room and waited for her to ask the bodyguard's question through the door, but she didn't do that either.

Something felt very wrong about this.

Confusion bred danger, and having all these people moving around made Hunter uncomfortable. All these deliveries meant strangers showing up and possibly entering the apartment.

He hurried toward the elevator and rode down to the main floor to find out exactly when this new furniture would be brought up. The doorman and security guard stood at their post just inside the front door talking like usual.

"Hey, I need to know when the second furniture delivery arrives. Alexis said she was in a hurry for her guys to move things around up there, so it should be any time. Can you check what time she gave you?"

The doorman, an elderly man called Chambers with silver hair and a long serious face, stared at Hunter. "Another delivery?"

"Yeah, yeah. I know. How does anyone fit that much furniture in one penthouse? Trust me. It's already piling up in the hallways up there," Hunter said, not even trying to hide his disgust.

How the hell had he been relegated to furniture delivery scheduler for some movie star?

The doorman flipped through the papers on the desk in front of him and then looked up at Hunter. "I don't have a second delivery, sir. Just the one earlier this morning. Miss Marchand didn't mention anything about another delivery when she left earlier either."

Hunter stood there stunned. Left? Why is Carla talking to her bedroom door then?

"When did she leave?"

"Right before nine. She and her assistant."

"Do you know where they were going?" he asked, his concern growing by leaps and bounds at every passing second.

"I don't know, sir. We were talking and saw them walk out and get into a car. Then they drove away."

Hunter turned to rush back up to the penthouse, but the doorman stopped him. "Sir, Miss Marchand received a letter right after she left."

Stopping dead in his tracks, he spun around. "A letter? Who brought it? Does the mail get here this early in the morning?"

The doorman held it up for Hunter to see. "No, it didn't come through the post office. This letter was hand delivered."

At that moment, Hunter's blood felt like it ran cold. A hand delivered letter? Had the stalker been here at the building today?

"Did you see who delivered it?" he asked as he took the white envelope from the doorman. "Can you give me a description of the person?"

He looked over at the security guard for some help, but he just shook his head. "No, I'm sorry sir. We were talking and then someone else in the building had a bit of an issue with a delivery, so we got tied up. We, unfortunately, didn't see anyone."

Damnit! If this letter was from the stalker, he or she had gotten entirely too close to Alexis. Christ, they may have been right next to her as she left to go God only knew where.

Hunter turned and raced through the lobby toward the elevator. Frantically pressing the button to return to the penthouse, he tried to keep calm as every fiber of his being raged at Alexis and Lauren's childish bullshit. The whole ride up, he stewed over Alexis leaving without telling him, and as each floor passed, he realized the whole thing with Carla earlier was just a way to distract him so the two of them could sneak out.

The elevator reached the top floor, and before the doors had even opened all the way, Hunter yelled, "Carla! Tell me where they went!"

She still stood outside Alexis's bedroom door acting like there was someone on the other side. He stormed down the hallway getting angrier with each step at seeing her still pretending. By the time he reached her, she stared at him with wide eyes filled with fear.

"I need to know where she went, Carla. Someone's stalking her and might see her alone and unprotected. She's in danger."

Carla's eyes filled with tears, and she looked down, avoiding his gaze. "I didn't know. She told me to keep you busy."

"Why? Where did she go, Carla?" he bellowed, tired of the games these people insisted on playing.

She looked up at him and sobbed, "Atlantic City."

Fucking Atlantic City! Alexis and Lauren alone without any protection in fucking Atlantic City.

God only knew how many people might have access to her there. The stalker could very well find her and Lauren all alone without even a single bodyguard there to protect her.

Hunter hurried to his room to get his cell. He needed her manager's help on this. He knew her better than anyone. Anyone but Lauren.

"Paul, I need a car right now. Alexis snuck out with Lauren and they're on their way to Atlantic City right now. They've got about an hour head start."

"Jesus Christ! Atlantic City? Okay, I got this.

I'll have a car there in less than thirty. Damnit, Lexi!" Paul said in utter frustration.

"Any idea why she went there?" Hunter asked. "Does she know someone there she's going to see?"

"No. I don't know why anyone would want to go to Atlantic City, to be honest."

"Maybe the beach?"

Paul sighed. "Maybe. She does miss living out in LA so close to the beach. Hell, she might want to gamble for all I know. What I don't understand is why she didn't just tell all of you. Why put herself in danger like this?"

"I have no idea. I just know the longer she and Lauren are alone, the bigger chance there is that someone could get to them. Someone like the guy stalking her. Just get me that car so I can find her before he does."

"Got it. I'll have it there in a few."

Hunter tossed his phone onto his bed and began to pace back and forth. Why the hell had she done something so reckless and stupid? He thought they'd connected on some level with their conversation during the night and then with the bedroom surprise. What the hell had happened to make her act like this?

Then he looked down at the envelope in his hand and knew this little stunt of hers could be much worse. Carefully, he opened the flap and slid the letter out. Ordinarily, he would have preferred to have gloves on to preserve any fingerprints, but if the LAPD hadn't found any on the previous letters, he had no reason to think there would be any on this new one.

Laying it flat on his dresser, his heart sank at the sight of letters jaggedly cut out from magazines in the stalker's latest letter to her.

I HOPE YOU'RE LOVING NEW YORK AS MUCH AS I AM. I LIKE LA BETTER, THOUGH. WHEN ARE WE GOING BACK THERE, ALEXIS? SEE YOU SOON.

Had the stalker been in LA when she lived there and moved here when she did? He flipped over the envelope and saw no postmark, so he had no way of knowing where the stalker was now.

If only the doorman and the security guard downstairs in the lobby hadn't been so fucking interested in talking about whatever idiotic topic they obsessed about that day, they might have been able to tell him what the person who delivered the letter looked like. Were they a male or female? Young or old? Was it the stalker himself or had he or she given it to someone else, say a delivery service, to drop off?

And even more, if Alexis hadn't duped her bodyguards to sneak out, those men may have seen someone drop the letter off. What the hell was wrong with her?

He didn't have the answers to any of his questions. All he knew was every minute she didn't have anyone protecting her, she was in real danger that her stalker would find her. The thought of that happening made his stomach twist into a knot.

And not just because Persephone would have his head if he lost a client.

Chapter Nine

THE CAR STOPPED about a block away from the Boardwalk and the driver looked up at the rear view mirror. Smiling, he said, "We're here, miss. You said you wanted to get as close to the beach as possible, so here we are."

Alexis looked out the window and saw the Boardwalk in the distance. Never before had she been so excited to see something so ordinary. She'd seen boardwalks before in California, but this one held a special feeling for her because it symbolized her first attempt at breaking free.

Free from her stalker. Free from her home. Free from everyone's rules about how she was supposed to act now that she might be in danger.

She didn't want to think about any of that today, though. This day was for fun with her best friend.

Turning to look at Lauren, she smiled in anticipation. "You ready?"

She nodded and straightened Alexis's long brown wig. "I guess. I'll follow you."

"We'll be back at this spot at three o'clock, Jeff. See you then!"

"Yes, miss," he said as they piled out of the backseat into the sunny day that awaited them.

The two women bolted toward their destination, their bags on their shoulders bouncing around as they ran. Alexis hadn't felt this free in forever. At least since she left modeling for acting. She loved the sense of independence that rushed through her as she and Lauren ran up the little street leading to the Boardwalk.

"The first thing I want to do is bury my feet in the sand!" she said with a giggle. "I need to feel the sand against my skin again."

"Alexis, slow down!" Lauren cried as she fell behind. "I'm not in shape like you are."

She stopped just as she reached the stairs to the Boardwalk and waited for her friend. Alexis didn't want to stop for anything, but for Lauren, she'd slow down a little.

Looking up, she watched people's feet and legs as they walked by. She shifted her weight from one foot to the other, anxious to get moving again, turning to see where Lauren could be. Still a few hundred yards away, she walked far too slowly for Alexis.

"Come on! We only have four hours!" she yelled to her.

"I'm coming. Give me a minute."

Too impatient to give up another moment, Alexis waved her on. "I'll meet you at the top. Don't dawdle. We have too much to get to today!"

She took the stairs two at a time and reached the top just as Lauren yelled up from the bottom, "Wait for me!"

Alexis scanned the scene in front of her, loving this place. The beach and ocean lay just a few yards away, closer than she'd been to the water in far too long. Looking down, she saw real wood beneath her feet. A real wood boardwalk like she'd seen in the movies. She'd just assumed that had changed and they'd gone to something vinyl instead.

Lauren joined her, and as she struggled to catch her breath, Alexis pointed down at the Boardwalk. "It's real wood! How cool is that?"

Confused by her excitement, her assistant didn't even bother to look down. "I thought they all were made of wood. Isn't that what makes them boardwalks, after all?"

"Let's go! I want to hit the beach first before we do anything else," Alexis said, tugging Lauren's arm to make sure she kept up this time.

They ran across the wooden planks and down the stairs to the beach, dropping their bags in the sand. Although the calendar said October, the temperature still hovered in the low sixties, warm enough for Alexis to dip her toes into the water just to feel it against her skin.

They slid their shoes off and tossed them behind as they stepped into the ocean. Both looked down in shock at how chilly the water felt, so after just a few seconds, they ran back to grab their shoes and head to where they dropped off their bags.

Flopping down onto the sand, Alexis buried her feet beneath it and laughed. "I haven't felt water that cold since we were kids in Minnesota. This definitely isn't LA."

Lauren covered her hands with the ends of the sleeves on her sweater and folded her arms across her chest. "Definitely not. I know it's probably above sixty now, but it's chilly."

"Oh, that's just because your feet are cold. Put them under the sand like I did. You'll get warm."

Alexis tilted her head back and closed her eyes to let the heat of the sun hit her face. This place wasn't LA, but it was still pretty damn wonderful.

"This feels so incredible. I'm so glad we did this. Aren't you?" she asked her friend.

When Lauren didn't answer, she opened her eyes and looked over at her sitting there nervously looking around instead of enjoying herself. "What are you doing?"

"I'm looking."

"For what?"

She didn't say anything, but Alexis knew what worried her. Lauren feared the stalker even more than she did. She loved her for that, but today wasn't the day for worry.

Tugging her arm so she'd lie down in the sand, she said, "Just relax. No one noticed us or even cares. Let yourself enjoy the sun hitting your face and the sand all around you. Pretend this is our very own private beach."

"I just worry. Maybe we should have told Paul or Hunter. What if someone sees us?"

"Then we talk to them. If they're hot guys, we definitely talk to them."

Lying there, she felt just like she used to back home in LA with the sun beating down on her and the sand between her toes. She'd missed that so much.

Lauren, however, couldn't seem to get comfortable. Nudging her, she said, "Those people over there are looking at us. What do we do?"

Opening her eyes, Alexis looked around but saw no one looking at them. "Jeez, Lauren. You're such a worry wart. Trust me. In this wig, nobody knows it's me, so we're just two girls relaxing on the beach. Stop acting guilty and no one will even care we're here."

She knew her friend likely wouldn't relax, but that's exactly what she needed. For as stressed as her life was, Lauren's sometimes seemed even worse. As her assistant, she helped Alexis with every aspect of her life, but even more, she worried about her more than anyone else in her world. Alexis wanted her to enjoy this day as much as she was.

Closing her eyes again, she let the stress of the past few months ebb away and wished her best friend could have the same relief. It felt incredible to sit out in the open under the sun and just let go of all the bad.

In truth, little of her life could ever be considered truly bad. She knew that. She had more money than she'd ever dreamed of. She could go anywhere and do anything she liked. She could buy anything her heart desired.

But more often than not, her fame kept her trapped in her home. It wasn't the worst hardship in the world, but it wasn't what she thought life would be like before she became famous.

She'd always dreamed of traveling the world and meeting glamorous people. She'd achieved all that and more. When she began modeling, she dreamed of becoming an actress and showing the world she was more than just a pretty face.

Nowadays, she dreamed of just being happy and not having to spend every day under the watchful eyes of people who believed danger lurked around every corner. Of having the chance to walk out of her house and simply go to the corner store or to the park.

Or the beach for a few hours with her nearest and dearest friend.

For fifteen minutes, she worked to empty her mind of everything. The stalker. Moving away from her home. Hunter. All of it. For the first time in too long, she truly relaxed.

Lauren touched her on the arm, rousing her from daydreaming about absolutely nothing. "We forgot to put on sunscreen. I think my nose is starting to burn, Alexis. Can we get out of the sun?"

Obviously, her friend hadn't been able to find a way to relax. Giving in, she sat up. "Fine. We'll go. Get your stuff."

Sad to have to leave the beach so soon, she grabbed her bag and headed back toward the stairs. Lauren hurried to catch up with her as she started to walk down the Boardwalk, reading each sign and inhaling the smell of greasy French fries and sugary sweet cotton candy as they passed a food stand.

"Where are we going?" Lauren asked breathlessly, still not fully recovered from running up the stairs.

Alexis took her hand and swung their arms back and forth. Smiling, she said, "I don't know, and that's the best part. All I know is I want to eat some popcorn and salt water taffy and drink lemonade. And after I do that, then I want to ride that rollercoaster next to the water and head into a casino to gamble."

Her explanation earned her a timid smile. Lauren always worried needlessly about things. But she wouldn't let that ruin their day.

"Don't worry. We're fine. We're on the Boardwalk in Atlantic City, and oh my God! Look at that!"

"What? What is it?" Lauren asked in a panicked voice.

She dropped her hand and pointed at the flashing lights on the Ripley's Believe It or Not sign about a block ahead of them. "That's the place where they have all those freaky things like bearded ladies and midget horses!"

"Bearded ladies? What are you talking about?"

"Yes!" Alexis squealed. Pulling Lauren down the Boardwalk, she said excitedly, "Come on! Let's go see some freaky stuff!"

A HALF HOUR later, they walked out of the Ripley's exhibit and back out into the sun. Seeing the shrunken heads and a wax figure of the world's tallest man, among other bizarre things, had calmed Lauren enough so she could laugh about how wild that place had been.

"That was the weirdest bunch of things I've

ever seen," she said.

Alexis looked down the Boardwalk for where to go to next. At that moment, a craving for something sweet and chocolatey came over her. Turning to face Lauren, she said, "I want fudge. Do you think they sell fudge anywhere here?"

"I don't know, but now I want some too," Lauren said as she headed toward the stores in front of them.

"I'm having so much fun," Alexis said as she peered into the store windows looking for candy. "I needed this so much. I'm so tired of living like a butterfly under glass."

She stopped in front of a white building and pointed at the window. "There's our fudge. I bet I can get some salt water taffy here too. See the boxes stacked up on the counter? I promised Carla I'd bring her some back."

They walked into the store and stopped dead in the doorway as the intoxicating smell of sugar and chocolate hit them. Alexis rarely indulged in sweet treats because once she had a little, she always wanted more. Today, she didn't care, though.

"Oh my God! This place smells like heaven!"

A group of tourists turned around and stared, so Lauren leaned over and whispered in her ear, "Let me get the fudge and taffy. We don't want anyone to recognize you. What kind do you want?"

Alexis craned her neck to look at the choices in the glass candy cases in front of them. "Get a pound of peanut butter fudge and a box of taffy for Carla."

"Okay. Wait for me over there near the shelves and keep your glasses on."

Lauren got in line and Alexis stepped back so she was out of the way of other customers. As she waited, she saw a couple come in holding hands. Around her age, they looked so carefree and happy, like they didn't have a trouble in the world. They talked and laughed about something, and she noticed how comfortable they appeared with one another.

She wanted to be in a relationship like that. One that she could feel comfortable enough to laugh and be herself with a man again. She hadn't been that way since the early days when she and Jackson began dating.

Tapping her on the shoulder, Lauren pulled her out of her thoughts. "Hey, let's go. If I stay here much longer, I'm going to gain ten pounds."

"Okay. Let's go back to the beach and gorge on peanut butter fudge."

The candy smelled so good they didn't even make it back to the beach before they opened up the little white box and each took out a piece of fudge. The sweet aroma of the chocolate and peanut butter combined with the salty scent of the ocean nearby to create the most incredible sensation as Alexis inhaled a deep breath of air.

And then the fudge hit her tongue and she knew she was as close to heaven as she'd ever been.

"Oh, this is so good," she said as Lauren nodded. "Who knew New Jersey had such great stuff?"

"No more until we get back down there and sit on the sand. I think I'm getting a sugar rush already," Lauren joked as she took the box of fudge and stuffed it back into the bag.

They hurried down the stairs and ran a little ways to a spot away from people playing Frisbee down closer to the water. Throwing their bags off to the side, they sat down and Lauren handed Alexis her third piece of fudge.

Like before, the moment it hit her tongue, the sweetness made her eyes roll back into her head. "That is so good. God, I could eat this all day."

"Me too, but we shouldn't," Lauren cautioned, putting the box of fudge away once again.

As they reveled in the decadent taste of the peanut butter fudge, a male's voice said, "Hey ladies! How would you like some company on this fine day?"

Lauren's hand clamped down on Alexis's

forearm, but Alexis opened her eyes and from behind her sunglasses looked up to see two young guys standing over them. One had blond hair that almost hit his shoulders and a great tan. She quickly let her eyes travel down from his head and liked what she saw. Great body with muscles and a nice face.

The other one had shorter, dark hair and wore sunglasses. Slightly thinner than his friend, he also had a nice tan, even if his body wasn't as good.

"We're just enjoying some fudge. What kind of company were you thinking of?" Alexis said with a smile, enjoying the flirtation with the two men.

Lauren looked over at her with horror in her eyes. "Alexis!"

The blond crouched down in front of them and touched her leg. "So your name is Alexis. A gorgeous name for a gorgeous woman."

Suddenly, fear began to overwhelm her. Her chest began to hurt, like someone was sitting on it, and she couldn't get enough air into her lungs. The blond was too close, his friend felt like he was looming over them, and Lauren kept squeezing her arm. It all became too much for her.

She pulled her legs up away from the blond and wrapped her arms around her knees. "No, thanks. We're going to be leaving soon."

"Yeah, we have to go," Lauren said nervously.

But neither man seemed to get the hint. The one standing in front of Lauren extended his hand to grab hers. "Come on. Loosen up."

She yanked her hand away from his hold as Alexis began to rock back and forth, burying her head in her knees to hide. "Just leave us alone."

A hand touched her chin to lift her head, and Alexis almost screamed. Swinging her hands in front of her to make him go away, she knocked her glasses off her face and her wig began to fall off. She knew instantly by the look of recognition on both men's faces that they knew exactly who she was.

As she frantically worked to straighten the wig and find her glasses, the blond said, "Holy shit! You're Alexis Marchand."

Everything began to spin out of control around her, and there on the wide open beach, she felt like the world was closing in on her. She put her head down and begged Lauren to make them go away.

"Leave her alone! Go away!" she shouted at the two of them.

"Can we get your autograph? We're huge fans. Just one autograph. And a picture. Nobody's going to believe we met you on the beach today if we don't get a pic," one of them said right next to Alexis's ear.

"Leave me alone!" she screamed, pushing her

hands out to make him go away.

Other people began to stop nearby and watch as the guys began to complain. Grabbing her hands, the dark haired one held her wrists tightly. "Don't be a bitch. We just want a picture and your autograph. You're not too good for that, are you?"

Then the other one began taunting her. "Chaz, I think she thinks she's too good to be seen with us. A big Hollywood actress too good to be hanging out with guys like us. Is that how it is?"

Alexis squeezed her eyes shut and shook her head, hoping they'd just go away. All she wanted to do was have a nice day at the beach with Lauren. She just wanted to eat some fudge and feel the sand between her toes. She never wanted to make anyone angry. She never wanted to even have anyone notice her.

Why couldn't they understand that? Why wouldn't they just go away and leave her be?

"Go away! We're not bothering anyone. Why won't you just leave us alone?" Lauren screamed.

"All we want is for her to not act like a stuck up bitch. Who does she think she is?" one of them snapped.

His words echoed in her head. *Bitch. Who does she think she is?*

With her face buried in her knees, she prayed

to God for someone to make them stop. She wasn't a bitch. She would never treat someone like they were treating her. Why didn't they understand she was a human being just like them?

Was it too much to ask for the world to understand she had feelings too?

Tears welled in her eyes as she rocked back and forth silently begging for it all to be over. Then she heard a third male voice and every muscle in her body tensed as she waited in terror for something to happen.

"Get away from her! Get the hell out of here!" the man bellowed.

She knew that voice. Looking up, she watched Hunter chase the two men off and then get rid of all the onlookers who had begun to gather around them. Embarrassed, she covered her face with her hands to avoid facing him.

This wasn't what she wanted to happen.

"We're going. Now," he said sternly.

Leaning over, Lauren whispered in Alexis's ear, "It's okay. Hunter's here. He made those guys go away. We're okay."

As she rubbed her back to make her feel better, she didn't know the truth, but Alexis did. Nothing was okay. All she'd wanted was a day away and to enjoy the sun at the beach for just a few hours with her best friend. She couldn't even have that now.

Chapter Ten

ALEXIS SAT HUDDLED over on the sand hiding her face as Lauren stood looking at Hunter with pure guilt in her eyes. She should feel guilty. An entire household had been sent into a tailspin because the two of them wanted to act like teenage runaways.

"Lauren, get her bag and start walking toward the car."

"Where is it?"

He pointed toward the street a block away and said nothing more to her. Everything he wanted to say wouldn't have been helpful at that moment anyway.

She ran off, and he crouched down in front of Alexis, who still hadn't said a word to him. She looked so frail, so broken sitting there hugging her knees to her chest, her face hidden so he couldn't see if she was crying.

"Alexis, we need to go," he said as gently as his mood would allow. "Don't worry. We'll get you out of here."

Scooping her up in his arms, he walked toward the steps nearby as he saw a few people point at them. Even with that brown wig, he would have known it was her, so it didn't surprise him strangers did too. Her face was too recognizable.

She curled up in his arms and hid her face in his shoulder as he walked silently across the Boardwalk and down the other set of stairs. Her body trembled against his chest, and every so often she let out a quiet sob. Other than that, she didn't make a move to fight him, something he was genuinely thankful for.

This moment didn't need to have an argument added to it.

They reached the car, and he set her down in the backseat before closing the door to see Lauren waiting to get in with her. Not this time, though. He wanted her alone for the ride back to the apartment.

"What are we going to do about the car that brought us here?" Lauren asked as she reached to open the car door.

Kyle and Malcolm walked toward him, so he pointed at her and told them, "Take Lauren and go with her in the car they came down in. I'll take Alexis. We'll meet back at the penthouse."

"But she needs me," Lauren said in a tearful voice. "It's my job to help her with this kind of thing."

"You already did enough, don't you think?" he said, barely able to contain his anger over what the two of them had done.

His accusation stunned her, and for a moment her mouth hung open as she struggled to find the words to say in response. Hunter knew this hadn't been Lauren's fault. He'd only been around Alexis for a short time, but he knew who called the shots.

Lauren followed. She didn't lead.

But at that moment, after hours of his emotions ping-ponging from angry to scared and then to furious when he saw them sitting there on the beach as two men harassed them, he couldn't separate his anger from his relief that he'd gotten there just in time.

As tears filled her eyes, she lowered her head and quietly said, "I would never do anything to hurt her. I swear I wouldn't, Hunter."

He felt for her. Of all the people in Alexis's world, Lauren saw as much of the awful parts of it as she did the good. If anyone deserved a break, it was her.

"I know. Just give me a little time alone with her."

She wiped her eyes and held out Alexis's bag. "Here. Give this to her. I put her fudge in there for her."

Hunter took the bag and tried not to be angry at her for still enabling Alexis even then. As he got into the car, he tossed it onto the passenger seat and looked up at the rearview mirror. Alexis sat curled up in a ball, her face once again hidden in her knees.

As much as he wished he could say something kind or sweet, all he wanted to do was lash out at her. She could have gotten herself hurt or even killed. Why wouldn't her stalker know she went off on her own without even a single goddamned bodyguard to fucking Atlantic City? He seemed to know her every move, and yet she ran off with no protection and just her best friend to shield her if anything happened.

Which, of course, it fucking did. What made her think she could just put on a brown wig and nobody would recognize one of the most beautiful women in the world? That unforgettable face had been on magazine covers in dozens of countries. How could she have thought she could ever just go sit on the beach like anyone else?

He drove off and headed up the Garden State Parkway, stewing over everything that had happened. As he settled into the drive, he looked up in the rearview mirror again and saw her still sitting there terrified. The sight of her curled up and rocking back and forth made his anger soften enough that he wanted to let her know she had him to protect her.

"It's okay. You're safe. You can relax now."

Alexis looked up and her gaze met his in the mirror. She stared at him with her big brown eyes still full of fear but didn't say a thing. She didn't look away before he turned back to focus on the road again, and as he navigated through traffic, he couldn't get the look in her eyes out of his mind.

The way she seemed so small and vulnerable back there did something to him he hadn't expected. Without even knowing when it happened, he realized now that he wanted to protect her more than just because it was his job.

The mere idea of her being hurt made his chest ache. That blond guy had his hands on her, and just the sight of that made him want to tear his head off.

As they slowed down for traffic, he grabbed her bag off the passenger seat and reached back to put it on the seat next to her. "Lauren said there was fudge in there."

She didn't say anything, and a few minutes later he looked back and saw she hadn't opened the bag either. Maybe he should have let Lauren come along with them. She seemed to be the only one who knew how to reach Alexis. Obviously, he couldn't.

The cars in front of him began to speed up as they passed a broken down car in the slow lane.

Hunter looked at his watch and saw it was two o'clock already. Most of his day had been spent either worried or angry.

Or a combination of both.

Now he felt strangely calm, like the relief of knowing she sat safely in the seat behind him made all the anger and worry fade away. Odd. He never thought of himself as emotional. In fact, back at the estate, he considered himself one of the more reserved of all the guys there. He certainly was no Gideon or Xavier with their yelling and arguing over sports all the time. And he definitely didn't act like Julian with his con man bullshit he liked to use to play tricks on people.

All this ran through his head, and he realized just how much being around Alexis had made him feel more of everything. First, it was disgust when he didn't know much about her. Then curiosity. Then worry and anger over her antics today. And now as he looked back at her while she slyly popped a piece of candy into her mouth and then looked around like she'd done something wrong, he felt protective.

He'd never felt that way about any other client, and more than one of them had been in far greater danger than her. Convinced the difference had to do with the circumstances of this case, he chalked up his changing emotions to her effect on everyone in her world. As soon as he finished this assignment, he'd go back to being his normal self.

At least he hoped he would. God help him, he couldn't continue feeling like this for much longer.

"I'm hungry. Can we stop somewhere?" Alexis asked in a quiet voice.

He looked up at her in the mirror. "This is the Garden State Parkway. You're not going to find a four star restaurant here."

She shrugged and then shook her head. "I don't care. I don't need that anyway. Just a burger would be great."

On the side of the road he saw a sign for the Forked River exit. "Two miles ahead we might be able to find something."

"Thank you, Hunter," she said softly.

She sounded so tiny he wondered if she was really okay after what happened back at the beach. As much as he wanted to know, though, he didn't ask.

He parked the car in the service plaza and turned around to face her. "It looks like you can have a hamburger, hot dogs, or pizza. They've got a Starbucks if you want coffee too. I'll get you whatever you want. Just stay here with the doors locked."

Alexis gave him a faint smile. "You don't have to worry. I'm not going anywhere."

"It's not you I'm worried about. It's everyone out here. Keep the doors locked while I'm gone, and I'll be right back. What do you want me to get you?"

"Just a burger, but tell them no pickles and no lettuce, please," she said after thinking about it for a moment.

"Do you want fries?"

"Oh, yeah. Definitely fries. I'm dying for French fries."

The way she sounded so thrilled to have fast food seemed almost charming. Hunter guessed she didn't get to enjoy things like that much, likely because if she ate like that all the time, she wouldn't have a gorgeous body like hers. Whatever the reason, the way her eyes lit up at the mention of fries made him smile.

"Anything to drink?" he asked with a chuckle.

"Just a diet soda, please."

"Okay. I'll be right back with all that. Don't open the doors for anyone but me."

And just as quickly as her mood had brightened, it darkened again. With a frown, she nodded. "I won't. Don't worry."

He didn't like seeing her sad like that, although he didn't know why it bothered him like it did. He barely knew her. Why should he give a damn how she felt?

"This is just a job," he said as he headed into

the service plaza building. "She's a client, and no matter what Persephone seems to think, my job isn't making people happy."

A busload of senior citizens milled around the doors, blocking access to the restaurants and making Hunter nervous. Alexis had already bolted one time that day. What was to stop her from doing it a second time?

In truth, he doubted she'd leave without someone to go with her. He'd had a sense from the moment he met her that being alone wasn't something she liked. If Lauren was sitting in that backseat with her, he'd have bet money on them taking off again, but alone?

No way. She wasn't stupid or even thoughtless. He had a feeling she was just tired of feeling trapped by her life. He could understand that, even if it pissed him off to no end that she'd forced an entire household of people to drop everything and search for her for hours.

As he pushed through the crowd of old people, he kept his eye on the doors. He may not have believed she'd run, but he put nothing past her. The woman had a free spirit he suspected didn't take to being caged like her life demanded.

Ten minutes later, he returned to the car with all she'd asked for and something for himself. Before he could hand her the food, she climbed into the front seat and sat down next to him.

Shyly, she said, "I thought it might be nice if I sat up here to eat."

She wouldn't look at him now, avoiding his gaze. Confused, he didn't give it much thought and handed her the burger, fries, and diet soda. "Bon appétit."

"Do you know French?" she asked as she unwrapped the burger and took a bite.

Hunter laughed. "No. I just know all the foreign words everyone else does and a few curses in Spanish. Well, more than just curses, but nothing I'd use around you."

"I'm not sheltered or ignorant, Hunter. You don't have to watch what you say around me. I'm a grown woman."

He took a bite of a French fry and washed it down with some soda. "I wouldn't say the things I know around you because it's not something a man should say around a woman."

His explanation stopped her talking until she finished her burger. After she crumpled up the wrapper into a tight ball and stuck it in the bag, she quietly said, "I'm sorry, Hunter. I shouldn't have run off like I did."

Residual anger kept him from responding to her apology, but out of the corner of his eye he saw her looking at him and waiting for him to say something. He didn't know what to say that wouldn't sound like he was scolding her, though.

Staring out at the parking lot in front of him, he asked, "How was the burger? I've had better. That's for sure."

"It's something. I think I used up all my energy when all that happened with those guys. I was pretty much running on a sugar high from the fudge anyway. If I didn't get something in my stomach, I was going to be sick in the back seat."

Her reference to what happened at the beach made him turn and look at her, and he saw she had a dab of ketchup on her upper lip. Unable to stop himself from smiling, he handed her a napkin.

"Wipe your mouth. You have ketchup on your lip."

She snatched the napkin from his hold and turned away to clean her face. A few seconds later, she glanced over at him again with a worried look.

"Is it gone?"

He studied her face for a moment and couldn't help but be struck by how beautiful she was. Even with that brown wig, she was gorgeous. He didn't know if it was her perfectly formed mouth or the straight nose that fit her face just right or the sculpted cheekbones. Or maybe it was a combination of all those and her deep brown eyes that made her such a knockout.

Whatever it was, he had a feeling he knew at that moment what Gideon and Xavier and all her fans saw when they looked at her.

"You're good."

They ate the rest of their food in silence. When he opened the door to throw the garbage away, Alexis gently touched his arm, stopping him dead. He looked down at where her pale pink fingernails sat against the tan skin of his arm and then up at her face as she stared at him with wide eyes and felt his heart skip a beat.

"I am sorry, Hunter."

He still didn't know what to say, so he fell back on what he'd been assigned to do. "I'm not around to control you or make your life miserable, but I can't protect you if I'm not around you, Alexis."

She hung her head and quietly said, "I know. I never meant to do anything to disrespect you or anyone else. I just wanted to go to the beach and be out of the house for a day."

Seeing her looking so sad bothered him more than he wanted to admit. He'd never felt trapped a day in his life. No matter how bad being a cop got, never once did he feel like he had no way out. He couldn't imagine how much she wanted to break free from so much of her life.

To everyone else, she looked like she held the world in the palm of her hand. The truth was much less glamorous. All her success meant the world controlled her instead of the other way around.

Reaching out, he pushed her hair off her shoulder. "Next time, just let me know. I'm not here to stop you from living your life. My job is to find out who's stalking you, but it's also to protect you. That doesn't mean keeping you locked up in your house, though."

She lifted her head and her smile lit up her face. "Okay. Thank you for understanding."

He didn't understand. He knew that. But he wanted to. He wanted to help her break free of this stalker and everyone else who thought it was their job to keep her under their control.

When he got back into the car after throwing away the garbage, he turned to face her and said what he should have said earlier that morning. "Thanks for what you did with my room. It was a really nice thing for you to do."

The smile he received in response for just those few words made him forget all the anger he felt toward her for so much of the day. She had a way of lighting up a space with her happiness that made him want to be around her.

"I'm so happy you like it, Hunter. I didn't want you to have to suffer on that couch. From one bad sleeper to another, you know? At least if you're going to be up half the night, you can be comfortable in a bed. And now you have somewhere to put your things, although I have to admit I haven't seen that you have much. You changed clothes, though, so you must have things, right?"

He turned the ignition and chuckled. "I'm pretty low maintenance, so I don't require much. Just a few change of clothes and a few pairs of shoes. I travel light, as a rule."

Alexis narrowed her eyes like what he said sounded completely foreign to her. He started to explain that he was like most men, but she said, "I bet you think I'm very high maintenance, right?"

Until just a few minutes before, he would have responded with a resounding yes. Any woman who acted the way she did with her bodyguards, forcing them to move rooms full of furniture on a whim and then sneaking away so everyone around her nearly lost their minds trying to find her, would definitely be classified as high maintenance.

Very high.

But now he saw her differently. True, she still came with a lot of maintenance required, but he understood why a little better. Plus, when you got past all the Hollywood diva stuff, Alexis Marchand wasn't that different from anyone else he'd met in this world.

"No more than any other woman, I'd guess," he said with a smile.

He began to drive again as she said, "Oh,

really? So you're one of those kinds of men who like only low maintenance women. I bet you like the kind who doesn't expect anything from anyone and looks great even when she doesn't wear makeup."

"No. I don't like that kind of woman. I'm not a fan of doormats, even if they do look good first thing in the morning," he answered honestly.

"Hmmm. So you don't like women who require work, and you don't like women who are low maintenance and will take whatever you dish out to them. So what kind of woman do you like?"

Merging into the passing lane, he glanced over at her and saw by the eager look on her face that she genuinely wanted to know the answer to her question. He didn't know exactly what to tell her, though. His history with women was nothing less than checkered, to say the least. That he didn't hesitate for even a minute when Nick first asked him if he'd be interested in joining Project Artemis was a good indication of how single he'd been and for a long time.

He and women didn't equal anything lasting, and his past was littered with ex-girlfriends who'd be happy to tell Alexis why he wasn't good for any woman.

But she waited for an answer, so he gave her the best he had. "I guess it depends. For me, a woman should be herself. She should be strong too. There's nothing sexier than a woman who knows what she wants and isn't afraid to go after it."

"So strong women don't intimidate you?"

Hunter shook his head and smiled. "Nope. It's a lie that strong men like weak women. We don't. Strong men like a challenge, and any woman who can show them she doesn't need a man even if she wants him is definitely a challenge."

"Really?" she asked, her voice full of surprise.

He stared straight ahead as he drove north toward the penthouse. "Really. Nothing sexier."

"Hmmm."

The conversation ended, but when he glanced over at her a few minutes later, she looked happy, smiling as she watched out the window.

CHAPTER ELEVEN

ALEXIS SAW PAUL waiting outside the building when they pulled up, and dread replaced all the happiness she'd felt because of her conversation with Hunter on the way back from Atlantic City. His deep frown and eyebrows drawn in like angry blond slashes told her she was in for a terrible lecture from her longtime manager. She knew she deserved it, but that didn't mean she wanted to hear anything he had to say after the day she'd just been through.

She took a deep breath right before she opened the car door and braced for the shit storm that awaited her. Paul had been angry before, but she'd never seen him look so furious with her. This would make that chewing out he gave her that one time when she foolishly answered a reporter's question about a director she didn't like much look pale in comparison. Her truthful comment about his being a little too friendly had created a weeklong drama with Paul practically losing his mind.

His expression now told her this one would last even longer. Great.

"I'll be up in a minute," Hunter said with a smile.

If only she had to just deal with him instead of Paul too. Suddenly, she had the desire to shut the door and tell Hunter to drive to someplace where she could hide for a day or so.

She looked over at him and wondered if she asked, would he do that for her? Studying his rugged face, she guessed he probably wouldn't. He was Paul's hire, after all, so no matter how pleasant he looked and how nice he'd been since that rest stop, he likely wouldn't understand why listening to her manager ream her out about her behavior once again was something she desperately wanted to avoid.

Stepping out onto the sidewalk, she made it two steps toward the front door before Paul rushed out toward her and took her by the arm like she was some kind of invalid. To the swarm of paparazzi nearby seeing his behavior, they might think he was someone who cared about how she felt.

"Miss Marchand! Alexis! Look this way!" one of the photographers ordered as she hid her face in Paul's jacket.

"How are you enjoying New York, Alexis? Where were you today?" another one asked, yelling his questions as the group hovered far too closely for her comfort.

Paul stopped walking and said to the group, "Gentlemen, give our girl some space. We all know how much she loves her fans, but with the recent problem with someone stalking her, you can't expect her to love what you all are doing right now. We ask that you respect her privacy, okay?"

His request fell on deaf ears, though, and they began hurling questions at her.

"Do you know the identity of the stalker? Have they contacted you again? What protections are being put in place for your safety, Alexis? How will this affect your filming schedule? Does this mean you'll have to take time off from your career?"

She pressed her face hard into the soft fabric of Paul's brown jacket as every question made her feel sicker and sicker to her stomach and tears welled in her eyes. Time off would be a death sentence for her career. God, when would this nightmare end?

Paul escorted her into the building, and as soon as the glass doors closed behind them, he pushed her away and started in on her. "What the hell were you thinking, Lexi? I've been pacing back and forth for hours sick about you out there on your own. Lauren's upstairs and she's a mess after all of this."

Stunned at how much anger dripped off each word he spoke, she stood staring up at him for a moment and then turned to head toward the elevator, desperate to escape from him and everyone else. The doorman gave her a tepid smile like he felt bad for her as she passed by him. Paul walked behind her and continued to rave on about how he'd practically worn a path in the hardwood floor by pacing and how big the knot in his stomach had grown because of what she'd done.

As the elevator doors closed, he grabbed hold of her hand and squeezed it. "Look at me, Lexi. You took ten years off my life today. You can't do this."

She hated when he talked to her like this. Nobody needed to tell her she'd made a mistake. She knew. And she didn't think he should treat her like she was some petulant child who deserved to be chastised for her behavior.

Turning to look at him like he demanded, Alexis apologized, just as she knew she needed to. Giving him big brown eyes full of sadness, she whimpered, "I didn't mean to upset everyone, Paul. I'm sorry."

But this time he didn't seem to be buying her sad girl act.

"Don't give me that look, Lexi. I know you

well enough to know just how much it's all an act. You think that's enough, don't you? You think giving me the sad face and that voice will make up for everything you did today. I work my tail off day and night to make sure your career doesn't derail, and then you pull this kind of stunt! Don't you give a damn about anyone but yourself?"

But her sadness wasn't an act. He just had a different opinion about why she should be sad.

The elevator reached the penthouse and the doors opened to Lauren standing there waiting for her with tears in her eyes. She ran to Alexis and wrapped her arms around her as she began to sob.

"I'm so sorry. Hunter told me I couldn't come with you. I didn't just leave, Alexis. I would never do that. Never."

Holding her best friend, she consoled her while she consoled herself. "I know, Lauren. It's okay. I'm fine."

"Yeah, she's fine. You're fine. Everyone's fine but me. I'm a wreck, but thanks for asking," Paul complained as he began to pace back and forth in front of the elevator doors as they closed, waving his hands around frantically.

"I really am sorry," Alexis said as she backed away from Lauren to face him. "I didn't mean to ruin everyone's day."

"What were you thinking, Lexi? Just tell me that so I can understand this whole damn thing.

You could have gotten yourself hurt, or even worse, killed! You've got a stalker out there. What if they found you? Was Lauren going to protect you? Does she suddenly have the strength and abilities of a bodyguard? Lauren, how about you show me how you planned to protect Lexi? Do you have a gun or anything to use to do that job? No, you don't!"

As he talked, his voice got louder and louder until by the end, he was screaming at them. His face grew redder and redder with every passing moment, frightening her. Paul had never been like this before, and Alexis didn't know what to do. Suddenly, all she felt like doing was curling up in a ball again and crying like Lauren was now.

Holding on to her friend's hand, Alexis tried to protect her. "It isn't her fault, Paul. Lauren would never put me in harm's way. I did this on my own. She just came along because I made her. I just wanted—"

He cut her off and began barking at her again. "You just wanted to have some fun. I know. Lauren already told me. But Lexi, you're not like other people. You can't just decide to take off for the beach any damn time you like. Even if you didn't have a stalker, you can't just go off on your own. And what would have happened if that stalker found you and did something to Lauren before kidnapping you? Would you be able to forgive yourself for her getting hurt or killed just because you did one stupid thing?"

The mere thought of Lauren being harmed because of anything she did made Alexis choke up with emotion. Of all the people in the world she'd never want to see hurt, Lauren was top on that list. She'd never get over it if she suffered for a mistake she made.

The elevator doors opened and Hunter stepped out into the horrible drama that had blown up in the past few minutes. Embarrassed and feeling like her emotions might unravel at any moment, she stepped back away from Paul and hung her head as she felt the tears begin to burn her eyes.

"I didn't mean to upset everyone. I would never do anything to hurt any of you."

Paul started to say something, but Hunter spoke up. "We've all had an exciting day. I think Alexis would like to be left alone for a while."

She looked up at him in amazement. Did he just say she should be left alone? She knew Paul was saying exactly what Hunter thought about all she'd done. Why was he defending her?

"Left alone?" Paul said, astonished at what he'd just heard from the man he'd hired. "I think we need to have a conversation about how she scared the living hell out of all of us, don't you think? Maybe some discussion about how she can never do this again?"

Hunter put his hand on the small of her back and began to gently guide her down the hallway toward her room. "We've already had that conversation, so let's give Alexis some time alone. If anyone needs anything from her, see me or Lauren and we'll take care of it."

Alexis looked back to see Paul standing there with his mouth hanging open in shock as Hunter led her away from him and the discussion he wanted to have. He opened the door for her and held it as she walked in and sat down on the bed, stunned by everything that had happened in the past minute.

"Let me know if you need anything," he said as he began to close the door.

"Hunter! Wait!" she yelled, not wanting him to go before she said something to him.

He stopped and looked back at her. "Something wrong?"

"I just wanted to say thanks. I know I deserve the lecture Paul wanted to give me back there, but thanks for getting me away from it."

He smiled a warm and sexy grin that made him even more handsome than usual. As he spoke, her stomach did a little flip. "I figured you're a grown woman. You don't need to be told something you already know."

A grown woman? Paul never treated her like

she was anything more than some head case he needed to constantly keep watch over. In fact, nobody treated her like a grown woman. Even Lauren.

Not that she made it easy to. She knew that. Her antics and ranting about things hardly created an environment where anyone would see her as an adult who deserved to be treated with respect.

But she liked how it felt when someone did.

Embarrassed by what she'd done that morning, she lowered her head. "Thank you. I guess I didn't act like a grown woman today, so thanks for treating me like one anyway."

"You're very welcome. Do you want me to have Lauren come in?"

"Yeah. Tell her to come in."

He turned to leave, and she added, "Please."

Looking back at her, he smiled in that sexy way again. It made her stomach flutter even more this second time.

"Okay. I'll be out here working, but if you plan to go out, just let me know, okay?"

"Thanks, Hunter."

As the door closed and he disappeared, she thought about how much she knew he agreed with Paul. That he didn't just stand there and let her get lectured on how stupid she'd been that day showed he really wasn't just another one of her bodyguards since none of them would ever dare to stand up for her to Paul before.

He defended her.

No one had ever defended her. People told her what to do and what not to do. They told her how to act. Fans told her how much they loved her. Critics told her what they thought of her work. Haters told her to give up acting and stick to being a dumb blonde who should do nothing but model.

But no one, not even her ex-husband, had ever stood up for her like that.

A tiny knock on the door she recognized as Lauren's roused her from her thoughts, so she called her in. She hurriedly locked the door behind her and rushed over to sit next to Alexis on the bed.

Wide-eyed, she said, "Oh my God! Paul was so furious when we got back. He was so mad. I thought he was going to stroke out right there when I got off the elevator. I wanted to cry he was yelling so loud."

Alexis didn't want to think about Paul now. Turning to face Lauren, she excitedly asked, "Did you see how Hunter stopped him from giving me chapter and verse about how I should have been more careful? I couldn't believe it! I thought the two of them were going to read me the riot act for at least an hour when I got here."

All the worry and stress faded from Lauren's expression, replaced by a huge grin that lit up her face. "I did. What happened in the car on the way back to make that happen? I figured they'd both pile on once you got home since Paul was the one who brought him here."

"I don't know. Nothing. I know he was as furious as Paul is when he found us, but he didn't yell at me or even scold me about it. All he said was if I wanted to go somewhere to just let him know."

"That was it? Nothing else? I thought you'd tell me he bitched you out all the way home."

Alexis shook her head, still stunned he didn't. "Me too, but there was no bitching."

"I guess, now that you mention it, he doesn't really seem like the bitching type. He's more of a quiet kind of person, but sometimes those are the ones who yell the loudest."

Thinking back, she went over the ride home in her mind and smiled. "Well, there was no yelling of any kind. I kept expecting it too, but it never came. For the first twenty miles or so, I just sat in the backseat curled up and waiting for him to start in on me about how stupid I'd been and how I could have gotten myself killed, but he never did that. He definitely wasn't happy with me, but he didn't yell like Paul."

Leaning in toward her, Lauren asked, "Well,

what did you guys talk about all that way if he wasn't explaining how stupid what we did was, which it was, you know."

"I know, but I'm not sorry we did it."

Alexis stopped and thought about what she just said. That wasn't exactly the whole truth.

"Well, I guess maybe I'm a little sorry. I never wanted you to be in trouble with Paul, so I'm sorry about that. And I could have been hurt by that stalker, so that wasn't so smart. And I would never be able to forgive myself if you got hurt because of what I made you do. But it was nice seeing the beach again."

Lauren hugged her. "It was. Maybe next time we go we don't cause a ruckus and freak everyone out."

"Okay. I can deal with that."

"So what did you guys talk about the whole ride home?"

"We talked a little about a lot of stuff. We stopped for hamburgers at a rest stop. He didn't treat me like I'd committed a crime just because I wanted to get out of the house for a few hours. He definitely wasn't thrilled at what we did, but he didn't act like I deserved to be punished for it like Paul did. I liked that."

She slid the brown wig off her head and tossed it on the bed behind her. Lauren immediately reached out to arrange her long blond hair over her shoulders and smiled.

"I probably look like a mess, don't I?" Alexis asked, self-conscious as always about how she looked.

Shaking her head, Lauren said, "No, you look like you always do. Beautiful."

"Then why are you smiling?"

Her friend shrugged while her smile grew even bigger. "It's just that I don't remember the last time I saw you look so genuinely happy like you do now. That little trip to Atlantic City seems to have done you a world of good, even if it did give Paul the worst scare of his life."

Alexis nodded, but she secretly thought it wasn't their trip to Atlantic City that made her feel so good. It was Hunter and how he treated her.

First, he protected her, and then he defended her.

And he liked what she did for him with his new bedroom.

But she didn't want to share what she thought just yet with Lauren, so she chuckled to herself and leaned over to get her bag from the floor to pull out the white box of peanut butter fudge.

Shaking it in front of her, she giggled. "This calls for some celebratory fudge, I say!"

"Definitely! To hell with the calories. We'll just have to spend more time at the gym," Lauren said as she stuffed a big piece of fudge into her mouth.

Her eyes rolled back in her head, and she moaned, "Oh, God. This is so good. We have to get back to the Boardwalk again just for this fudge."

"Agreed," Alexis said, taking a bite of the candy. "But we do have to find a gym too. I haven't done anything in all the time I've been here in New York. If I keep slacking off, I'm going to blow up to the size of those balloons they have in the Macy's Thanksgiving Day parade."

Grabbing another piece of fudge, Lauren said, "Well, we can always ask Paul for where to find a gym. That would probably smooth things over with him a little. You know how he loves to be in control."

Alexis didn't want to deal with Paul at the moment. Now that she'd been treated like an adult, she wasn't in any hurry to go back to being treated like some kind of responsibility he had to worry about all the time.

Ignoring her friend's suggestion, she took another bite of fudge. "First, I have to find a gym that doesn't require a three hour trek to get there. Just another reason I miss the house in LA."

"Yeah. There's no way you can fit a home gym in this apartment. Well, unless you redo that bedroom you gave Hunter into one," Lauren said.

Shaking her head, Alexis vetoed that idea immediately. "Nope. That room is his, so he can keep it. We'll just have to find a gym somewhere around here."

"Okay. I can do that today. I'll find a few close by and we can go look at them to see which ones have what you want," Lauren said before swallowing her piece of candy.

Moving the box of fudge away from her, Alexis joked, "Maybe you should look for gyms a couple miles away too. That way, we can get a run in before our workout because we're going to need it if we keep stuffing our faces with this fudge."

A guilty look washed over her assistant's face. "Okay. You're right. No more. My stomach already is beginning to feel distended."

"As soon as you get the names and directions to those gyms, we'll go check them out. We'll take Hunter too," Alexis said, looking forward to getting out again and with him.

Her mention of Hunter surprised Lauren. "But what about Kyle? He's always the one to go to the gym with us when we're not in LA. He knows what to look for in the equipment since he used to work at a gym himself."

Alexis shrugged, not caring much about who came other than Hunter. "I guess he can come too, but it's not like we can't figure out if there's a treadmill or stepper machine in a gym. It's not rocket science. I'll probably give him a break from going with us every day, though. If Hunter's going to be there anyway, I don't see any point in dragging another person along every time."

"Okay. Give me an hour and I'll get you the names of those gyms," Lauren said as she stood from the bed.

When she got to the door, she turned around and looked at Alexis with concern in her eyes. "You were kidding about running to the gym and then working out, weren't you?"

"Sort of, but just find any in a ten block radius. That way we can be warmed up by the time we get there every morning."

"You do remember we're in New York, Alexis. In just a couple months, it's going to be too cold to walk ten blocks first thing in the morning. Think Minnesota, not LA."

She had forgotten the dreaded winter that lay before them in just a short time from now. Running or even walking ten blocks in frigid temperatures, or God forbid snow, made her cringe.

"Well, don't exclude ones closer by. If it turns out I like one further away, we're going to have to get rides to and from there when it gets too cold to walk. Sound good?"

Lauren still didn't look completely convinced, but she nodded and faked a smile before leaving to go start her research on the local gyms. She'd never been as fond of running as Alexis, but ten blocks wasn't much.

Plus, it would be good for both of them to get to know the neighborhood while at the same time getting some exercise. At least until the temperature dipped below fifty.

Then again, she could probably handle forty degrees.

As all of this ran through Alexis's mind, she thought back to them growing up in Minnesota and how they used to be so used to the cold and the snow. Back when they were kids, they spent hours ice skating and happily building snow forts until their fingers grew numb. It was nothing to stay out in the frigid cold for an entire day having a good time. They always knew a cup of hot cocoa waited for them when they finally decided to go inside to warm up.

Those were good days for both of them. Now as she sat in a luxurious townhouse in the Upper West Side of Manhattan, she knew they'd gotten spoiled by living in LA all that time. But they weren't delicate flowers who couldn't handle a little tough weather. They were two women who'd braved the winters of Minnesota for the first seventeen years of their lives.

They could handle a couple blocks in chilly New York City.

Chapter Twelve

"Hey, Hunter, can we talk?" Paul asked as he approached him in the kitchen. He'd only wanted to grab a drink, but it looked like he'd have to deal with questions about Alexis too. Of all the hassles on this assignment, not being able to escape the people who lived in this penthouse apartment was quickly becoming the worst.

He was starting to understand why Alexis wanted to get away.

Opening the refrigerator, he stuck his head in to look at his choices. "Sure. Give me a sec, okay?"

Paul mumbled something as Hunter stood staring at the containers on the shelves. Milk, orange juice, filtered water, tea bags, and coffee. None of them thrilled him, so he grabbed the pitcher of water and poured himself a glass. He knew Paul stood anxiously waiting to begin his spiel about how Alexis needed to be more careful and how he worried about her, but he intentionally made him wait, preferring to put off the conversation until he couldn't anymore.

The reality was that Paul wouldn't be telling him anything he hadn't already thought himself. He just had a different tactic to make her take more care with her security than Paul. He preferred a less confrontational approach, one that didn't include blowing up every time something happened that he didn't like.

Two glasses of water later, he turned toward her manager and smiled. "Ever get so thirsty that you could drink a gallon of something? I swear it's like I'm dehydrated. I wasn't even in the mood for water, and here I've downed two glasses of it and could do two more."

Preoccupied with the topic he wanted to discuss with him, Paul shook his head. "No, not really."

Hunter set his empty glass in the sink and turned around to lean against the counter. Folding his arms across his chest, he decided he'd tortured Paul for long enough. Five minutes of having to stand there and wait hadn't calmed him down any, but it had amused Hunter a little.

"So, what did you want to talk about, Paul?"

His mouth dropped open and his eyes grew big, like he couldn't believe Hunter didn't know what he wanted to discuss. "Lexi, of course. Something has to be done about her. I can't go through another day like today."

"I agree. We definitely don't need another day like today."

Even agreeing with Paul didn't seem to make him happy, though. He shook his head back and forth like some kind of crazy blond bobblehead doll and flailed his hands around in front of him.

"Well, I'm glad we're in agreement on that, but what are we going to do about it? She can't just go running off to Atlantic City whenever she damn well feels like it!"

Hunter took a deep breath and nodded. He didn't necessarily agree with Paul's exact statement, but he agreed with the sentiment. He had a feeling how they'd ensure what happened that morning didn't happen again is where they differed.

"I've got it under control. Trust me. I don't believe she's going to be sneaking off with Lauren again."

That promise didn't serve to lessen Paul's exasperation. If anything, it only made it worse. But Hunter wasn't just bragging. He trusted that if Alexis wanted to leave the house again, she'd let him know. He didn't know if that trust was misplaced or not, but he had a feeling he'd find out soon.

Either way, his style didn't include emotional outbursts and threats he couldn't or wouldn't back up. Unfortunately, that seemed to be all of what Paul had to offer. Hunter may not have known Alexis well at all, but he understood human nature and treating her like some misbehaving child wouldn't get them anywhere.

"What do you mean you've got it under control? You don't even know her. Trust me. This isn't the first time she's done something like this, and it won't be the last. One of these days she's going to make some damn foolish decision and pay the ultimate price for it."

Hunter patted him on the shoulder, hoping to get him to calm down. "Relax. It's all under control. I swear you have nothing to worry about. Now about this stalker. She got another letter today after she left. Alexis doesn't know about it yet, but I want you to take a look at it and tell me what you think?"

His announcement that another letter had come completely shifted Paul's focus from Alexis's poor choices that morning, so now he sagged against the counter next to Hunter. His excited expression drooped along with his body, giving him a defeated look.

"Another one? I had really hoped they'd stop once she moved here. I guess I'm lucky Persephone could send you when she did. Between Alexis and this madman, I'm going to be grey by the end of the month."

Hunter pulled the letter out of his back pocket and laid it on the counter in front of them. "Take a look and tell me if anything jumps into your mind about this."

Leaning over, Paul studied the letter for a minute as Hunter re-read it for the fifth time that day.

I HOPE YOU'RE LOVING NEW YORK AS MUCH AS I AM. I LIKE LA BETTER, THOUGH. WHEN ARE WE GOING BACK THERE, ALEXIS? SEE YOU SOON.

He let out an audible sigh and shook his head. "What is with this guy? Now he's sending her letters about the weather?"

Hunter tapped on the note to get Paul to focus on what the stalker had told them through his words. "Look, I think we have to consider the idea that the stalker was in LA when he started and now is here in New York. I wasn't sure at first with the snow globe, but I think this shows us he's travelled with her."

Paul stood up and stared at Hunter with wide eyes. Whispering, he asked, "Are you saying he's someone on her staff here?"

"I don't know. Was each one of them thoroughly checked out before they were hired?"

"Of course. I checked each of their backgrounds myself. I would never let anyone who could harm Lexi get anywhere near her."

His tone became increasingly defensive, so Hunter quickly moved to calm him. "I'm not saying you would, Paul. That's not what I'm thinking. I just wanted to ask to cover all the bases."

Shaking his head, Paul repeated himself. "I would never let anyone harm her. She's more than just my client. She's like the little sister I never had."

Hunter folded up the letter and stuck it back into his jeans pocket. "I know you wouldn't. Don't worry. I'm going to find this guy and stop him. In the meantime, you don't have to worry about Alexis running off anymore either. I think she and I have come to an understanding."

"I hope so. She's a handful, Hunter, but I love her like she's family. I know you think I was tough on her earlier, but that was more fear talking than anything else. If anything ever happened to her…"

His voice trailed off, and Hunter gave him a light pat on the arm as he moved to leave the kitchen. "I know. Don't worry, though. Things are going to be better from this point on."

From behind him as he walked toward his room, he heard Paul quietly say, "I hope so. My heart can't take another day like this one."

HOPEFUL HE COULD focus on the case without any more distractions, Hunter closed himself in his new bedroom and called Gideon back at the estate for some help on finding out about a few people around Alexis.

"Hunter, how's the life of the working man?" Gideon asked when he answered the phone.

"Fuck you. Don't you know how to answer a phone call, for fuck's sake?"

His friend laughed out loud in that way that made Hunter smile. Gideon was nothing if not a good time.

"Well, hello, Hunter. Aren't you a ray of fucking sunshine today?"

"Yeah, yeah. Speaking of work, I need you to check out a few people for me. I want to know everything you can find out on them."

"What am I? Your guy Friday, for God's sake? I'm in the middle of something right now, but I can probably get to it later," Gideon said dismissively.

"Whatever you're in the middle of can wait until later. Just DVR the damn game, for Christ's sake!"

"It's not a game, and I think I have you to blame for that. Did you tell Persephone that all Xavier and I do is shoot pool and watch sports? Because she's got me doing what amounts to busy work and it started right after you went to see her the other day. For fuck's sake, she's got him doing something with her office computer. He's pretty insulted, actually," Gideon complained.

Hunter had to chuckle. He had mentioned something about the two of them having it pretty easy lately. Not that he'd intended for Persephone to necessarily change that. He'd just been blowing off steam. Now that she had put them to work, though, he really couldn't feel bad for either one of them. They still got to sleep in their own beds every night, even if they did have to do something other than hang out all day.

"I'm sure she just finally noticed that out of all of us, you guys are always sitting on your asses watching some game lately. She does have eyes, you know."

"I don't just sit on my ass, you son of a bitch. I'm up at five every day and in the gym before your sorry ass is even out of bed."

"That's only because it's a habit for you from your time in the Navy."

Gideon huffed his disgust. "Actually, it's from my high school football days, but it's neither here nor there. The point is that while you are still lying in bed giving your cock a few nice tugs, I'm up and getting shit done."

"Yeah, I know. You do more before eight am than other people do all day. I think someone took that slogan, though, so you're going to have to come up with a new one."

Before he came to Project Artemis, Gideon had been a number of things. He'd been a Navy SEAL, and he'd spent a few months on a search and rescue team right there in New York. But he still seemed like that high school football player more often than not.

Hunter had to admit the guy was a hell of a physical specimen, even if he did seem to spend most of his time recently watching some sport or another on TV in the game room at the estate.

"So you called me to hear me say fuck you to the favor you want me to do for you?" Gideon snapped.

Hunter knew the time for busting ass was over. "Come on, man. I need your help with this. Alexis Marchand has someone stalking her, and I need to clear everyone around her so I can move on to who might be doing this to her. You've got the ability to find out anything about a person there. I barely got a bedroom here."

His mention of Alexis made Gideon's whole attitude change. "What's she like? Is she full of herself or a bitch to everyone? Typical Hollywood diva like you thought she'd be?" he asked.

For a moment, Hunter thought about what he'd learned about Alexis so far. She'd treated her bodyguards like lapdogs, had one of her assistants lie for her, and she'd snuck out and worried the entire household needlessly.

Still, he couldn't say anything bad about her. He looked around the room she'd furnished for him and smiled. "Not really. She seems to be like everyday people."

"I like that. Is she as hot in person as she is in her movies?" Gideon eagerly asked.

In that, he and Xavier had been right. "She's definitely gorgeous. No doubt about that."

"I knew it! No way a woman that gorgeous on our TV could be a dog in person. Oh, that body…the way that ass looks when she walks away in a skirt…"

"Steady dude. You sound like you're going to blow any second. How about we get back to what I need you to find out for me?"

"All right," Gideon said, sounding disappointed. "Text me the names and I'll get on it as soon as I can. But will you at least answer one thing for me?"

"Why do I have to text you the names? Can't I just tell you them?"

Christ, why did he have to be so difficult?

"I don't have a photographic memory like Julian, you jackass. Just text them to me."

Hunter grumbled, "If you had a photographic memory, you'd want me to text them to you. Photographic means you have to see them."

"Christ, Hunter! It's one damn text. Now tell

me. Does she sound the same as she does in her movies?"

What the hell was Gideon talking about?

"How would I know?" Hunter answered, already frustrated by this call. "I've never seen any of them."

"Christ, you're a Philistine. Her voice sounds soft, but you get the sense when she's not acting that there's something more underneath it. I have this fantasy that when she's in the middle of—"

The time had come for Hunter to cut this conversation off right now. "Whoa! I swear to God, man, you are oversexed. Maybe you need to get out of that chair and away from the TV for a little while. Just assume she sounds like any normal woman. I'm sending you the names of the people I need everything on. And the next time I call you, try to keep that shit to yourself."

Gideon chuckled. "I'm a red-blooded American male. By the way, just so you know, I'd have that in my bed before the end of the assignment. Hell, I'd have had her by now," he bragged.

"Bye, Gideon. You need to get yourself some soon before you explode there."

"Don't you worry about me getting some. I do just fine, thank you. What I need is to not have to do busy work. But at least I get to partner with Tess on the things Persephone gave me to do. Jealous?" Gideon said, taunting him.

At any other time, Hunter thought about how he would have been a little jealous Gideon got to work with Tess. Now, though, he wasn't bothered at all.

"Nope. Just get me that information ASAP."

"Yeah, ASAP. Got it. Later, Hunter."

Tossing his phone onto the bed, he shook his head at Gideon. That guy needed to get out more. But maybe he had something about Alexis. Not the sound of her voice when she…fuck, now he'd have that in his head the next time he spoke to her.

No, maybe he had a good point about knowing more about Alexis. Hunter wondered if he should watch some of her movies. It couldn't hurt.

A knock at his bedroom door pulled him out of his thoughts. He opened it to see Alexis standing there in front of him in a pair of pink jogging pants and a t-shirt. As his gaze floated down her body, he noted that even in workout clothes she looked incredible.

Quickly directing his attention to her face, he asked, "What's going on?"

"I need to find a gym. Lauren's rounded up the addresses of a few. We're going for a run to check them out. You told me to let you know when I wanted to leave the house. We're going with Kyle if you don't run, so we won't be alone."

She smiled and raised her right hand. "Scouts' honor. I promise."

He hadn't expected her to be a runner. Not that he'd put much thought into what she did to keep her body in such good shape. But her running surprised him. She had a way of doing that, it seemed.

"I could go for a run. It'll clear my head. I have to admit I didn't peg you for a runner, though."

Alexis gave him a huge smile. "Good! Be ready in ten. The four of us will go for a nice run."

"I'll let Kyle know he doesn't have to go since I'm going."

"Well, he's the one who goes to the gym with me every day when we're not at home. Since this house doesn't come with a place to work out, I figured he'd be coming with us."

"No need. I'll be there. Let Kyle have some time off," Hunter said as he thought about four definitely being a crowd.

Alexis shrugged. "Okay. He'll probably be happy to get an extra hour of sleep every day since he won't have to come here from the hotel every morning to go to the gym with me. You let him know, and I'll see you in a few minutes."

Hunter watched her jog down the hallway and had to admit Gideon was right. The view from behind was spectacular.

He found Kyle downstairs in the building's lobby and pulled him aside. "Alexis tells me you usually go with her when she works out, but now that she's here, you're relieved from that. Enjoy the extra hour of sleep every morning."

At first, he didn't seem to understand what Hunter had just said, but then his expression turned dark as his meaning became clear. "I'm Alexis's trainer. She's never let anyone else do the job but me."

"Well, you don't have to do it anymore," Hunter said flatly, already wondering why this conversation had gone on this long.

Kyle shook his head but said nothing more. Sensing something more was going on, Hunter took a hard look at the man. Slightly shorter than him, the bodyguard had a thicker look courtesy of hours more in the gym, he assumed. He wasn't a bad looking guy, though. Dark hair with brown eyes. Hunter had a feeling he had no difficulty with the ladies. Then he remembered the story Lauren had told him about that night Kyle had spent with Alexis right after her divorce became final.

"Is there some problem I don't know about?" Hunter asked.

"No. I just don't appreciate the fact that Alexis didn't tell me this herself."

"She's got a lot going on, Kyle. I'm sure you understand that."

But he didn't seem to understand. All Hunter saw in Kyle's face was hurt, oddly enough. Why the hell would he feel that way about getting extra sleep time every morning?

"What's going on here?" Hunter asked, and this time he watched Kyle's expression carefully. This guy's reaction to a simple change in his responsibilities seemed strange, to say the least.

The words barely made it out of Hunter's mouth before the bodyguard's entire body language morphed into the definition of defensiveness. He grimaced and puffed out his chest like some gym rat preparing for a fight.

"What are you saying? You don't know what you're talking about, dude. Stick around a while and you'll see what's what."

Hunter took a step toward Kyle, decreasing the space between them until he almost bumped into his bulging pecs. Whatever this guy was feeling, he was reacting way out of the ordinary to something so insignificant.

And Hunter planned to find out why.

Leveling his gaze on the man's face, he said flatly, "I'm saying that you don't have to get out of bed early every day because Alexis doesn't need you to go to the gym. Nothing more. You're not being fired or even demoted. You're just being given a break every day. Is there a reason this means so much to you?"

Kyle stared back at him for a long moment before he shook his head. "What are you implying?"

"I'm not implying anything. I'm asking straight out. Why is being relieved of having to go to the gym every day with Alexis a problem for you?"

While he waited for Kyle to answer, Hunter wondered if the man standing in front of him could be the stalker. He clearly felt upset about something regarding Alexis, and he had a feeling the man harbored far more feelings about that single night he spent with her than she did. Had he been the one terrorizing her so she would turn to him for protection?

"It's not a problem for me. I just don't like being treated like some second-class citizen just because some new guy shows up on the scene."

"You're not. Nobody is saying you're not a valuable member of Alexis's security team. You're just not needed to accompany her to the gym. Nothing else has changed."

Hunter stopped for a moment and then added, "Is there anything I should know, Kyle?"

Still unhappy, the bodyguard stepped back and shook his head. "Nope."

"Good."

But Hunter made a note of how upset he'd been about something so incidental. Whatever his problem was, Kyle had jumped to the head of the line of possible suspects in Hunter's mind.

Chapter Thirteen

The first gym on Lauren's list was located about eight blocks away. Alexis started running as soon as they walked outside the building's lobby, thankful to see no photographers milling about and desperate to put some distance between her and that apartment. She'd only been there a little more than a week, but every moment she spent inside felt like the walls were beginning to close in on her. She feared when the construction crews began taking down some of them and opening up the space like the designer suggested it still wouldn't make the place anywhere she wanted to live.

Half a block away from the building, she looked to her left and saw Hunter there beside her. Kyle always ran behind her. For a moment, she didn't know how she felt about this change.

Curious to know why he thought he should be there next to her, she said, "I'm used to Kyle staying behind me on my runs."

Hunter turned to look at her and then looked

away at the sidewalk in front of them. "I guess he and I have different styles. I can protect you better being at your side instead of trailing behind you."

Everything about this man said control, something Alexis had never liked much. Paul continually tried to exert control over her, whether it was what parts she chose or what events she attended. Her ex-husband had been a big fan of control, deciding on everything from what clothes she would wear to how long she should keep her hair.

And with both of them, she rebelled every chance she got.

Now that she had yet another man in her world who seemed so determined to have control, she wondered if maybe she had been wrong about that touchy subject. Maybe that's why Jackson had left her for an even younger woman after just a few years of marriage. Maybe if she'd been more amenable to taking direction from him off the set as much as on the set, he wouldn't have cheated on her.

Oh no. To hell with that.

Nobody—not Paul, not Jackson, and not Hunter—was going to control her ever again, and she'd never torture herself with the idea that if only she let them have what they wanted that maybe she could make them happy. Now, she wanted to be happy.

Just before she took off into a sprint across the intersection, she glanced over at Hunter and smiled. "Well, let's see if you can keep up then."

Long legs and a lean body that had always lent itself to running had made Alexis a natural sprinter, so within a block, she'd left Hunter and Lauren behind her. She knew this technically broke her promise not to leave without having him right there with her, but she didn't care. For the first time since she moved to New York, she felt independent. Even the trip to Atlantic City hadn't given her that.

She reveled in how great she felt running in the nearly sixty degree temperatures while the light breeze hit her face and the sun warmed her cheeks. As she rushed by the trees planted along the sidewalk, she saw the leaves had changed to show their vibrant reds and oranges for autumn, something she hadn't gotten to enjoy in years. For a moment, Alexis wondered if New York wouldn't be that terrible after all.

Just then, she heard Lauren cry out behind her, "I've got a Charlie horse! Cramp! Cramp!"

Alexis stopped and turned around to see her assistant about a block away hopping around on one foot in front of a brownstone and nearly falling into the shrubbery that lined the sidewalk. Hunter waved her back to help poor Lauren, who looked like she was in agony.

She ran up to her and put her arms around her shoulders to hold her up. "What happened? Are you okay?"

Wincing in pain, she kept her right foot suspended in the air and groaned, "I think I overdosed on fudge and my body's rebelling. I don't think I can run any further. I'm sorry."

She suspected Lauren's cramp, while it may have existed, likely didn't rate all this trouble. She'd never liked running, but since she'd already gotten in trouble for helping with the jailbreak earlier that morning, Alexis felt like she deserved sympathy.

They could walk the rest of the way.

"It's okay. We'll get there. We can walk instead."

Lauren stood up straight and shook her head. "No, you don't have to stop on my account. You two go on ahead. You guys love running, and you aren't injured, so you should. Get your run in. I'll get there. Just a little slower."

Alexis looked over at Hunter and saw he was waiting for her to make a decision. But she couldn't just leave Lauren there to walk the rest of the way alone, no matter how much she wanted to challenge Hunter to another sprint race.

"I'm not going to abandon you. We'll stay with you."

As they made their way toward the first gym,

she said to Hunter, "I guess we should have brought Kyle after all."

He grimaced at her comment and nodded. "I guess."

"Well, all the better for you since I was going to challenge you to a race. You should be happy Kyle isn't here," she teased.

Hunter flashed her that sexy grin she'd seen a few times that day already. "You'd probably win. Even though I'm at least four inches taller than you, I think you have the longest legs I've ever seen on a woman. That gives you an advantage. Plus, my friend likes to tease me that I don't do enough to stay healthy, so that's another thing you have going for you."

His use of the word friend made her curious, and even though she didn't understand why, it bothered her. Was this friend a male or female? It had never occurred to her that Hunter could be with someone. Who was she? How did she feel about him staying at her apartment while he worked to solve who was stalking her?

Even more, Alexis wondered why she suddenly cared if Hunter was single or not.

Lost in thought, she tripped over her own feet and careened into him. He caught her as she fell, his muscular arms steadying her, and she had to admit she liked how they felt against her body.

But she didn't know if she should let herself

think about him in that way. If he was taken, she had no business being anything other than respectful. Stepping away from him, she smiled politely.

"Thanks. I guess I need to pay more attention to where I'm going."

He smiled like he wanted to say something, but Alexis quickly looked away to focus on Lauren. "Let's keep going. At this rate, we'll be lucky if we get to any gyms at all today."

Grabbing her assistant's arm, she hurried her down the sidewalk, leaving Hunter behind. When they got far enough away that she didn't think he could hear her voice, she whispered to Lauren, "Pretend like we're talking about something funny."

Confused, she looked around like she'd missed some part of the conversation. "Why?"

"Don't look back at him. Just act like we're having fun."

Hunter kept his distance behind them, not too far so he couldn't protect her but far enough that she could speak with some privacy. For her part, Lauren seemed genuinely unhappy and hurt.

"I'm nursing a Charlie horse and I think all that fudge I ate today feels like it's going to come up at any minute. If this is fun, I really don't want to experience misery."

"I know. I know. Just laugh like we're having

a good time and I promise you won't have to go running unless you want to ever again."

"Trust me. I don't want to ever again. Okay, here goes." Throwing her head back, Lauren laughed loudly. "That's hysterical!"

Alexis nudged her in the arm as she looked back to see what Hunter was doing. "Go easy. I said good time, not you after three shots of tequila."

They stopped at an intersection, and she glanced back again as Lauren asked, "Why are we pretending to have the time of our lives walking to the gym?"

The light turned green, and they started walking again. Leaning in, Alexis said, "Because I want to."

She couldn't explain why she wanted Hunter to think she didn't need to have him around to be happy. It was stupid and probably meant nothing to him anyway, but she'd rather pretend not to think about him at all than give him any hint of the truth.

A truth she couldn't really believe herself.

TWENTY-FIVE MINUTES LATER, the three of them reached the first gym on Lauren's list, a place called Dynamics. Looking through the windows that made up the front of the building, Alexis joked, "This gym sounds like something L. Ron

Hubbard would be part of."

The manager, a man named Ricardo, rushed over to greet them as they walked through the door, instantly fawning over her and praising her for her acting work on his favorite film of hers. She smiled and dutifully nodded as she watched where Hunter walked away to.

"Miss Marchand, it is such an honor to have you here at Dynamics. When your assistant called earlier, I must say a chill ran up and down my spine at the thought that one of my favorite actresses would choose our gym to workout in," the man said, smiling broadly like he'd just won the lottery.

"I'm sure you get many famous people in here," Alexis said politely as she looked around to find Hunter.

"Well, if you come this way, I can show you the machines, the sauna, and all we have to offer."

She followed him but continued to look for where Hunter could have gone off to. The place wasn't that big that he needed to leave her side. What could he be doing?

Then she spied him talking to a female worker over near the tanning rooms. She couldn't hear what he or she was saying, but the brunette with the perfect gym body and big boobs seemed to be having an awfully good time chatting with Hunter.

Jealous, even though she couldn't put her finger on why, she cut off the manager of the gym in the middle of his pitch and said, "My assistant will contact you. Thank you."

Turning on her heels, she walked outside without saying a word to Lauren or Hunter. Her stomach had twisted itself into a tight knot, and standing on the sidewalk, she tried to get a deep breath of fresh air into her lungs, hoping it would make her feel better.

She'd sworn she would never again feel jealous over a man after what Jackson had done to her. Never again would she let herself think she was less, but as she stared at Hunter talking to that woman and watched her touching his arm in that way flirtatious women did when they wanted to let a man know they wanted him, that old familiar jolt of pain from being jealous shot through her chest.

It embarrassed her to feel that way. He hadn't given her any indication he thought of her as anything but the spoiled pain in the ass he'd been assigned to help. Yes, he'd treated her like an adult, but now as she thought about how he'd looked talking to that woman in there, she realized that he hadn't looked that comfortable and happy at any time he'd spoken to her. It felt like when he treated her like a grown woman, he'd been patronizing her instead of respecting her. That brunette had gotten his respect even as a complete stranger to him, but as she replayed his defending her earlier, she knew he hadn't given that same respect to her.

He'd handled her, just like everyone else in her world except Lauren did so she'd do exactly what they all wanted her to do, when they wanted her to do it.

While she stood there on the sidewalk punishing herself, a man approached her and excitedly said, "You're Alexis Marchand! I'm a huge fan! Oh my God! You're Alexis! Can I have your autograph?"

Caught off guard, she stammered out, "I…I don't have a pen. I'm sorry."

His face grew dark and he glowered at her. "Oh, come on. I'll just ask someone for a pen and then you can sign my shirt. It will just take a minute."

Unnerved at how close he was to her, she turned to walk back into the gym, but the man grabbed her arm and clamped his hand down on her wrist to stop her. Alexis looked down in horror at the man's fingers pressing into her skin. Who was he? Was he her stalker? Why was he holding her arm so tightly?

"Let me go!" she cried as she tried to pull away from him. "Get off me!"

He began to say something about her not

caring about her fans, but everything around her began to spin and she fell back toward the glass windows behind her. She didn't know when Hunter appeared and got in between her and the man, but she heard him begin to yell at him.

"Hey, buddy! Let her go. She's just stopping by the gym. Back away, man."

The man released his hold on her arm and held up his hands in front of him. "I just wanted an autograph. Nothing else. I wasn't trying to do anything to her. She should be used to fans wanting autographs by now. What's the big deal?"

Lauren took hold of Alexis as she began to shake, and Hunter pushed the guy away so he fell down on the sidewalk. Raising his voice, he barked, "Get the fuck away from her! She doesn't owe you a damn thing, and that includes an autograph!"

The guy ran off as Lauren hugged her close. "It's okay. Forget him. Let's go home."

Hunter turned back toward her, and with concern in his eyes, he looked at her like he was examining her for damage. "Are you okay? Did he hurt you?"

Alexis shook her head but couldn't get the words out to tell him she wasn't hurt. Behind her, Lauren said, "We need to go home now. Can you get us a cab?"

Hunter nodded. "Yeah. I got it."

He hailed them a ride a few seconds later, and when they were safely inside the backseat of the car, Alexis closed her eyes. She didn't want to cry. Not even when she began to realize that she would be trapped in that apartment forever.

God, she missed LA. She missed the sun and the beach. She missed home.

She missed being normal.

No one said a word as they rode up in the elevator to the penthouse. Lauren held Alexis tightly in her arms, her left hand gently stroking her hair to calm her. It didn't work, but she couldn't blame her friend for trying.

Once again, Hunter didn't chastise her for running off or blame her for putting herself in the situation where someone could get to her. She didn't know if she deserved either. Before this whole stalker thing started happening, she could walk out in public like a normal person, even though Paul always told her that the day would come when she couldn't.

But it never did. Never once did anyone accost her. Not until the stalker started terrorizing her.

Alexis knew she bore some of the responsibility for what happened with that man back there at the gym. Before she grew fearful of everyone and everything, she would have joked with him about not having anything to write with and he would have seen she was a good person he just caught at a bad time. She might have even walked with him to a local store to borrow a pen from the clerk behind the counter, even signing something for that second person, if they asked.

That's who she used to be. That's the woman these people wanted an autograph from. Not the terrified mess she'd become after only a few months of her stalker sending those damn letters.

She didn't want to be this way. Each day that passed without anyone stopping him, she retreated a little more into the safety of her own world. Sure, she broke out from time to time, but each time she did, she was shown exactly why she couldn't trust people.

Everything Paul had always warned her about was coming true. She'd moved from a home she loved to a city she knew nothing about and still she couldn't walk freely down the sidewalk. But it wasn't the place.

It was her.

The stalker had succeeded in trapping her not only in her home but inside herself.

The elevator doors opened, and Alexis walked directly toward her room. She didn't want to be around anyone now. Neither Lauren nor Hunter could help her. That had been proven back there on the sidewalk outside the gym.

No assistant or bodyguard could protect her

from the danger outside or the fear that grew by the moment inside her.

They followed her down the hallway, but she waved them off. "I want to be alone."

Chapter Fourteen

HUNTER WATCHED AS Alexis walked slowly down the hall toward her room. With her shoulders drooped, she didn't look like the confident and strong woman he'd come to admire over the past few days.

"I feel so helpless. I want to help her, to protect her, but even going to the gym is becoming impossible because of this stalker. Before this all started, that guy at the beach and the one at the gym wouldn't have been a problem," Lauren said sadly next to him.

He turned and looked at her in confusion. Hadn't Alexis always had to deal with unwanted attention from her fans? Hunter just assumed all stars did.

"What do you mean?" he asked.

"She was never afraid like she is now. When fans came up to her when she was out in public, she chatted with them, took selfies, and signed autographs. She never felt like she was in any danger. But now even one fan approaching her she just gets paralyzed with fear."

"I can't imagine her that way," he said, surprised to hear Alexis used to be so at ease with her fans.

Lauren shook her head. "She was so open to meeting people, but this stalker has changed that. Every day she goes inside herself more and more. She wasn't even like this after she and Jackson broke up, and that was bad."

"What happened then?"

Frowning, she explained what he'd guessed about the breakup. "She took it hard. Jackson didn't even have the decency to tell her before he began strutting around with that girl. And I mean girl. She's three years younger than Alexis, for God's sake. He had a beautiful woman who loved him, and he threw her away for the flavor of the month. I'm waiting for the announcement that he's moved on from her and hooked up with a teenager, the pig. Alexis had to pretend for the whole world that she was fine with being humiliated, and she did. She held her head high and people applauded her for taking the high road on the whole thing. But she stopped wanting to go out, and when someone would invite her to a party, often she'd come up with an excuse not to go. She started hiding from her life."

"So what brought her out of that?"

Lauren's face softened as she smiled at him. "I

like to think I had some part in that. I never let a day go by without reminding her how strong and talented she was. I know assistants are supposed to do that, but I meant every word. I know Alexis since we were little kids, and she's the strongest person I know. That's why seeing her retreat into herself like this is so upsetting. This time it isn't just a person she loves betraying her. This stalker isn't someone she can look at and say, 'I can do better than what you gave me.' He's hidden, so that means she's all alone in it this time."

"She's not alone, Lauren. She has you and she has me. I'm going to find out who's behind this and give her the life she always wanted back."

With tears in her eyes, she looked up at him. "Please do it quickly. I feel like she's slipping away more and more every day."

Lauren left to go to her room she shared with Carla, so Hunter headed to his own room. Maybe Gideon had already made some progress on those names he'd given him. Even just one lead would be better than sitting around feeling helpless.

As he sat listening to his phone ring, Hunter thumbed through the reports from the LAPD and the private detective he'd gotten from Paul. Nobody seemed to ever get a good bead on this stalker. He sent letters regularly, but they never came through the post office and somehow they always got to Alexis, no matter if she was in LA or

New York.

This told Hunter whoever the stalker was, he had to have someone on the inside helping him. But who?

Hopefully, Gideon would be able to help answer that. Assuming he ever answered his goddamned phone.

Finally, he heard his friend's voice in his ear saying, "Twice in one day? You must miss us back here at the ranch."

He didn't have time for his jokes. "Hey man, tell me you found out something."

"In like four hours?" Gideon asked in amazement. "Are you kidding? I need at least a couple days, dude. You gave me a list of like twenty people."

"I know. I just hoped something popped right off the bat. You are working on it, right? Because this is way more important than that busy work Persephone has you doing."

Gideon didn't answer as Hunter's thoughts wandered to Alexis down the hall and if she was okay.

"Hunter, what's going on?"

"What do you mean? I'm doing my job. What are you talking about?"

"I've never heard you like this. You sound worried, man. That's not like you."

Hunter lay down on his bed and covered his

eyes with his arm. "I'm fine. Same as always."

"I don't think so. What's going on there? Do you think you know who's stalking Alexis?"

Hating that he didn't have even one goddamned solid clue yet, he said, "No. I've got nothing. Not a single damn lead."

"They can't expect miracles. Rome wasn't built in a day, man," Gideon said, trying to be supportive.

"Nobody's saying anything. I just want to get to the bottom of who's doing this to her as soon as I can," Hunter lied.

It wasn't just that he wanted to catch Alexis's stalker. It was more than that. He wanted to see that open soul that Lauren talked about. So far, all he'd seen from Alexis made her seem so closed off. If he could get the stalker and end that torment for her, he hoped he might be able to see her open up again.

Of course, Gideon didn't know any of that, so he naturally assumed Hunter just wanted to get this case over and done with so he could head out on vacation. "I know you want to get back so you can get some time off. I get it. Give me some time and I'll get everything down to the last time each person had sex and if they enjoyed it. How's that sound?"

"Is everything about sex with you, man?" Hunter asked with a laugh. "We're talking work here, and you have to stick sex in the middle of it."

"I'm not the one who just said stick sex in the middle, dude."

"It sounds like you need to get some, Gideon. I'm not kidding here. This is the second conversation that you interjected some mention of sex into. I'm just saying if all you're doing is busy work, you might want to get out and clear your head, if you know what I mean."

"You do realize who you're talking to, right?" he asked, sounding offended. "Trust me. There is no problem on my end here. Life is just as it always has been for me, so don't worry. I'm a perfectly healthy American male. As for you, I'm guessing you still haven't taken Alexis Marchand to bed, right?"

"I didn't call you for a lecture on how to sleep with women, man," Hunter said with a chuckle, amused by his friend's growing obsession with his not sleeping with the client.

"No, but you have to admit I took your mind off your worries for a few seconds there. Give me a little more time and I'll find out everything I can for you about all the names you sent me. Until then, just enjoy the fact that you're protecting one of the most beautiful women in the world, Hunter."

He'd always been able to count on Gideon to

focus on the big picture. At least the big picture according to him.

"Thanks, man. Call me as soon as you find out anything."

"You got it. And relax up there. She's safe and sound with you around. Hey, I like that. I think I'm going to suggest that for the group motto to Persephone. Maybe it will get me out of all this goddamned busy work she has me doing."

"Bye, Gideon."

Hunter ended the call and shook his head at his friend's suggestion. Persephone would likely double his workload after hearing that idea of his.

Tossing the phone onto the bed, he mentally ran through every person on that list he gave Gideon. None of them had exhibited even the slightest behavior that would indicate they were behind the letters and packages Alexis had received. The LAPD had no real leads on any possible suspects either. And his suspicion about Kyle was nothing more than that. Suspicion.

Mumbling to himself, he said, "How is it someone could do this and no one would know who it is?"

Frustrated, he headed to the kitchen where he found Carla hurrying back and forth between the oven and the counter preparing dinner. He couldn't help but be surprised since no one had cooked much of anything since he'd been there.

At least nothing he'd been offered.

He leaned against the doorframe and watched her for a minute. "What are you making?"

Carla looked over and a sheepish look came across her face. "Lauren thought it would be nice if Alexis had her favorite food. She can rarely eat it, especially when she's filming, so now's a perfect time to make it. And since she's…"

She didn't finish her sentence, but she didn't have to. Hunter knew what she meant. Lauren was having her make Alexis comfort food.

Hunter scanned the countertop. Fresh carrots, peas, and green beans sat cut up and in bowls. Baby red potatoes waited for Carla's knife to cut them up, and various spice jars sat lined up next to the cutting board. Perhaps comfort food for movie stars meant vegetables. This was Alexis's favorite food?

"What is all this?"

The assistant opened up the oven door and took out a pan. "Pot roast with glazed carrots and baby peas. The green beans are for Lauren. She loves them with garlic."

She smiled as she tossed the vegetables into the pan around the pot roast that sat in the center on a metal rack. "And I always throw in potatoes for good measure."

"You weren't her cook back in LA, though, right?" Hunter asked, seizing on that point as he remembered Alexis telling him about another woman who stayed behind when they all came east.

"No. I just fill in sometimes. I learned how to cook from my mama, so whenever Alexis needs a home cooked meal, I do my best."

"Hmmm. Go figure. I would have never guessed her favorite meal would be something so common. I would have thought someone famous like her would like fancier food. I'd guess she could have anything her heart desires. Who'd think pot roast would be what she wanted?"

Carla ripped off a sheet of aluminum foil and began tenting it over the pan. "It comes from growing up in Minnesota, I think. Alexis is from ordinary people. She wasn't born with a silver spoon in her mouth."

"I had no idea," Hunter admitted as he watched her continue to make the meal with loving care. But he noticed her hands were shaking.

She nodded and gave him a smile. "Yeah. That's why she's so down-to-earth."

Grabbing a piece of carrot, Hunter bit into it. "Carla, you've been with Alexis for three years, right? In that time, is there anyone you can think of who would want to hurt her?"

She stopped covering the pan with foil and shook her head. "No. Until all this started with the letters and packages, I would have said everyone loved her."

"Okay, thanks." He watched her for a few more moments and asked, "Is anything wrong? Your hands are shaking."

Carla quickly shook her head. Wiping her hands on a dishcloth, she forced a smile. "No. No, nothing's wrong. I probably just need to eat something."

"Okay. I'm here if you have anything you want to talk about."

Hunter grabbed another slice of carrot and started to leave, but Carla touched him on the sleeve to stop him. Turning around, he saw she had something else to say.

"I'm sorry about lying to you earlier, Hunter."

"I understand, Carla. You have to do what your boss tells you to do."

With sadness in her eyes, she forced a smile. "Thank you. I just want you to know I would never do anything to knowingly hurt Alexis. I hope you find out who's doing this to her so she can get back to living her life. She deserves it."

"I will," he said as he walked out of the kitchen.

Glancing down the hallway, he thought about knocking on Alexis's door to see if she was okay but decided to let things lay as they were. He likely couldn't say anything to help her feel better anyway.

Chapter Fifteen

A LONE IN HER room, Alexis enjoyed the pot roast dinner Carla made for her, wishing she felt like being out in the dining room where everyone else sat enjoying themselves. She heard Lauren and Hunter out there laughing about something, but even their happiness didn't cheer her up.

Honestly, she wondered if anything would ever make her truly happy again.

Carla's meal worked just like Lauren knew it would. Whenever she felt sad, Alexis could always count on her best friend to make sure she had something to help her through it, and comfort food that reminded her of her childhood never failed to make her reminisce about growing up in Minnesota.

Life then was easier, and not just because they were kids. People could be trusted back home. Caring about one another meant something important to the people she grew up with. Back in high school, no one would have ever bothered to stalk her. She was just one of the girls in those days.

Lauren knocked lightly and said in her worried voice, "Honey, are you okay in there? Do you want me to come in and hang out with you for a little while?"

As she stared at the bedroom door, she shook her head, even dreading having to see the person closest to her in the world. "No, thanks. Please just tell everyone I want to be left alone tonight. The bodyguards can go home. I'm not going anywhere tonight, so let them have a night off."

She heard her friend sigh before she said, "Okay. I'll be around if you want me. It's only eight o'clock, so I won't be going to bed anytime soon. Just yell for me if you need anything, okay?"

"Okay. Thanks, Lauren."

Nothing she could do would make her feel better, so Alexis doubted she'd need anything that night. What she needed was for her life to go back to a time when she didn't fear everything in her world.

Alexis set the tray of food on the dresser and lay down on the bed. She curled up in a ball and closed her eyes, praying that sleep would come and take her over until the next morning.

SHE AWOKE STILL curled up in her bed and looked around, wondering if she'd gotten her wish and she'd made it all the way to the morning. Craning her neck, she looked out the window on the other side of the room and saw the sad truth in the darkness. Whatever time it was, it wasn't morning yet.

Checking the time on her phone, she saw she'd only slept two hours. Disappointed, especially since that probably meant she'd be up most of the night tossing and turning, she quietly opened her door and listened for any indication that Lauren or Carla were still around. The last thing she wanted was to talk about what was bothering her. She'd done enough talking to last a lifetime.

She crept down the hallway as silently as she could and went to the kitchen to get a drink. Looking across at Hunter's door, she wondered if he had gone to sleep yet. Unsure if she should bother him, Alexis tapped on his door lightly and waited a minute. When he didn't answer, she figured it was for the best and began to walk back toward her room.

"Are you okay, Alexis?" she heard behind her about halfway down the hallway.

Turning around, she nodded. "It's nothing. I was just wondering if you were still awake."

He smiled and she couldn't help but notice how sexy he looked at that moment. Still in his jeans and a dark blue t-shirt, he seemed so comfortable just standing there in his doorway.

"I'm not Lauren or Carla, but I'm still awake. What's up?"

She walked to where he stood, and for a moment, neither one of them said anything. It didn't feel awkward, but there was no denying the sudden silence. Not that Hunter had shown himself to be a big talker. That was one of the reasons why she knocked on his door. She didn't want to talk so much as not be alone, and out of everyone in her world, only he seemed to fit the bill for that.

Hunter stepped back out of the doorway to welcome her into his room. "I'm not doing anything much at the moment. Come in."

As he closed the door behind her, she looked around at the room that used to be her office. It felt foreign to her now. Masculine. As her gaze settled on his gun sitting on the dresser, Alexis couldn't even remember what this room had looked like as her office such a short time ago.

Then she noticed she hadn't thought to get him anything to sit on other than the bed, so she stood in the center of the room as he sat down and cleared away papers he'd been reading.

"I'm sorry I didn't get you any chairs, Hunter. I don't know what I was thinking. I should have gotten you a desk too. I can take care of those things tonight and have them here tomorrow," she said, hoping he didn't notice how embarrassed she felt.

He tidied up the papers and set them on his nightstand. "That's not necessary. I can work like this."

She smiled at his attempt to be gracious but made a mental note that she needed to get him a desk and at least one chair.

After a few moments, he asked, "Do you want to sit down?"

Alexis looked around awkwardly wishing so much that she hadn't been such an idiot when she bought the furniture for this room. The only place to sit would be on the bed with him, but she didn't want to stand the whole time she stayed there.

"Yeah. Thanks," she mumbled as she sat down on the side of the bed opposite him. Still feeling out of place, even though this was a room in her own home, she said, "This feels comfortable. I'm glad. I wasn't sure which mattress to get."

He didn't say a word to her silly mention of the bed, which only added to her awkwardness, so she mumbled, "These are nice sheets. Very masculine. Grey and black. Lauren has great taste. I think she said they're five hundred thread count."

"I wouldn't know. I don't know about those

things," he said in a low voice.

She ran her fingers over the flat sheet next to her. "Yeah. I think these are five hundred."

Even Alexis didn't think he should respond to her idiotic yammering on about thread count, so she wasn't surprised when he didn't. It only made it crystal clear that she shouldn't have knocked on his door in the first place.

As she pondered the idea of leaving, he said, "Carla made a great pot roast dinner. Did you have any?"

She turned to face him, happy for a topic about something other than the thread count of sheets. "I did. It's my favorite. I love when she makes it for me."

Unfortunately, the conversation fell silent again, and she knew it was time for her to leave. Standing up, she said, "I guess I'll go. Have a good night."

As she walked toward the door, he asked, "Did you want to talk about anything in particular?"

Turning back, she looked at him. "No, I just..."

She didn't know how to say she didn't want to be alone without sounding pathetic. No matter how she tried to phrase it in her head, it still came out the same.

Pathetic.

Hunter swung his legs off the bed and stood up. "What do you say we go out for a little while? Maybe just go for a walk, or if we find a quiet bar, we could have a drink?"

The idea of getting out sounded wonderful, even as that tiny voice in the back of her mind warned her that she might run into a guy like the one at the gym earlier today. But she didn't want to be afraid of everyone in the world anymore. She just didn't know how not to be.

She wanted to try, though.

"Okay. I'll grab a sweater and be right back."

"Good. Meet you in the hallway in a couple minutes."

As she stepped out onto the sidewalk, the chill of the night air surprised her. Wrapping her sweater around her, she tried not to look as cold as she felt.

But Hunter noticed immediately. "Do you want to go back in? You look cold."

Alexis shook her head, eager to be out of the house for even a short time. "No, I'm fine. My blood just hasn't gotten used to New York weather yet. My body still thinks it's in LA."

Satisfied by her lie, he pointed up the block. "Looks like your adoring fans with the cameras went home to bed. Let's walk up there. We went south this afternoon, so what do you say about trying north?"

"Sure! North it is."

Hoping once she got moving she'd warm up, she happily kept up with Hunter, who walked much faster than she usually did. Probably another throwback to her time in LA where no one seemed to ever be in a huge hurry.

Outside the apartment, he seemed far more talkative and asked her about her films and her favorite parts. She could tell instantly that he'd never seen any of her movies, but his effort flattered her.

After that conversation died down, though, they didn't seem to be able to restart another one, so Alexis took the chance that maybe he'd like to talk about himself for a little while. He hadn't given her any indication of his life at all before moving in to work on her case, so she couldn't help but be curious.

"You mentioned, or maybe it was Paul who told me, but someone said you used to work for the LAPD. You look too young to be a retired cop. What made you leave LA and that job to work for this Project Artemis group?"

"They recruited me. I wanted to do something new with my life, so I said yes. But even before that, I wanted something new, so I turned in my badge and moved east to Virginia since I knew a few people in the DC area. I've been there ever since."

She listened as he talked about what he did for Project Artemis, and she couldn't help but notice he never mentioned a girlfriend or wife. But she never asked, and he never offered any information other than about his work.

He sounded noble when he talked about helping people, and as they walked the streets of the Upper West Side, she had to admit that as attractive as the outside was with Hunter, the inside was appealing too.

Curious how many women like her he'd helped, she asked, "So how many of me have there been?"

He turned to look at her and smiled, making her stomach do that flipping thing. "What do you mean?"

"I mean, how many women like me have you helped?"

A look of recognition washed over him, and he nodded. "Oh. You're my tenth assignment."

So he'd helped nine other women before her. Had he slept with any of them? Her tendency to be jealous reared its ugly head and made her want to ask, but she couldn't find the right words. How could she phrase that anyway? Hey, by the way, how many clients have you taken to bed?

That didn't sound right, and in all honesty, she didn't want to know. She didn't care how many women he'd been with. She just liked being near him, walking around at night like two normal people living in a big city. He gave her that, even if he didn't realize it.

Normalcy. He had no idea how wonderful a gift that was, and Hunter gave her that in those two hours they walked around talking about his work and her films and a hundred other commonplace things she hadn't talked about in ages.

She couldn't remember the last time she laughed and really meant it. She didn't pretend once the entire time, and being genuine felt better than she'd actually remembered it feeling.

When he suggested they go back to the apartment, she smiled and said yes, but she could have stayed out there in that chilly night air for hours more just talking and walking without a care in the world. For the first time in far too long, she'd gone out and had a good time.

As they rode up in the elevator to the penthouse, the reality of her life came rushing back, though, when he turned to her and said, "You don't have to worry, Alexis. I'm not going to let anyone hurt you. I'm going to find out who's behind this and I'll be out of your hair in no time."

She didn't want to focus on the stalker or anything to do with him. Shaking her head, she quietly said, "I don't want to think about that now. I just want to think about how much I enjoyed walking around the neighborhood and talking with you like a normal person. Please don't make me think about how much I won't have that when you leave."

The elevator doors opened, and without a word, they each walked to their own rooms. As he closed his bedroom door behind him, she knew she had to apologize. Hunter had never done anything but try to help her. He didn't deserve to be dumped on like that.

Embarrassed yet again, she knocked lightly on his door as she stood there nervously trying to come up with the right words to say. For far too long, she hadn't truly told anyone she was sorry and actually meant it. Maybe she was a diva after all.

He appeared in the doorway and smiled like he was happy to see her. "Something wrong, Alexis?"

"Can I come in?" she asked nervously.

Nodding, he stepped back so she could walk in. She cleared her throat and hoped she hadn't forgotten how to sincerely tell someone she was sorry.

She expected him to stand at the door holding it open so after she said what she came to say she could make a quick escape. Instead, though, he closed it and then walked back to sit on his bed like before.

Alexis once again felt awkward and out of place while he looked as comfortable as ever in his own skin. As she worked up the courage to say she was sorry for what she'd said back in the elevator, she couldn't help but appreciate that way he had of always seeming to fit in perfectly, no matter where he was.

He didn't speak, likely thinking not saying a word would be polite, so she had no choice. She took a deep breath and did what she knew she had to do.

"I'm sorry for what I said back there. It wasn't right to unload on you like that. You haven't been anything but helpful, well, other than that first time we talked and you were rude. But that doesn't matter. I shouldn't have been like that when you were simply trying to reassure me. So I'm sorry."

She didn't give him time to respond and turned on her heels to leave as quickly as possible. As she reached for the doorknob, he finally spoke and his words cut straight to her deepest fears.

"Why did you come in here before? What did you want?"

She closed her eyes and let out a heavy sigh, unsure how to answer. Should she tell him the truth, or should she simply pretend like she always did?

Did she dare show him the real Alexis or should she continue to pretend to be just the actress she showed the rest of the world?

Chapter Sixteen

S HE DIDN'T ANSWER, but as she stood there silently staring straight ahead at the bedroom door, Alexis heard him get off the bed and walk over to stand behind her. Even if she hadn't heard him move, she would have felt him there. He exuded a sense of power that was unmistakable, and something deep inside her craved what she sensed in him.

"Alexis, why did you come here tonight?" he asked, his voice a husky whisper.

Closing her eyes again, she made her decision to not pretend with him. Quietly, she said, "Did you like her?"

"Who?"

"The brunette at the gym with the perfect body."

"No."

Alexis winced at how hard he was making this for her. "Why? She was beautiful and I saw how you acted with her. She looked so perfect standing next to you."

Hunter took a step closer to her and touched the ends of her hair with his fingertips, sending chills down her spine. "I didn't even notice her. I was too busy looking at the most beautiful woman in the room."

As if she'd been holding her breath from the moment he first asked why she'd come to him, she exhaled and all the fear inside her evaporated. Slowly, she turned around to face him and saw not that sexy grin she'd expected but something darker, more sensual in his expression now.

"You were all smiles with her," Alexis said, looking up into his dark green eyes for some hint of how he felt at that moment.

"I didn't care. I was doing my job," he said as he took another step forward, staring intently at her while he closed the last few remaining inches between them.

Now as he stood so close to her, she noticed how big he seemed, even next to her. Power and strength radiated off him in waves that washed over her. Never before had she known any man who made her feel so confident one moment and so weak the next.

"Are you doing your job now?" she asked in a shaky voice, unsure she wanted to hear the answer.

Hunter shook his head and slowly dragged his tongue over his bottom lip. "No. You're not in any danger from the stalker here, so you don't need anyone to protect you right now."

Need of a different kind coiled inside her. She watched his mouth move as he spoke, desperate to feel his lips press against hers in a kiss. Aching to feel his body next to hers, she tentatively reached out and rested her hand against his muscular chest.

His eyes narrowed, making him look hard, so she pulled her hand away, afraid she'd misunderstood the signs. But before she could apologize, he leaned in and grazed his lips against hers, so lightly that it felt more like teasing than a kiss.

And then he spoke, and she felt like all the air had been sucked out of the room.

Looking deep into her eyes, he whispered against her lips, "Alexis."

Her name had never sounded like that coming from anyone else's mouth before. Sexy and sensual, like a promise of something delicious only he offered.

God, she wanted him to kiss her with all the power he possessed. To kiss her and take her breath away like she knew he could.

But he simply stood there letting his mouth touch hers just enough to make her want so much more.

"Why won't you kiss me? Don't you want

to?" she asked, terrified of what his answer would be.

"Because if I kiss you we're not going to stop there, and I don't know if I can hold myself back," he said in a low voice tinged with an emotion she recognized all too well.

Need. The kind of need that forced you to choose between wanting something so badly it hurt and fearing something so much it paralyzed you.

The kind of need that threatened to burn you up inside if you didn't satisfy it.

"Don't hold back," she whispered into his mouth.

He slid his hand up the column of her neck and stuffed it into her hair, tugging her head forward until his mouth crashed into hers. He kissed her hard, like he wanted her to know he'd given up on holding back, and she welcomed it, returning his kiss with one full of as much need as his.

His body pressed against hers, letting her know he wanted her for more than just kissing. She felt his hard cock push into her hip, and even without seeing it, she knew she would give anything to feel him inside her.

Hunter moaned against her lips as their tongues mixed to ratchet up the need the two of them felt. She could listen to the sound of him moan for the rest of time. Low and deep, it hit a part of her deep inside she'd only hoped existed before this moment.

Then suddenly, he pulled back and stared at her in a way that made her feel empty and alone. "Alexis, I don't want to hurt you."

"The way you're looking at me now hurts more than anything you could physically do to me. Don't let doubt ruin this."

"I don't doubt how much I want you. You shouldn't either."

She tugged on his shirt to pull him closer. "Then show me," she said in a voice that verged on begging.

His mouth covered hers as his hands roamed over her body, pulling her jogging pants down past her knees. She wriggled her leg out as he slid his fingertip under her panties to lightly touch her tender skin.

Her body craved so much more than he'd given her so far, but part of her loved the slowness and teasing. It made her want him so badly.

She playfully bit his lower lip when he slid his finger over her needy clit, making her wish he'd just fuck her with his fingers so she could have some relief from this need that burned inside her.

Dragging her fingernails down his neck and over his shoulders, she closed her eyes and moaned, "Please…"

"Look at me, Alexis," he ordered in a voice low and deep that resonated in the room around her.

She opened her eyes and saw him focused on her. He was so close, so intense right there in front of her, and then he slowly slid his finger over her clit, sending waves of pleasure rushing through her entire body.

A single finger pushed inside her and then another, making her eyelids flutter closed as a feeling of ecstasy washed over her. All she needed was a little more and she'd come.

But Hunter stilled his fingers inside her and leaned in next to her ear. "I want you to look at me, Alexis. I want to see your eyes as I fuck you."

She did as he commanded, staring directly into those mysterious dark green eyes that never showed any emotion. "Why do you want me to keep my eyes open? What are you looking for in them?"

"I want to know what you look like when I get you off fucking you with my fingers."

Oh, God, how she wanted that too! She kept her gaze fixed on his as he began to pump his fingers into her, grazing every nerve just how she needed. He inched her close to coming and then backed off, all the while staring into her eyes with a look that transfixed her.

It made Alexis want more, so she slid her

hands down over his hard abs and undid his belt and then his jeans. Opening them, she pulled the fabric apart by the zipper and reached in to touch the grey cotton covering his cock.

He twitched as she ran her fingernails down the length of him through his boxer briefs. Cupping him through the fabric, she felt an ache in the pit of her stomach she recognized and reveled in.

Kissing him long and deep, he thrust his fingers into her, gliding in and out as she inched toward orgasm, but she craved something even more than that. Lowering herself to the ground in front of him, she pulled the cotton back to reveal his long, thick cock. Never before had she wanted to please a man as much as she did at that very moment. Never before had she wanted to hear that sound a man made at the first touch of a woman's tongue to his cock.

She closed her eyes and slid her tongue over her lips to wet them. Taking hold of him at the base, she held him erect and flicked the thick vein that traveled up the side of his cock.

And then she heard that sound that made her pussy run wet. That moan at the first touch of her tongue to the silky skin of his cock. It came from somewhere deep inside him, a place she wanted to know and be welcomed in.

"Fuck."

The word came out in a rush, drawn out for two seconds and then three as Alexis finally reached the swollen head and sucked it into her mouth. Above her, she heard his sharp intake of breath and looked up to see Hunter staring down at her in awe. Now she didn't need to be told to keep her eyes open because she didn't want to miss a moment of her effect on him.

She took as much of him in as she could, using her hand to stroke him the rest of the way, all the while watching as he struggled to follow his own command. It thrilled her to know she could mesmerize him like he did her. It made her feel powerful and strong.

Suddenly, he pulled her up to him and kissed her hard. Breathlessly, he whispered against her lips, "No."

His rejection reverberated through her brain, making her want to lash out, but before she could say anything in protest, he tore her panties off and roughly pushed her legs apart with his knee. Then he hooked his arm under her knee and lifted it in one smooth motion, so quick that she stared at him in surprise.

He stopped for just a moment, and she whimpered, "Don't worry. It's fine."

The last thing she wanted to do was explain to him what birth control she'd chosen long before she ever met him. She wanted to live in this moment, to relish it and let herself truly feel it, as raw and as real as it would be with him.

Hunter groaned, "Give me your hands."

She did as he commanded, placing them in his left palm. His strong fingers closed around her wrists, and he lifted her arms above her head before pinning them to the door.

Holding her left thigh up, he pushed his hips forward and filled her completely in one thrust. Her eyes rolled back in her head as he began to pump into her.

"You feel so fucking good. Christ, take every inch of me."

She tilted her hips to take all of him, and she heard him moan low in her ear. Alexis wanted to touch him and pushed against his hold on her wrists. He stilled inside her and leaned back to look at her.

"Let me feel you."

Hunter's eyes narrowed as he let her hands fall from above her head, and she slid her arms around his neck. He didn't need to be told what to do next and lifted her up, pressing her back against the door.

"Fuck me, Hunter," Alexis moaned against his lips.

He gave her a wicked grin, like he'd been waiting to hear those very words, and began pumping into her with abandon. Every thrust of his cock sent ripples of pleasure rolling through her body, until Alexis teetered on the edge of an orgasm.

"Don't stop...God, don't stop..." she whimpered as she watched the muscles in his neck tighten with each thrust.

Just as she asked, he continued fucking her like she'd never been fucked before. Her body surrendered to his willingly and forcefully, and she loved every second of it. When she finally felt her release begin to unspool inside her, she silently prayed to God Hunter wasn't like other men and would go until she finished. Her orgasm rushed through her like a force of nature, leaving her weak in his hold.

Panting, he pressed his forehead to hers and stared at her like he needed to know what she experienced and the answers lay in her eyes. It was the most intimate act she'd ever experienced. She couldn't pretend a single emotion like that, so he got all of her.

The vulnerabilities she kept hidden from the rest of the world. The unvarnished and untouched real image of who she was.

And in return, she saw in front of her the man she'd wished all her life for. Raw, hard, and animalistic, he possessed her body like it was his to take. But she also saw more than that.

As Hunter's release roared through him, the

guttural noise of a satisfied man escaped his throat, and then his body stilled. Alexis gently ran her hands over the back of his head and down his neck, feeling the dampness of the sweat from their lovemaking.

Placing a soft kiss on his lips, she sighed and smiled. "That was…"

He kissed her and finished her sentence. "Incredible."

"I was going to say phenomenal."

"That too."

As pain began to course through her hips, she groaned and said, "I'm not sure I'm going to be able to walk tomorrow. I think I need to get down."

Setting her on her feet, he pulled up his pants and zipped them, leaving them unbuttoned and his belt undone. As he sat down on the bed next to her, Alexis couldn't help but think Hunter looked just as comfortable at that moment as he had before they had sex. She admired that in him.

"Why so quiet?" he asked, leaning over to kiss her sweetly as she still worked to recover from their rendezvous.

"No reason. I was just noticing how comfortable you always are in your own skin. I wish I could say I was like that, but I think it must be something you're either born with or not."

Hunter ran his hand over the top of his head to catch a few beads of sweat. For a moment, he didn't say a word, but then he smiled in that way that made her stomach do flips and tucked her hair behind her ear.

"You're one of the most beautiful women in the world, Alexis. Don't try to be anything you're not. You're perfect just like you are."

Perfect.

No man had ever called her that. Not her ex-husband. Not a single photographer who fawned over her. Not a director on any of her films.

No one else in the world.

And yet, in those dark green eyes, she saw he truly meant that. He thought she was perfect.

"Thank you, but I don't feel perfect."

Hunter slid down the pillows and pulled Alexis over next to him. Wrapping his arms around her, he kissed the top of her head.

"Well, you are to me," he whispered and hugged her to his body.

Alexis curled up against him and lay her head on his chest. So much bigger than her, he held her in his strong arms as his words echoed in her head.

Perfect. You're perfect to me.

She didn't want to make more of what they'd done than it truly was. He wouldn't be staying in her life forever. As soon as he found her stalker, he'd leave and go back to his life.

A life she knew almost nothing about.

As she lay there in his protective arms, she felt safe, and for the first time since moving to New York, she didn't feel trapped in her home. She wasn't hiding now. The apartment didn't feel like a prison anymore.

Because of Hunter.

But how hard it would be when the day came when he had to leave. Alexis didn't want to let herself feel attached to him. She wasn't an inexperienced girl who knew nothing of the world. She understood the difference between sex and love, and all they had between them was sex.

Despite all that, as she lay there listening to him breathe in and out as he held her to him, she knew what they had between them was more than sex. He'd given her something she needed so desperately and hadn't been able to find on her own.

That strength she'd always believed she held inside.

It had been pushed down by life, by love, and by her career, but in just the short time Hunter had been in her life, she'd found that strength once more.

And she never wanted to lose it again.

CHAPTER SEVENTEEN

HUNTER SLOWLY AWOKE and opened his eyes, still not used to his new room. As he eased into consciousness, he saw a blond head resting on his chest.

Alexis.

They'd had sex hours before. Mind blowing sex, the kind you never forget. Three times. And now she lay curled up next to him sleeping with her head on his chest.

But they both had clothes on. Craning his neck, he looked down her body and saw that wasn't exactly the case. While he was fully dressed, she wore nothing other than a t-shirt.

He smiled, thinking to himself that he could get used to waking up and seeing those gorgeous legs and ass every morning. His cock twitched in his pants, as eager as the rest of him to go for round four.

A noise outside in the hallway tore him from the fantasy he'd begun to construct about enjoying an early morning lovemaking session.

Looking down at Alexis, he stroked her hair and smiled, still having a hard time believing what they'd done last night.

Not regretting it, though. No, he definitely wasn't unhappy about sleeping with her. He just hadn't planned on it. But now that they'd gone there, he certainly wanted to continue what they started.

And now seemed like a great time to do just that.

Sliding his hand down her back, he cupped her firm ass and inhaled deeply. The image of her riding him while he squeezed that ass made him want to get down to business right now.

Alexis lifted her head and looked up at him sleepily. Smiling, she said, "Hey, good morning."

"Good morning. Did I wake you or did the noise out there do that? There's something going on in the hallway," Hunter said with a smile, loving how sweet she looked first thing in the morning.

She really was perfect.

And just as he began to pull her up on top of him, she suddenly sat up straight, yanking the sheet off the bed to wrap it around her and cover that beautiful ass and those sexy legs. Clutching it just above her breasts, she said frantically, "Oh my God! I didn't expect to sleep so late. I never sleep until morning. God, of all the days for my body to finally figure out how to sleep, why did it have to be today? Everyone's up already!"

"So? You slept in a little. You deserve it," he said as he looked down at the bulge in his pants. "I say we go for another round right now. Trust me, I'm ready."

Her gaze zeroed in on his pants and then she looked up at his face. "Another round? This is no time for joking. Everyone is going to know we were together!"

Hunter stood and pulled her to him to kiss her. "I wasn't joking, and what's the problem with your assistants and your bodyguards knowing we spent the night together?"

Alexis wriggled out of his hold and began looking around the room. "I don't want them to know. That's the problem. Where the hell are my pants?"

With each moment she looked horrified to be there with him, his ego grew more and more bruised. "Is there some problem with us being together?" he asked sharply, not caring that she may think he was overstepping his bounds.

She stopped and looked at him, frowning. "No. That's not it at all, Hunter. I just prefer to keep my private life private."

Living with two assistants and having bodyguards around at all times made any kind of privacy unlikely. How she thought she could ever keep any part of her life private he couldn't understand.

Her face lit up, and she lifted the pink jogging pants in the air. "Found them! Will you go out there and distract them for me? I need to be able to get to my room unseen."

"You mean like Carla did with me?" he asked pointedly.

As she got herself dressed, she looked confused by how he was acting. "Why are you being difficult like this?"

"Because I'm not used to women I've just slept with being ashamed to admit they've been with me."

Alexis let out a huge sigh and frowned. "It's not like that. I promise. I just don't feel like gossiping with Lauren and Carla about how you were in bed because that's what's going to happen if they find out."

"Really?"

"Yes. I know we look like adults, but the reality is that sexy time with a hot man brings out the teenage girl in all of us. It's not pretty, but there it is. There's no way I'm going to escape talking about how you were in bed, Hunter."

"Okay. I get it."

Happy again, she smiled. "Thank you. So you will distract everyone long enough for me to get back to my room?"

"On one condition," he said with a chuckle as he sat back down on the bed.

"What? One condition? Fine. What is it?"

Hunter leaned back against the headboard and put his arms behind his head. "Tell me what you would have said if they asked you how I was in bed," he said with a grin.

"What?"

"You heard me. What would you tell them?"

She huffed and marched around the bed to stand in front of him. "That you're fine in bed but difficult outside of it."

"Just fine?" he asked, stifling a chuckle at how cute she was when she got angry.

She put her hands on her hips and scowled down at him. "I'm not going to compliment you just because you're fishing for them. Now please distract everyone like you said you would so I can run to my room."

Happy to hear she enjoyed herself, he stood up with a hard-on that was visible in his pants and smiled. "We're missing a perfectly good opportunity here."

Fixing her gaze on the bulge in his pants, she shook her head. "Are you always ready like that?"

Hunter walked over to her and kissed her on the neck just below her ear. "I am when I'm around a gorgeous woman like you."

She closed her eyes and sighed. "Please don't

make this more difficult for me than it has to be. I just need to get to my room so no one knows I was in here."

"So I'll run interference while you go to your room. Nobody will be the wiser."

Opening her eyes, she looked him up and down. "Button your pants and get that smile off your face. Everyone is going to know you did something."

"I'm a grown man. I get to have sex. If I'm lucky, I get to have great sex with a beautiful woman."

A knock at the door startled her, and she shook her head, her eyes wide with fear. "Don't let them know I'm here!"

He mouthed, "Okay," and opened the door a crack to see Lauren standing there looking frazzled. "Morning, Lauren. What's up?"

"I'm worried about Alexis. I've knocked on her door twice, but she hasn't answered. After yesterday and how she stayed in her room all night, I'm scared."

"I'm sure she's fine, but let's gather everyone in the kitchen. I'll be right there. Do me a favor and round everyone up."

"Okay. Thank you, Hunter."

"Don't worry. We'll make sure she's taken care of. I bet she just slept in after an excitable night."

"I hope so. I worry about her."

Lauren ran off to do as he told her to, and Hunter closed the door. Turning to look back at Alexis, he said, "Operation Distraction is underway. Give me a couple minutes and then I think you'll be in the clear."

"I slept in after an excitable night?"

The memory of how good their sex had been made him smile. "Well, I couldn't very well tell her you slept late because I kept you up having mind blowing sex."

His joke didn't make her smile, so he asked, "What's wrong? I was just teasing. I'm sure Lauren didn't know what I was talking about. Everything's going to be fine."

Looking down at her feet, Alexis quietly asked, "Are you with someone, Hunter? Did you cheat on someone last night?"

Surprised at the question, he shook his head. "No. Why?"

"No reason," she said, avoiding his gaze. "Just that you said you have sex with beautiful women, but earlier yesterday I got the feeling you had someone waiting for you."

He dipped his head and kissed her softly on the lips. Tilting her chin up, he looked into her eyes and told her the truth.

"There's no one waiting for me anywhere. As for sex with beautiful women, you're the only woman who qualifies as that in a long time."

"Oh. Okay," she said with a little smile. "Okay. Let's do this. Operation Distraction is underway."

"I'm on it. Give me a minute and you'll be safe to go to your room. And by the way, feel free to knock on my door anytime."

She blushed in such a cute way he wished they could have another few minutes alone together. Disappointed they couldn't, he left her standing in his room and walked out to the kitchen where everyone already waited for him.

"Morning everyone."

He turned his back on the group of people and poured himself a cup of coffee while he tried to get the smirk Alexis had chastised him about off his face. He couldn't help it. Why shouldn't he smile? It wasn't everyday he could say he woke up with one of the most beautiful women in the world beside him in bed after a night of phenomenal sex.

Damn. His body was still interested in another go, even though he had to address an entire household of people about the very woman he wished he could be burying his cock inside at that moment.

Well, Operation Distraction couldn't wait for him to go soft. Time for him to put on his show.

Turning around, he leaned against the

counter and tried to look as casual as possible. "You all know what my job is here. I'm going to find out who's behind the letters and packages that have terrorized Alexis for months. I've begun my investigation, but I want to know if any of you who are closest to her have any opinion on who might be doing this."

Hunter didn't have a sense that any of them would necessarily give up that information even if they knew it, but he watched each of their reactions to what he said. Carla didn't look surprised, likely because he'd just spoken to her last night, but Lauren looked utterly baffled as to why he'd chosen this very moment to make this point since her concern revolved around the fact that she still hadn't been able to get Alexis to answer her that morning, even after two attempts.

The bodyguards didn't look particularly surprised, either. Malcolm nodded and looked around at the rest of the people around him, while Kyle simply scowled at him. The other two, Kevin and Mark, looked angry, but he had the feeling it was more because they felt protective about the woman they worked for instead of something else.

Believing he'd given her enough time, he abruptly said, "Okay, well, if any of you want to tell me something privately, please don't hesitate. Thanks and have a great day!"

Lauren waved at him from behind Carla and

said, "Hunter, I still don't know what's going on with Alexis. I can't get her to let me in this morning. Has anyone seen her yet today?"

He'd almost forgot that poor Lauren had gotten herself worked up into a nervous mess about not being able to reach Alexis yet, so he said, "Oh, yeah. Has anyone seen Alexis today? Any of you bodyguards see her go toward the elevator? I certainly hope we don't have another situation like yesterday."

Everyone in the room shook their heads and murmured that they hadn't seen her yet that day. None of that helped Lauren, though, so she hurried off to try Alexis's bedroom door yet again. He felt a little bad about messing with her feelings, but it had to be done.

Operation Distraction a success, Hunter took his coffee and sat down in the living room. A few minutes later, Alexis walked into the kitchen with Lauren in tow.

"Then you're okay?"

"Sure," Alexis said. "I just overslept."

Visibly relieved, Lauren's shoulders dropped from where they'd sat up near her ears. "I knocked and knocked but got no answer. I got scared. I even went to find Hunter because I thought something might have happened. You always answer. What happened? You never sleep like that."

Shrugging, Alexis smiled at her. "Nothing. I was soaking in the tub. It's the only thing I love about this place, so I wanted to enjoy it."

"But your hair isn't wet. How did you get it all up on top of your head without my help?" Lauren asked, confused and a little more than curious this morning.

Her questioning flustered Alexis, who seemed unable to come up with a good lie to cover her first lie. "I don't know. Honestly, you'd swear I did something wrong. I didn't leave the apartment like I was told not to, and I just enjoyed a bath. Everyone needs to calm down. There's no crisis. Just a woman starting her day a little late. Do me a favor, Lauren, and go get the script on my bed I was up late reading. I want to finish it so I can talk to Melanie about it later today."

Distracted by her boss's request, Lauren gave up asking any more questions and ran off down the hall. Hunter waved Alexis into the living room and smiled.

"Good morning! How did you sleep?" he asked as she sat down on the couch opposite where he sat in a chair.

"Pretty good, actually. First time in a long time. Whatever I did, I think I should do it more often. I don't remember having a night as good as that in a long time," she said with a sly smile.

"I think you should."

"And you?" she asked with a slight giggle, looking around to see if anyone was listening to their conversation.

"I got a bit of a workout right before I fell asleep, but I woke up feeling better than I have in a while. Must be the new bed. Thanks for that, by the way."

"You're welcome."

A second later, she leaned over toward him and whispered, "Thank you."

"My pleasure. Anytime."

A confused look settled into her features, and then she shook her head. "I didn't mean for that. I meant for distracting everyone."

"Oh. Well, anytime for that too."

A blush came over her, making her cheeks turn a sweet shade of pink. Hunter watched as she sipped her coffee and couldn't help think no one in the world knew how special Alexis Marchand truly was. Whatever they saw in her up on the screen couldn't compare to what she showed him sitting cross-legged drinking her morning coffee.

He'd been wrong about her being a Hollywood diva. She was just the girl next door deep down.

Smiling to himself, he thought about how Gideon and Xavier would kill to see Alexis like this. Then again, he suspected they liked the movie star. For his fantasies, though, he'd take the person he knew she was.

Sensual, sweet, and even thoughtful. He'd take that Alexis any day.

Chapter Eighteen

Alexis couldn't remember the last time she slept with a man and it didn't feel awkward the next time she saw him. Of course, since Hunter lived less than fifty yards away from her, the situation with him was a little different.

Still, that they could sit in the living room together and drink their morning coffee without strangeness creeping in between them made her happy. She didn't feel embarrassed about their time together, even though every time she thought about how incredible he made her feel as he slid in and out of her body, she blushed a little.

Her cheeks grew warm, so she placed her coffee cup on the table in front of her and covered her face with her hands. The last thing she needed was Lauren thinking she was getting sick. She'd hover over her like a mother hen, which would make getting to Hunter's room again tonight difficult.

That she already had a plan in her mind for how she'd sneak down the hall to be with him made her feel lightheaded. She hadn't experienced the thrill and exhilaration of a new romance in so long, she'd forgotten how wonderful it felt.

Looking across the room, she saw him pretending to focus on whatever was happening in the kitchen, but a closer look told her he was paying attention to her. She liked that. Alexis hadn't forgotten what he'd said about her being perfect. She doubted she'd ever forget that. What woman could? The world probably thought she heard that compliment every day, but acting turned out to be more like living under a microscope. People always seemed to be looking for flaws and imperfections, so it ended up that not only had she never heard anyone say she was perfect, but she'd heard the exact opposite enough times to start believing the critics and naysayers.

"Alexis, did you hear me?"

She turned to see Lauren and Carla standing next to the couch looking down at her like they were waiting for an answer. Unfortunately, in her daydreaming about Hunter and their time together, she'd completely dazed out.

"I'm sorry. I was lost in thought. What's up?"

"Are you okay?" Lauren asked in that concerned voice she used so often lately.

"Yeah. Why?"

"Your face looks red. You're all flushed. Should I call the doctor?"

She and Carla leaned in as if to examine her flushed skin further. God, she loved them, but they really were part of that whole microscope life she could do without.

Reaching over, she grabbed her coffee cup and took a sip. "For a flushed face? There are people in the world who are on death's doorstep who can't afford to see a doctor. I'm not going to bother one because you two worry too much. I'm fine. I had a great night, and I'm feeling better than I have in a long time."

Lauren gave her another long stare like she wanted to see if her claim would hold up and then sat down on the couch next to her. "Okay. That's good. So what's on the schedule today?"

"Well, I went out for a walk last night and the neighborhood is really great. I'd like to get out again today too."

Out of the corner of her eye, Alexis saw Hunter smile as Lauren's and Carla's mouths dropped open in surprise.

"You went out last night?" Lauren asked in a shocked voice. "I thought you were in your room all night."

Turning toward Hunter, she smiled. "I had a case of wanderlust, so Hunter was good enough to accompany me on a little walk. The neighborhood is pretty nice."

Lauren looked over at him and then at Carla

before turning back to face Alexis. "Wow! I'm so glad you got out. I thought after what happened outside that gym that you wouldn't go out for a while."

Alexis waved off her concern. "No way. I'm not going to spend the rest of my life scared."

While her assistants seemed surprised by her newfound strength, Hunter wasn't. All she saw was pride now as he smiled at her. She liked how it felt to see someone look at her like that for something other than acting. That she could do easily. Steeling herself and forcing down the fear in real life was much harder.

"That is so great!" Lauren said, genuinely happy to see her confident again. "See, I told you this move was going to be good for you. It just took a little time to get used to the place."

"Well, maybe you're right. I still miss the sun in LA, but maybe New York won't be so bad. What do you say to checking out another gym today?"

She looked over at Hunter and chuckled. "You up for another run?"

His eyes lit up at her offer of another challenge. "Of course. Just say when."

"Later this morning, then. I just need to get a shower and I'll be ready to go."

As the words left her mouth, she saw Hunter's eyes grow wide. A split second later, she realized what she'd done as Lauren looked at her and shook her head.

"A shower? You told me you took a bath this morning."

Quickly, she tried to cover up her mistake. "Oh, well, you know how baths feel great but then you never feel clean? That's what I meant. I want to feel clean when I go for a run. That's all."

Yeah. That made sense. Showering before she went running. At this rate, she'd be lucky if Lauren and Carla didn't want to rush her off to a doctor to have her head examined.

Thankfully, one of her bodyguards walked into the room at that moment and said, "Miss Marchand? Sorry to bother you, but you just got this special delivery."

In his hand, he held an oversized manila envelope. Just seeing it made Alexis's entire body tense up. She'd been having such a good day so far, and now this had to happen.

Hunter quickly took the envelope from Mark's hand and examined it, gingerly holding it by the edge and turning it over to look at the back before saying to her, "It's from a Melanie Dannon. Do you know her?"

As if the tension and stress of seeing that envelope melted away at the mere sound of her agent's name, Alexis smiled. "That's my agent."

Holding out her hand, she added, "It's okay.

She probably sent something I need to sign. I think she mentioned something the last time we talked the other day."

He relaxed and nodded as he handed it to her. "Okay. As long as you recognize the name. I didn't think this would be from him anyway. None of the others had a return address on them."

Alexis let out a sigh of relief. "Oh, that's good. I didn't think about that. I just got a little freaked out there, but once you said my agent's name, I knew it was okay."

She eagerly opened it and pulled out a sheet of paper. Suddenly, it felt like her coffee would come up as her stomach twisted into a tight knot. This wasn't something from Melanie she had to sign.

"It's…it's from…" she stammered out, shaking her head in disbelief.

Her hands shook in terror as Lauren asked, "What's wrong? What did Melanie say?"

The paper fell from her hands, and Alexis pulled her knees up to curl into a ball to protect herself. She'd promised herself she'd be strong, but now the stalker had come into her home once more and all she wanted to do was crawl into bed and hide.

Hunter hurried over and crouched down in front of her to pick up the horrible letter. She wanted him to take her into his arms and tell her he would protect her. That everything would be okay because he'd make it okay.

But he didn't.

He stood up and said to Lauren and Carla, "You two take care of her. I'll be right back."

She watched as he walked out of the room, leaving her there with nothing but her fear and the helpless words from her two assistants. Closing her eyes, she hid her face in her knees and wished for this all to be over.

But would it ever end? Would she ever be free of this mystery person who tormented her with his letters?

Chapter Nineteen

H UNTER MADE A beeline for his room and slammed the door shut behind him. In his bag, he grabbed a plastic baggie and slid the letter and envelope inside, knowing all too well that any check for fingerprints would find his and Mark's. Hopefully, though, they'd find another person's.

He called the estate and heard Gideon answer. "Hey man! What's up?"

"I'm sending you a letter that just got delivered to Alexis. It was supposedly sent from her agent, Melanie Dannon. It's from the stalker. I need you to check for fingerprints and see if there's anyone around the agent we can connect to this. You'll find my prints and one of her bodyguards' prints, Mark Driscoll, so keep that in mind."

Gideon blew the air out of his lungs into the phone, making a whooshing sound. "Jesus. She got another one? That was fast. What does it say?"

Sighing, Hunter read the letter through the plastic covering it. "I know. They're starting to come more frequently since she got to New York. Damn, it sounds like this fucker thinks they're best friends. Listen to this. 'Alexis, I see you spent some time enjoying the beauty of the Upper West Side last night. Did you see me too? Someday soon, we'll meet and you'll finally get to know your #1 fan.' Gideon, I was with her last night when she went out. How the hell did I miss this guy?"

"Hunter, you're in the middle of one of the largest cities in the world. You can't be expected to have eyes on every person in New York, for Christ's sake. God only knows how many apartment windows you passed just getting a cab."

His words were supposed to be helpful and supportive, but they weren't working.

"We went out for a walk too. Fuck. He could have been anywhere. Damnit, I'm failing at this assignment."

"Don't do this to yourself, man. Just don't. She's safe, and he hasn't gotten to her. Don't forget that," Gideon said sternly like he was scolding him.

Hunter began to pace around his room. "She's practically a prisoner in her own home. I haven't done a goddamned thing to fix that since I got here. Persephone should have sent someone else on this assignment. She chose the wrong one of us this time."

He tossed the letter on the bed and lay back against the pillows, covering his eyes with his arm. "I'm sending the letter as soon as I get off the phone. Do me a favor and find whatever you can on it."

"Okay. I'll get on it as soon as I get it this afternoon," Gideon promised.

"Thanks. Call me as soon as you have anything."

His words were met with silence for a long moment before his friend said, "Hunter, you're tying yourself into knots over this. I've never seen you like this on an assignment. What's going on?"

He didn't want to admit that what he felt for Alexis might be clouding his judgment on this case. Even if it was, that wouldn't be so bad. Caring for a client didn't hurt his efforts.

"Nothing's going on. You try working on as many assignments as Persephone and Nick have dumped on me in the past few months. If I'm on edge at all, it's because I'm fucking overworked. Call me when you get something."

Before Gideon could say anything more, Hunter pressed END and threw his phone onto the other side of the bed. He should have found out who was behind these damn letters coming to Alexis by now.

And what the fuck was taking Gideon so long with checking out twenty fucking names? It wasn't like he had much else to do other than watch football, and those games didn't take up every minute of the damn day.

Hunter took a deep breath. This wasn't Gideon's fault. This wasn't anyone's fault but his own. He had to solve this case, not anyone else in Project Artemis.

The problem was he had no leads. Everyone who worked for Alexis either had a clean record or couldn't be connected to the letters in any way, according to the LAPD and a private investigator Paul had hired. Even the ones Hunter had vague suspicions about might turn out to be okay when Gideon finished his search.

Fifteen minutes later, the envelope with the latest letter from the stalker was on its way to Gideon. Hunter stood in the lobby of the apartment building watching the security guard and the doorman as they went about their business and wondered how anyone had gotten into the building to leave the envelope. He understood how Alexis and Lauren could get out because they'd already been inside, but the doorman let no one in he didn't recognize. Just in the time Hunter had been standing there watching him, Chambers stopped two people from coming in already.

Hunter walked outside to where the man stood helping a woman into a car. The October sun felt warm on his face as he waited for him to have time to speak to him.

Turning around, Chambers smiled. "Mr. McKary, can I get you a cab, sir?"

"No. I wanted to speak to you about something. Miss Marchand received an envelope today. It didn't come in the mail, so how would someone have gotten in to deliver it to you at the desk? I've noticed you don't let anyone in who doesn't have a reason to be here."

The doorman puffed out his chest in his very formal doorman's uniform and nodded. "That's true, sir. Unless it's a courier service like the one you just used or someone who we know will be coming to see one of the residents, we don't let anyone in who doesn't belong, especially those damn photographers who seem to be lurking around all the time since Miss Marchand moved in."

A sheepish look crossed his face, and he added, "I know we didn't see Miss Marchand and her assistant leave the other day, but I can assure you no one gets in if they don't have business being here."

"Then how did she get that envelope this morning?"

Chambers looked confused. "What envelope, sir? Miss Marchand didn't receive any deliveries this morning."

"Yes, she did. One of her bodyguards brought her a large manila envelope. Didn't he get it from you? Wasn't he down here all night?" Hunter asked, his mind racing.

"I only work seven to seven, sir. At night, a security guard is in charge of the door and we keep it locked so no one can just wander in off the street. As for Miss Marchand's guard, sir, I didn't see him this morning when I came on. No one was down here."

"They're supposed to be on every day and night. When was the last time you saw someone stationed in the lobby, Chambers?"

The elderly man thought about the question. "Yesterday afternoon, sir."

Hunter's mind raced. Why hadn't her bodyguards followed his explicit instructions to be in the lobby around the clock?

He thanked the doorman and rushed upstairs to find out what the hell had happened. All four bodyguards sat in the living room chatting like nothing important was happening. What the fuck was wrong with these people?

Thankfully, Alexis had gone back to her room, so she wouldn't have to hear what he had to say to the men. Folding his arms across his chest, he worked to keep his voice calm as he asked, "Why aren't any of you downstairs like I told you to? I said that there needed to be at least one of you in the lobby at all times. Why isn't one of you down there?"

The four men looked at each other and then back at him. Malcolm, the head of her security team, shook his head. "We were told not to do that, so that's why we're all up here in the penthouse."

"Who told you to go against the very thing I told you to do?" Hunter asked in amazement.

No wonder this stalker believed he could get to Alexis.

"Paul. He said we needed to stick close by her at all times we're in the building after she ran away to Atlantic City. That's why we're all up here."

Hunter's mind raced. Why would Paul go directly against his orders and tell the bodyguards to leave the lobby unsecured?

Lauren walked into the living room as he said to Malcolm, "Forget what Paul said. I want one of you in that lobby at all times. Round the clock! Do you understand me?"

The men nodded and Malcolm stood to leave. "Got it. I'll take the day shift. Kyle, you take the night shift tonight."

"Hunter, Alexis wants to speak to you. She's in her room."

As much as he wanted to comfort her, he needed to investigate that letter first. "I have work to do, Lauren."

Frowning, she answered, "She wants to talk to you, Hunter. I think it's important."

"Fine. I'll be right there."

Lauren hurried off, but Hunter had one more person to question. He saw Mark walking toward the kitchen and yelled, "Mark, I need to speak to you."

The man stopped, and as he turned around, Hunter saw his face told the story that he'd been hiding something. Damnit, they didn't have time for secrets.

"Mark, who gave you that envelope to give to Alexis?"

His blue eyes grew wide, and then he looked down at the floor. "Nobody gave it to me. I found it in the elevator."

Jesus! Did none of these people understand what was at stake here? It was like none of them realized the danger they kept putting Alexis in.

"What the fuck is wrong with all of you? Do you want to see Alexis hurt?" Hunter asked, barely able to keep himself from lashing out at Mark.

The man looked up and shook his head. "I didn't think telling a white lie about where I found it would hurt anyone. It was from her agent, so I didn't think it would be a problem. I didn't want to see Carla or Lauren get in trouble because they dropped it when they went down to get the mail. I didn't mean any harm."

Hunter watched as Mark explained himself and had to admit that he didn't seem to be acting guilty. And the envelope had looked like it had been from Alexis's agent. Nonetheless, he joined Kyle and Carla at the top of Hunter's list of who might be the stalker or his helper on the inside.

"Fine. Join Malcolm downstairs in the lobby, and if anyone—and I mean even a single soul—comes with anything for Alexis, I want you to hold him there and alert me immediately. Understand?"

Mark nodded and left without saying another word. Hunter closed his eyes and tried to calm down, knowing he had to go talk to Alexis. He couldn't let her see him worried, no matter how much this morning had unnerved him.

Standing in front of her door, he hesitated before knocking. He didn't know what to tell her because he felt like he was failing at this case. Finally, he knocked and she quietly said, "Come in."

Bracing himself for what he'd find, he expected to see her a mess. He opened the door and saw her sitting on the grey loveseat in the corner of the room. Her eyes weren't red from crying, and she looked okay.

But appearances might be deceiving.

He closed the door behind him but didn't go

any further into the room. What he wanted to do he couldn't—take her into his arms and make her forget the world beyond them.

"Do you know why I'm sitting over here?" she asked in a low voice.

He heard defeat in her words. Defeat because the stalker had once again upended her life, and he hadn't done a damn thing to stop him.

Hunter shook his head but didn't answer.

"I've convinced myself that this is the only spot in the room where someone can't get to me through the window. I bet you think that's crazy. I mean, we're on the top floor, the penthouse."

"It's not crazy," he said, remembering how ridiculous he'd thought Carla had been with her concern about the windows the other day. "I don't think you're crazy Alexis."

She forced a smile that only accentuated the pain in her eyes. "I want to be strong. I do. And then I fell apart out there. I hate that."

Taking a step into the room, he stopped. "You didn't fall apart. You reacted the way anyone else would."

"Thanks, but it's such a drama. I hate that. It probably sounds bizarre—an actress who hates drama—but I do. I just want to live my life. Do you know I haven't done anything but worry about this stalker since I moved here? Well, other than stupidly running off with Lauren and freaking everyone out."

"Don't beat yourself up about that. Everyone needs to break out sometimes."

Alexis shook her head. "But Paul was right. I can't do that. I can wish all I want, but even with all the money I have, I can't buy the kind of life I wish I could have. Not and be the person I am now. It's like I have to choose between doing something I love and having a life I can be happy with. It's not fair."

Hunter suddenly wanted to give her that life, at least for a few days. It was crazy, but he didn't care.

He walked over to where she sat and crouched down in front of her. "Let's go. Right now."

Looking down at him with eyes full of surprise, she asked, "Where?"

"We can get away from here. We can go anywhere we can find privacy. I can work from wherever we go. We'll keep it a secret so no one will know. Not Lauren or Carla or the body-guards or even Paul."

Alexis leaned forward and clasped his hands. "Are you serious?"

"Yes. Tell me where you want to go and we'll drive there. Name the place. I think getting you away from here will do us both good."

What he hoped was his hunch about who might be behind this whole stalker thing would come to light once he had her in a secret place.

Maybe they could go to a cabin in the mountains somewhere. Or the desert. Or a secluded beach house. Anywhere she wanted, he'd take her.

"Take me to where you live. I want to see where you were before you came here."

Of all the places she could want to go, the estate was the last place he knew he should take her. Persephone had a rule that only he and the other employees were allowed there.

But he didn't want to refuse her this, so he quickly devised a plan where she could stay on the estate since his room was out of the question. The estate had a guest house on the other side of the property, so they could go there.

Nick and Persephone would just have to understand he had his reasons for doing this.

"Okay, I'll take you to the estate."

"Really? But should it just be the two of us? I've never been without Lauren since she became my assistant, Hunter."

Standing, he shook his head. "It has to be just the two of us."

Worry settled into her face. "You don't think Lauren could be behind this stalker's letters, do you? Is that why you want to get me away from everyone?"

In truth, he didn't think Lauren was part of it,

but he didn't know about Carla or the rest of the people Alexis surrounded herself with. His gut told him no matter how much they all said they loved her, someone knew more than they were telling.

"No, but I don't know about everyone else," he admitted, hoping he didn't frighten her.

The idea that someone you trusted with your life may want to hurt you could terrify anyone.

"So you don't want me to tell anyone where we're going?" she asked with hesitation in her voice.

He held his hand out to take hers. "Do you trust me, Alexis?"

Without a hint of reluctance, she placed her hand in his palm and let him pull her to her feet. Looking up into his eyes, she said, "I do. I'm sure a lot of people would say I shouldn't because we haven't even known each other for long at all, but I do trust you, Hunter."

"Then tell no one where we're going. I'll get a car and text you when we're ready to leave. Take the elevator down to the garage alone. Just be sure no one comes with you."

"But what if someone asks where I'm going?"

"Tell them I'm waiting downstairs in the lobby."

She bit her lip like this worried her, so Hunter gently cradled her face in his hands and looked into her eyes. "I promise I won't let anything hurt you. You can trust me. Just make sure to follow those instructions to a T and don't tell a soul we're going anywhere."

"I won't. I promise."

He bent down and kissed her softly on the lips. "Remember, no one. I'll see you in a little while."

Even though he saw worry in her eyes, she smiled and nodded. "Okay. I'll be waiting for your text."

Hurrying out of her room, he headed toward his room to make arrangements to take her to the estate. Nothing like this had ever happened to him on a case, but then again, Alexis Marchand wasn't like any other client.

Or any other woman, for that matter.

Chapter Twenty

THE THOUGHT OF going off with Hunter frightened Alexis as much as it thrilled her. Had she made a mistake telling him she would leave and not mention it to a single person? What did she actually know about him other than Paul had hired him and he came from some group called Project Artemis that helped women?

Maybe she should at least tell Lauren. Just in case.

Just then she realized she couldn't even tell her best friend exactly where they were going to. Swinging her legs off the loveseat, she began looking for a bag to pack a few things in. Wherever this place was he was taking her, she'd need her things.

As she stuffed a brush and some makeup into her bag, she mumbled, "This is crazy. I'm running off with a man I barely know."

Then again, she knew him a little more than barely, didn't she?

Her cheeks grew hot as the memory of their

time together in his room the night before rushed through her mind. Smiling, she admitted to herself she definitely wouldn't use the word barely to describe how she knew him sexually.

But did that mean she should leave the security of her home and drive somewhere all alone with him? At least when she went off with Lauren she was with someone she knew and trusted.

Tossing more makeup into her bag, she said, "I must be out of my mind. I'm crazy. This is crazy."

A gentle knock at her bedroom door tore her out of her thoughts, and she yelled, "Come in!"

Lauren's face appeared, and she asked, "Are you okay? Can I come in?"

Alexis waved her in. "Come in! I want to talk to you." She sat down on the bed and patted it next to her. "I need your help with something."

Her assistant eagerly nodded, happy to help, of course. "Whatever you want. What's up?"

"Hunter is getting me out of the city for a little bit. I don't know how long I'll be gone, but I need you to make it look like I'm staying in my room the whole time. I don't want anyone to know I'm gone."

He'd told her to not tell a soul, not even Lauren, but she had to let her know. She couldn't worry her best friend needlessly like that. Not after everything she'd done for her.

Lauren's mouth dropped open in shock at her announcement. "You barely know him. Do you think you should go off alone with him? I mean, I know he's here to help catch the stalker, but he hasn't been around that long."

"I know, but I trust him. It might sound crazy, but I need to get away from here. I feel like I'm just waiting for the next letter to show up and terrorize me."

As always, Lauren worried about the rest of her life like any great assistant would. "But what about that part Melanie was talking about last week? What if they want you to go read for it? You want this part, don't you?"

Alexis thought about the part, a character who struck out on her own after being abused as a child and worked her way up the corporate ladder. She loved the idea of finally playing a strong woman who controlled her own destiny, but as much as she wanted to play that character, she needed to get away more.

"It will probably only be for a few days. I don't think it will be a problem, and if it is, then that part wasn't meant to be."

Frowning, Lauren said, "Okay. I mean, if this is what you want to do, then I guess you're going to do it."

She looked into her friend's dark eyes and

hoped she saw the truth in hers. "I do need this. I can't explain it, but I trust him."

"I'm just curious about your going with Hunter. You barely know him. Are you sure about going away with him?"

Alexis looked away, avoiding her gaze now. "Well, I know him a little better than you think."

Lauren sat silently for a few moments before pushing hard on her arm and exclaiming, "Shut up! When? How? Where was I when all this was happening?"

As much as she wanted to gossip with her, Alexis didn't have the time. Hopping off the bed, she returned to packing her bag.

"I don't have time to tell you all the juicy details. It was last night, though."

"You have to give me something! You can't leave me in the dark like this."

Lauren bounced on the bed like a kid dying to hear where she was going that day. Alexis stopped packing and shook her head.

"We're not in high school anymore. We should be more adult when we talk about sex."

"Nonsense! Now give me the dirt."

Whenever she thought of Hunter now, Alexis couldn't help but smile. "It was different from everyone I've ever been with, and yes, I know. I haven't been with that many men. Don't remind me, okay? I can tell you this. He was a thousand times better than Jackson."

Eager to hear more, her assistant leaned forward toward her. "Go on. And don't worry about not having a lot of past lovers. I didn't need to eat that fudge the other day more than once to know it was heavenly. Some things you just know when they're good."

She always had a unique way of bringing her back to the focus of her thoughts. She loved that about Lauren.

"You know what it was? For the first time, I was with someone who didn't care who I was to the rest of the world. I liked that."

"I love that! Okay, I need to know more. What was it like? What does he look like under those clothes? I bet he's got a great body, right? Come on! You have to tell me more."

But Alexis ignored all her pleas for more details about her time with Hunter. It wasn't that she didn't want to share things with Lauren like she always had, but something felt different this time.

With this man.

Just as she stuffed her favorite pink sweater into her bag, she heard her phone vibrate in her pocket. It was Hunter telling her it was time to leave.

"I have to go. I need you to get everyone away from the elevator doors so I can get out of here."

Hopping off the bed, Lauren headed for the bedroom door. "Okay, I'm on it. Just promise me you'll let me know you're safe. Don't make me worry, Alexis."

"I promise."

That didn't feel like enough, though, so Alexis rushed over to the door and hugged her best friend. "I can't believe I'm doing this! Tell me I'm not crazy."

"I've never thought you were crazy. It's not crazy to want to live your life the way you want to. Just be safe, okay?"

Squeezing her hand, Alexis smiled. "I will. Together we'll make everyone think I'm spending the next few days hiding out in my room. Temperamental actresses do that all the time, right? Sounds like something someone like me would do."

Lauren cradled her face as she shook her head. "You're nothing like that, and you know it. Leave that nonsense in the tabloids. Now go and have some fun. I'll be here playing my role."

"Now who's the actress?" Alexis joked as she watched her best friend walk out into the hallway.

THE ELEVATOR DOORS opened, and Alexis looked around the garage for any sign of Hunter. Alone, she stood nervously waiting as the smell of engine fumes made it hard to breathe. After about a minute, she began to wonder if she'd made a mistake. She hadn't been alone for more than a minute or two in so long that she didn't know what to do. What if someone approached her? She'd have no way to protect herself.

With every second that passed, Alexis became more and more frightened. She never should have agreed to do this. She barely knew Hunter. What if he was behind the stalker and just wanted to get her alone in this garage?

As every horrible possibility ran through her mind, a grey sedan drove toward her. She strained to see the driver but couldn't through the tinted windows. Frozen in place, she didn't know if she should run back to the elevator or stay there.

The car stopped, and she held her breath, praying to God she could run away fast enough if it was someone who wanted to hurt her. The darkened driver's side window slowly lowered, and she saw Hunter smiling at her.

"Ready to go?" he asked with that sexy smile she loved.

Exhaling, Alexis nodded, eager to get into the car and away from the city. "I didn't know if that was you. I wasn't sure what to do. I was all alone here."

He waved her toward the car. "Come on! You're with me now, and we're getting the hell away from this place for a few days."

That's exactly what she needed to make her remember how much she wanted to go with him, so she hurried over to the car and jumped in, tossing her bag into the backseat. She didn't want to think or worry anymore. She just wanted to be free.

Hunter turned to look over at her and asked, "Ready?"

"Let's do this!"

"Okay. Until we get out of the city, I need you to get down so no one can see you. Everything taken care of upstairs?"

As she slid down onto the floor in front of the passenger seat, she nodded. "Lauren is going to make sure everyone thinks I'm hiding out in my room for the next few days."

Suddenly, Hunter's expression darkened. "I told you not to tell anyone, Alexis."

Just the sight of him upset with her made all the worrying return. She didn't have a choice. He didn't understand that if she didn't appear for a few days, someone would wonder what was wrong.

"I had to tell her. People will start to ask questions if there's no explanation why I'm not around for more than a few hours. Lauren will take care of that. Trust me, she'd never do anything to hurt me. We can trust her. She'll keep this a secret."

"And if Paul forces her to tell him, you don't think she will?" he asked, not believing in the woman who had watched over her forever.

Alexis shook her head. "She won't tell a soul. You can trust her. She loves me like a sister. Sisters don't betray one another."

"And you think anyone is going to believe that you're staying in your room for days on end? Lauren's sweet, but I'm not sure she can carry off that lie."

"I'm an actress. I think most people believe I act like that most of the time."

He pressed his foot down on the gas and smiled. "Well, they'd be wrong. Hold on. As soon as I get us out of the city, we'll be in the clear."

"I brought my wig in case."

The car quickly swerved left and then right, and Alexis grabbed onto the seat after nearly bashing her head on the bottom of the dashboard. She hadn't anticipated getting away to be like this.

Hunter reached over and touched her arm. "You okay? I had to take that turn a bit hard. I promise I'll try not to do that again."

Touched by his concern, she smiled up at him. "I'm fine. It's just nice to be out of that apartment, even if it's this way."

"Well, I don't think the world would forgive me if I hurt Alexis Marchand. I'd be the most hated man on the planet."

She giggled at his ridiculous claim. "Just a little exaggeration, don't you think?"

Focused on the road, he smiled. "Well, then I wouldn't forgive myself. Hang on."

The car swerved again and she closed her eyes. Who would have imagined it could be so scary in a car speeding down the road, but not being able to see where they were going or what was ahead of them made it truly harrowing.

No matter how frightened she got, though, she knew she was safe with Hunter. Opening her eyes, she looked up at him and even in her fear, she couldn't help but smile. He really was very good looking, and he had a real knight in shining armor way about him.

She didn't know how long it took or how many times the car swerved left and right, but it didn't matter. For at least a short time, she'd escaped her world, but it didn't feel like when she and Lauren ran off to Atlantic City.

No, this time was different. She didn't feel so much like she was running away but moving toward something. She didn't know what it was, but she liked the anticipation that came along with it.

A few minutes later, Hunter tapped her on the top of her hand. "We're out of the city. I think you can get up now."

She sat up in the seat and gave her legs a badly

needed stretch. "Should I put on my wig?"

Hunter turned to look at her and shook his head. "No. I like the way you are naturally."

Out of habit, she put her hand up next to her face to hide herself. "But what if someone sees me?"

"Not to worry. I can outdrive anyone."

She relaxed and slowly let her arm come back down to her side. "I'm not worried. I trust you, Hunter."

Looking over at her, he smiled, and her stomach did that flipping thing she loved.

CHAPTER TWENTY-ONE

AFTER FIVE HOURS of driving, Hunter pulled up to the guard shack at the entrance to the Blackmore Estate and rolled down the window. Freddie, the man on duty, made some small talk about it being nice to see him again and how the weather had been nice in the past few days. Then he leaned down out of his shack and his eyes nearly bugged out of his head when he saw Alexis.

"Is that…are you Alexis Marchand?"

Before she could answer, he started rattling off every movie of hers he'd ever seen and telling her which of them was his all-time favorite. Hunter wondered if he was the only man on the planet who hadn't seen even a second of any of her movies.

As he tried to explain to Freddie that they needed to get onto the estate for official Project Artemis business, she leaned over and rested her head on Hunter's shoulder.

"It's so nice to meet you," she said. "I'm so happy you enjoy my films. You've made my day,

Freddie."

The guard beamed his happiness, but still he continued to hold them at the estate entrance. Pointing toward the road in front of him, Hunter said, "We really need to get in there, so if you could just open the gate, we'll be on our way."

Alexis nudged his arm, and he turned to see her scowling at him. "We really need to get going. I'm sure we could have the Alexis Fan Club meeting some other time," he whispered.

"You really don't get how this whole movie star thing works, do you?" she asked with a smile.

Just then, the gate opened and Hunter quickly pulled the car through. "I guess I just don't see you that way, so when something like that happens, I don't really understand it. To be honest, I wasn't sure you'd deal with that as well as you did."

She nudged him again and moved back over onto her seat. "I don't know. I just did what I always used to do. I didn't even think about it."

"See what a little time away will do for you?" Hunter asked with a grin as he drove toward the guest house at the back of the property.

Alexis stared out the window at the main house in the distance, saying very little and obviously impressed with Persephone and Nick's place. He had to admit the estate was pretty damn nice.

Certainly better than everywhere else he'd ever lived.

"How many of you live here?" she asked.

"Seven of us. Well, six of us since Roman and Kate moved out of the house I'm taking you to. And then there's the other staff and Persephone and Nick."

"Wow! This place is stunning. The grounds are so beautiful. I wish I could have moved to somewhere like this instead of a penthouse apartment in Manhattan."

Hunter heard sadness in her voice and turned to see it all over her face. Hoping to cheer her up, he joked, "Trust me. If you asked any of the guys here, they'd probably take your place over living here any day. Once you leave the estate, there isn't much to do, unless you want to go into DC."

"I'd love it here. It's so peaceful and beautiful," she said in a faraway voice. "It sort of reminds me of my house in LA, except mine wasn't even half the size of this."

He stopped the car at the rear of the guest house that until about a month before had been the home of Roman and Kate until they bought a place a few miles away. Hunter knew Persephone wouldn't be happy that he'd brought Alexis to the estate, but he hoped she didn't make a big deal out of it.

If he knew her, she'd be all sweetness and light

to Alexis, but he'd pay for his decision after the case ended. It was all worth it if Alexis got to relax for a few days, though.

The guest house on Blackmore Estate would technically be called a cottage, but as Hunter escorted her inside, he thought about how many of his homes had been even smaller than this place. Calling it a cottage made the three bedroom, eight room house sound quaint, but in truth, most people lived in more modest places than this one.

Alexis turned around in awe as he set her bag down on the coffee table in the living room. Obviously happy, she smiled like he'd never seen her do before.

"This is so nice, Hunter! I love this house! If the main house is anything like this one, I can't believe anyone would want to ever move away from here."

"Living with six other men and a bunch of other people isn't as great as it sounds. I would think you'd know that."

She spread her arms and twirled around in the middle of the room. "But it's so wide open and charming. It's nothing like the penthouse where all the rooms are like little boxes."

"Well, imagine it with Lauren, Carla, and the bodyguards and it doesn't sound so charming anymore."

The smile slid from her face. "Well, when you put it like that, I guess not. But I still love this place."

The knock at the front door he'd been dreading since he pulled away from the guard shack came a second later. Hunter knew Freddie would tell anyone who would listen who he'd seen in the car with him, but he'd hoped he and Alexis would have more than a few precious minutes alone before the rest of the estate descended on the cottage.

No such luck, though.

Alexis looked over at him wide-eyed, so he took her hand in his and kissed her softly. "I had a feeling we'd have guests. You're pretty popular with a few of the guys here. I can send them away, but I've got to answer the door at least."

"Oh, they're fans of mine?" she asked in a surprised voice.

"Yeah. It seems I'm the only one who's never seen any of your movies. I need to get out more, I guess."

She smiled at his tepid attempt at a joke. "I like that you haven't. It means you like me for me."

"Well, I do, but brace yourself because these guys like you for entirely different reasons."

As he walked toward the front door, he just hoped the men he worked with would behave themselves when they met her. Something told him they wouldn't.

Opening the door, he saw Xavier and Gideon standing there wearing shit eating grins and behind them stood Persephone with a far more serious look on her face. In the distance, Julian hurried across the lawn to join them.

"Hi, everyone. What's new?" he asked casually.

"We heard you brought a friend home with you. We just came to welcome her," Xavier said as he leaned around Hunter to peer into the cottage.

"It was a long drive, so maybe later. You know, after we have a chance to relax a little," Hunter said, trying to put them off.

The way Persephone's eyes narrowed to slits told him it was no use. They would be coming in, whether he wanted them to or not.

"It wouldn't be very polite of the owner of this estate to not at least introduce herself and make one of her guests welcome, Hunter," Persephone said icily.

Gideon and Xavier grinned even wider when he said, "No, I guess it wouldn't. Please, come in everyone."

He stepped off to the side and watched as they filed past him directly toward Alexis. Closing the door, he hurried over to help her as they descended on her like a pack of wolves, but she handled them easily. In fact, Hunter felt proud of her as he watched her deal with them with grace and confidence.

Persephone pushed the men who towered over her aside and smiled at Alexis. "It's very nice to meet you, Miss Marchand. My name is Persephone Gilmore. I'm a huge fan of yours, as are my employees, clearly. What brings you to our little corner of the world?"

Everyone but Alexis picked up on the edge in Persephone's words. Smiling, she shook hands with the head of Project Artemis.

"Oh, please call me Alexis. I asked Hunter to take me to where he lives, so we got in the car and drove down here from my new apartment in New York City. Your home is gorgeous, Persephone. Thank you for letting Hunter bring me here to see it."

Hoping his boss wouldn't turn on Alexis's kind words, Hunter waited to see Persephone's reaction and breathed a sigh of relief when she smiled in that way he knew meant she genuinely liked Alexis. What she thought of him he suspected tended toward another emotion entirely.

"Well, I hope you enjoy your stay here. Please come to the main house so I can give you a tour before you leave. It's not Hollywood, but it's home."

"Oh, I will, for sure. Thank you."

"I need a few minutes of Hunter's time, so I'm sure you'll be in capable hands with Gideon, Xavier, and Julian here."

And with that, Persephone's sweetness turned as she spun around to look at him while he cringed at her mention of any of the guys having their hands on Alexis. The leader of Project Artemis walked toward him with a flinty look in her dark eyes and her mouth set in a straight line across her face.

"Come with me," she said in a low voice before walking outside onto the back porch of the cottage.

He followed her, and closing the door behind him so no one would hear what she had to say to him, he walked over to where she stood with her arms folded across her chest. She grimaced at him and didn't say anything for a long moment as Hunter braced for what would come when she finally did begin to speak.

Her body language alone practically berated him.

"I let you get away with things I shouldn't because of what Nick thinks of you. But he's not here at the moment, and I'm going to tell you right now this whole thing is unacceptable, Hunter. You are a good man who I've come to rely on, but this is too much. You've endangered everything we do here, and for what? So some movie star can enjoy a few days away? Why aren't you working on the case you were assigned in the place where it's happening?"

"I work hard for this mission. You know that," he said, careful in his defense not to anger her more. "You don't have to worry about Alexis. She won't tell anyone about this place. I promise."

Persephone looked into his eyes, studying him for a moment and then shaking her head. "I see you've been breaking the rules all over the place. You're too close to her. Too close to the client. I think maybe Gideon should take over this case. I know he's been working on it anyway from here, and he's had more than enough time watching TV with Xavier."

Jealousy coursed through Hunter, making his fists clench at his side at the mere thought of Gideon protecting Alexis. "No, don't do this. I can finish this job."

Persephone pointed her finger at his eyes. "Do you think I don't recognize that look in your eyes, Hunter? I remember that look in Nick's eyes. You aren't thinking clearly because you care for her."

"So what if I do? Why was it perfectly fine for Nick to care about you when he was saving you but not okay for me to care about her?"

"That was different, and you know it."

"Well, it doesn't matter because I'm thinking

just fine. Let me find the person who's doing this to her and finish this case. I think I'm close to solving it, so let me do my job."

"And our secret? This place?"

"You brought Kate back here to the estate when Roman's assignment went sideways. Why is that okay but me bringing Alexis here isn't?"

"She was shot, Hunter! Or did you conveniently forget that detail?" Persephone said angrily. "How are you going to make sure she doesn't tell anyone?"

He didn't worry about that. Alexis could be trusted to keep this place and all they did to herself.

"She'll be fine. She won't say a word. I'll make sure of it."

Persephone looked up at him and smiled. "You never doubt that your charm is going to get you what you want, do you, Hunter?"

Charm wasn't what he relied on with Alexis. He hadn't used that on her. He trusted she would keep their secret because he trusted her.

"She won't say a thing. I promise. You have my word."

"You better hope she doesn't. Be careful, Hunter. Movie stars aren't like other people. You're supposed to help her find out who's stalking her, and that's it. Whatever else you're doing is only going to make this case harder. I can see in your eyes you already have stepped over the line. That's not good."

"I'm fine. I know how to do this job. You know that. Nick knows that."

"Nick sees too much of himself in you, I think. By the way you were looking at Miss Marchand in there, I think he must be right. You're too close to her, and you know it."

Hunter didn't answer her, so she nodded, knowing she was right. "Don't lose perspective, Hunter, or you'll endanger her life and yours. I don't want to lose one of my men any more than I want to lose a client."

"I've got this handled, Persephone. Assuming Gideon did what I asked him, I should be able to find her stalker and wrap this case up in no time."

The fact that just saying those words made his chest contract let him know Persephone was right. He was too close to Alexis, but there was no turning back now.

Persephone smiled and patted him on the arm as she walked back into the house. "Be careful what you wish for."

He followed her inside and watched as she moved the men away from Alexis so the two of them could talk. Xavier and Julian sulked for a few moments before leaving, but Gideon headed toward him with a look on his face that told Hunter he had something to say.

Hopefully, he had news about those names he'd given him.

"Did you get me anything on that list I texted you?" Hunter asked impatiently.

Shrugging, Gideon shook his head. "I found nothing. They're all clean. No records, no pending charges, or even a parking ticket. One of the assistants owes a little too much money for most financial planners' comfort, but other than that, nothing."

"Which assistant?" he asked, silently hoping he wouldn't have to break Alexis's heart if he found out Lauren was behind the letters.

"Carla. Not enough to convince me she's up to no good, though."

"What about the envelope and letter I sent you?"

"I just fucking got it like a half hour ago. You know, you could have just brought the damn thing with you," Gideon said, busting his ass.

"Yeah, yeah," Hunter said as he looked over his friend's shoulder to watch Alexis and Persephone talking. "I didn't know I was coming here until after I sent it by courier."

"Hey, what's going on here?"

Hunter looked at him, confused. "What are you talking about? I'm trying to find the person who's stalking her. Did you forget what the hell we're working on?"

"That's not what I'm talking about," Gideon said, staring at him with a strange look in his eyes. "You can't stop looking at her. Are you two…"

"Stop. This is the job. I'm supposed to keep my eye on her, remember?"

Gideon turned to look at Alexis, and Hunter saw her glance over and smile, knowing she probably wanted him to come over. He didn't want his friend to think anything was going on between them, though.

Turning back to face him, Gideon studied him for a moment. "I'm seeing something here, man. She looks at you like you're some kind of hero to her, her knight in shining armor, and you're practically climbing out of your skin with the need to go to her. What's going on with you two?"

Looking away to hide how he truly felt, Hunter said, "Nothing. Don't be stupid. I'm doing my job."

In a voice he was sure both Alexis and Persephone heard, Gideon said, "Holy shit! You slept with her? You dog!"

Hunter cringed at how loudly he said that. "For Christ's sake, keep your voice down."

"Damn! You didn't even know who she was before you got this case. I'm impressed, man. I wasn't sure you had it in you. So what's going on?"

He couldn't help but roll his eyes at Gideon, who at the moment sounded more like a high school kid than a grown man. "Nothing. Just do your job and stop acting like a teenage girl. She doesn't need you getting into her business."

Gideon's smile spread until it practically reached from ear to ear. "You sound pretty protective there, buddy."

Hunter looked over at Alexis and she smiled at him. He couldn't help but be happy, but then Persephone turned around to face him and scowled.

Gideon watched the whole thing and mumbled under his breath, "Damn, she looks pissed."

Why wouldn't she be? Hunter understood he'd broken one of the group's cardinal rules. It was bad enough that he'd gotten involved with Alexis, but by bringing her here, he'd definitely stepped out of line.

And he knew he'd pay the price for it.

Persephone patted Alexis on the arm and then turned toward the two men. "Gideon, I think you've had enough time to get Hunter caught up on what you've found out so far. Time to get back to the lab and see what you can find from that delivery we got. Alexis, it was a pleasure to meet you. Please be sure to stop at the main house before you leave so we can have that tour I promised."

With that, Persephone motioned to Gideon that he needed to leave, and Hunter was finally alone with Alexis, at last.

CHAPTER TWENTY-TWO

"YOUR BOSS SEEMS really nice. She obviously thinks the world of you," Alexis said sweetly.

Hunter arched a single eyebrow and chuckled. "I think she was putting on her nice face for you. I'm guessing I'm one of her least favorite people right about now."

"Is she angry we're here?" Alexis asked, worry making her frown.

Shaking his head, he smiled and pulled her to him. "No, she'll be fine. Her boyfriend likes how I do the job, so even if she's upset, Nick will smooth things over."

That wasn't exactly the truth, but she didn't need to know just how much trouble he was in.

She looked up at him with hopeful eyes. "I'd hate it if you got reprimanded because of me, Hunter. Why didn't you tell me no when I asked? I wouldn't have been mad. We could have gone anywhere. I wouldn't have cared. As long as I was away from that penthouse…"

Alexis didn't finish her sentence and looked down, avoiding his gaze before adding, "...and with you, that's all it would have taken to make me happy."

As he watched her cheeks grow pink, he knew Persephone had been wrong. He wasn't the only one too attached. For now, he wanted to let himself enjoy the fact that a beautiful and famous actress wanted to be with him as much as he wanted to be with her. They'd deal with the reality of their lives later.

This moment was reserved for them to be happy.

Tilting her chin up, he looked down into her dark brown eyes and felt himself begin to get lost in her beauty, both inside and out. If he'd found out he'd been right about her being just another Hollywood diva, it wouldn't have mattered how stunning she looked. But in the short time they'd spent together, he'd seen something in her he hadn't expected.

A sweetness and goodness he didn't think existed in people anymore. All she wanted was to be happy and make movies her fans would love. That girl from Minnesota Lauren told him about right after he arrived at the penthouse still lived inside Alexis. Unlike with other stars, she hadn't shed who she was before she became famous.

And even though he knew it would sound

crazy to the Hunter McKary who walked out of that elevator just a week ago, he loved that woman.

"Is something wrong, Hunter? You look like you want to say something."

He did want to tell her something. That he'd fallen in love with her, no matter how insane that sounded since they'd only known each other for such a short time. He wanted to say all the things he'd kept inside for so long, hoping that one day he'd find a woman who he would willingly give his life to protect because he couldn't imagine living without her.

But he didn't say any of that. Instead, he just shook his head. "No, I'm just happy you're here with me."

"So what should we do now?" Alexis asked with a sexy smile.

Teasing her, he looked around the cottage's living room. "Well, we can watch TV. Or we can make something to eat. I'm sure there's something in the refrigerator. You're probably hungry after that long drive."

She slid her hands down his stomach and began unbuckling his belt, still staring up into his eyes. "I ate at that rest stop, remember?"

Nodding, he smiled as she slid her hand inside his pants to palm his cock. "Oh, yeah. That's right. The most fried chicken I've ever seen any one woman eat at a rest stop in my lifetime."

Her mouth dropped open in shock at his description of her lunch a few hours earlier, and she pushed him back onto the couch. Climbing onto his lap, she kissed him and giggled. "I didn't eat that much, and I'm trying to seduce you here, so if you could quit with the chicken talk, that would be nice."

Hunter looked down at where her hand lightly pressed against his already hard cock. "I don't think there's much need for that since I'm obviously up and ready to go."

"That's good," she said with a wickedly sexy smile that turned him on even more.

Sliding his hand around her neck, he pulled her mouth down to his and kissed her deeply, letting his tongue linger as he slipped it over her lips. Alexis rolled her hips to rub her pussy against his cock, and his eyes rolled back in his head.

"No fair. You made me keep my eyes on you last time," she whispered against his lips.

He opened his eyes and let his gaze slide down from her face to her beautiful but still fully clothed body. He'd had enough of foreplay. Now he wanted to be inside her.

Tugging at the top of her pants, he groaned, "These need to come off."

Alexis wriggled out of them as she stripped out of her shirt and bra. When she sat naked on his lap, except for her white cotton panties, she took hold of his hands so he couldn't touch her.

"No fair ripping off another pair. I need to have something to go home in," she said with a smile.

"Then you take them off because I can't promise they'll be in one piece if I get at them."

Sliding off his lap, she stood up and pulled her beautiful legs out of the panties before setting them off to the side with her pants. There, in front of him without a stitch of clothing on her, she looked like a goddess. Toned and long, her legs made him think about the last time they'd been together. Wrapped around him, she'd nearly made him come in those first moments when she tilted her hips and took every last inch of his cock inside her.

Alexis tugged his pants and boxer briefs down his legs as he lifted his shirt up over his head so he could be naked too. He pulled her down onto his lap and felt her wet pussy glide along his cock, sending ripples of need through his body.

Leaning down, she kissed him long and deep, making it impossible to wait any longer. Grabbing hold of the base of his cock, he directed it toward her entrance and lifted his hips off the couch to slowly slide into her until there was no space left between her body and his.

A soft moan escaped her throat, and she

leaned forward to whisper in his ear, "Fuck me. Make me yours."

Reveling in the feel of her body around his, he didn't move his hips for a few moments. Just having her there taking all of him made him want to freeze this moment in time. Before he started pumping into her and she started rolling her hips and before either one of them came, this moment of the two of them together as one was what he wanted to relish.

Alexis ran her tongue along the shell of his ear and whispered, "Is something wrong, Hunter?"

In his mind, he couldn't imagine anything he'd ever felt in his life being more right. Easing her back so she sat up on his lap, he watched a look of worry wash over her face.

"No, nothing's wrong. I want to see you ride me."

Bracing her hands on his shoulders, she rolled her hips and began to do as he wished, fucking him like a goddess riding his cock. He grasped her waist to keep her in place once she found her rhythm and watched in awe as this beautiful woman sensually bounced up and down on his lap. With each time she rose up, his cock nearly left her body, but then she rammed him back into her in a rush that nearly took his breath away every time.

The sweet and tender soul who made him fall

in love with her rode him better than he could have dreamed of, fucking him with abandon like no other woman ever had. Her body surrendered to his with every time his cock invaded her. Her moans of pleasure echoed around him, exciting him even more as she drew him closer to that edge of ecstasy.

Lost in her own pleasure, she didn't realize how much seeing her so sensual got him off. This was the woman millions of men dreamed of when they fantasized about Alexis Marchand, and now she was riding him toward a release he craved more than breath itself.

"Oh, God..." she moaned as she dug her fingernails into his shoulder. "This feels so good. Don't stop."

He couldn't stop even if he wanted to. With her, he had no choice. Making her happy made him happy.

Her body clenched around his cock, and Alexis pitched forward, pressing her face into the couch cushion. Her fingernails dragged from his shoulders to his biceps, raking the skin, but no amount of pain could take away the feeling of pure pleasure as she began to milk him, her orgasm taking him to his release.

He thrust hard into her over and over until the two of them couldn't move anymore. Exhausted from their lovemaking, they sat there silently, the tremors from sex still pulsing through their bodies.

Hunter ran his palm down her back and felt the thin glaze of sweat on her skin. "That was quite a workout. I think round two could be ready any minute."

She leaned back and looked down at him, smiling as she shook her head. "You're always about the round two, aren't you?"

"Two, three, four…I'm up for as much as you want."

"I guess I haven't been with anyone who knows how to treat a woman because I'm used to one and done."

"One's just a start," Hunter said with a grin. "I don't even want to think about the sex you've had if it's been one and done."

He didn't want to think about her sleeping with any other man, before him or after. And there was the problem. There would have to be an after him. He and Alexis weren't like Roman and Kate. She would always be in the public eye, so they could never hope for that little house in the country where he could continue to work for Project Artemis.

"Hey, what's wrong? You looked like you were a million miles away, and then you got a look on your face like you were unhappy," she said quietly as she wove her fingers through his.

He shook the thought of what would happen later out of his head and forced himself to smile. Looking up at her, he didn't want to ruin what they'd just had with reality and bring sadness to those beautiful dark eyes.

"I thought I heard a noise outside. Maybe we should get dressed before one of the people I work with comes barging in. Trust me. They'd kill to see you even half dressed. Literally, I mean kill."

Alexis giggled and kissed him. "You're crazy, but…" She stopped and shrugged. "Guess it's time to get up and into some clothes, huh?"

He wanted to hold her there with him for a little longer, but he knew he couldn't. Or more truthfully, he shouldn't.

"Just until round two," he said, hating that his words might be a lie.

She smiled and climbed off him before grabbing her clothes and hurrying off to the bathroom. "I'll be right back. I have a feeling I should fix my hair after that little rendezvous," she yelled out to him. "I must look like a banshee."

His first instinct was to tell her she looked as beautiful as always. That no matter how tangled her hair got, she still took his breath away every time he laid his eyes on her.

But he said nothing and simply got dressed again. As he slipped his pants back on, he caught a glimpse of Persephone and a man walking across the grass toward the cottage. Straining to see if it was Nick with her, he instead saw Paul by her side.

Alarm bells went off in his head, and he hurried to the door to head them off before they walked in. Through the window, he saw Paul's expression and knew what he'd come to do.

He planned to take Alexis back to New York with him.

Chapter Twenty-Three

STARING INTO THE mirror, Alexis tried not to cringe at how she looked after a five hour drive, too much fried chicken at a rest stop, and another round of incredible sex with Hunter. Eyeliner sat below her eyes, making her look like some blond version of a raccoon, and her hair looked ratty, like she hadn't brushed it in days.

God, she'd looked like that the whole time she and Hunter were making love. No wonder the man didn't want to go for round two yet.

She heard a noise out in the living room and hoped he wasn't coming in. After waiting a few seconds, she returned her focus to cleaning herself up, mumbling, "No man wants a woman who looks like a train wreck, even if she is in love with him."

And there, for the first time, she admitted the truth. She loved Hunter. She stared at her reflection in the mirror and wondered when that had happened. One day she was living her life and wishing she could find the happiness that had eluded her, and the next he walked in and a few days later she couldn't imagine her world without him.

He'd let her be her. No scolding her when she did something stupid like run off and endanger both her and Lauren's life. No lecturing her she couldn't when she wanted to try to live a normal life.

And because he did that, she finally saw that she didn't want to be a person who spent her time throwing tantrums or running away. He gave her that freedom, and she never wanted to give it up again.

She knew what the world would think. They were rushing things. They barely knew each other, so how could it truly be love? This relationship would end like all her others had.

But she didn't care what anyone else thought. For the first time since Jackson, she felt love and didn't want to be afraid to admit it.

With one last glance at the mirror, she turned off the light and headed back out to the living room. She didn't get halfway down the hall before she saw they weren't alone anymore.

Surprised to have Paul standing in front of her, she looked over toward Hunter, confused. Had he called him at some point? Why? They were supposed to be getting away from everything in her world for a few days, and that included her manager.

"What's going on? Hunter, why is Paul here?" she asked, searching his expression for the truth.

He stood near the couch and shook his head. "I'm sorry. Somebody obviously called him."

Looking over at Persephone, she asked, "Is that true? Why wouldn't you just tell me to leave instead of calling my manager?"

"I didn't call, Paul. He knew you were here and came down to see that you're okay," Persephone said, sounding more than a little defensive.

Her manager stepped forward toward her and held out his hand. "I just wanted to make sure you weren't hurt. You left without telling anyone, so I had to make sure you were fine."

Persephone walked out of the cottage quietly, leaving the three of them alone.

Anger swirled inside Alexis at what Paul must have put Lauren through to get the details about her leaving. "If you made Lauren cry, I swear to God, Paul, I will never speak to you again. I bet you threatened her, didn't you? That's the only way she'd tell you that I left."

"Maybe it wasn't her, Alexis," Hunter said as he walked over to take her hand. "Maybe it was Carla. Is she your mole at the house, Paul?"

She turned to look at Hunter and shook her head in disbelief. What was he saying? "Carla wouldn't do that to me. She's loyal. And what do you mean his mole in my house?"

Hunter squeezed her hand and quietly said, "I didn't figure it out until this morning. Paul told your bodyguards to not follow my instructions about one of them being in the lobby at all times. He had no good reason to do that, so why did he?"

Alexis turned to face Paul. "Why would you do that? Hunter wanted to protect me. You hired him to protect me, so why would you tell the men not to follow his instructions?"

Paul shook his head so vigorously that his blond hair swung left and right. "It wasn't like that. I knew you were never in any danger. I just told them to ignore that part of what he told them."

"Why? What if the stalker came to the building and dropped off a letter? One of the guys would have seen him."

As her head began to swim with questions about the man who had spent the last four years guiding her career and her life, Hunter pulled her close to his side and said, "There was no stalker. There was only Paul. He's the one who's been sending you the letters and packages. The only question he needs to answer is why before I tell the cops."

Alexis turned to look at Hunter, stunned that

he was accusing Paul. "What are you talking about?"

Before he could say a word, he pushed her behind him and she saw her manager standing there with a gun in his hand pointed at the man she loved. Terrified, she closed her eyes and cried, "Why are you doing this, Paul? What's going on?"

"What's going on is Hunter here was supposed to show up, do some checking, and then the letters would stop. We'd get some great press from the whole thing, the world feeling completely sympathetic for poor Alexis Marchand, and you'd have your pick of films in the end. I was doing my job, but he got out of hand."

Hunter stood as still as a statue in front of her, holding her hand tightly as he protected her. "And there I was thinking Carla was behind it because she's in so much debt. It was you all along."

"Oh, Carla helped. She got a few bucks every time she told me how Alexis was feeling. Then I'd tell the press and she'd be in the headlines again. Nobody got hurt, and everyone won in the end. But then you got in the way because you wouldn't just let it go the way it should have. I guess I shouldn't be surprised. Of course you'd fall for her. You've got that protective thing and she's a damsel in distress. So when the tracker I put on her phone after her little trip to Atlantic City told me you took her here, I knew I had to follow you and take her home. But I'm not going to jail for a little letter writing to help her career. Not going to happen."

Rage coursed through Alexis at that description of her. A damsel in distress. That's all her very own manager saw her as!

"How the fuck do you think this is going to end, Paul? You planning on killing her and ending the gravy train you worked so hard to keep going? Or is it me you plan to shoot? Because that gun says you think this is going to end that way."

Paul chuckled, and for the first time, Alexis looked around Hunter to see her manager for the man he truly was. All this time she'd thought he cared about her, but all he'd cared about was money and fame. No matter that the stalker's letters had made her practically a shut-in afraid to go out into the world around her. All he cared about were headlines to keep her in the news.

"I don't have to use it. I can just take her out of here and back to New York, and she and I can go back to making her the biggest star in the world."

Hunter shook his head and held tightly to her hand. "She's not leaving with you."

Pointing the gun directly at Hunter, Paul said, "Then I had to come here to rescue her from a jilted lover who kidnapped her and brought her to the one place he knew he wouldn't be found out. And if my friend Persephone wants to keep this project of hers quiet, she'll cover the whole thing up. You'll disappear and no one will know the truth."

Alexis couldn't let him do this to Hunter or to her. She wouldn't live her life under the control of a madman. She could be strong when she had to be.

Knowing Hunter always kept his gun near him when he didn't have it in his pants, she quickly scanned the room for any sign of it. God, why hadn't she paid attention when they arrived here? If only she could have some way to find out where it was without letting Paul know.

Hunter moved a step to the left toward the fireplace, and she zeroed in on it sitting on the mantle. It was now or never, and there was no way she planned to just stand by while Paul killed the man she loved. So she tore her hand from Hunter's hold and raced over to grab the gun.

Her hands shook almost uncontrollably as she wrapped her fingers around it and pointed it at Paul. She'd only held a gun once before, and that was for one of the first parts she'd ever gotten after leaving modeling. All she remembered about how to shoot was the safety had to be off. She had no real experience other than that since that gun had been nothing but a prop, but she didn't care.

She was an actress, so she needed to act like she knew what the hell to do as she pointed the gun at Paul.

But it wasn't her manager who spoke first. Hunter looked at her with fear in his eyes and shook his head. "Alexis, what are you doing? Don't do that. He's not going to shoot me. Put the gun down, honey."

"Lexi, watch yourself. You don't know what you're doing," Paul said in that patronizing way he always did when talked to her.

Tears welled in her eyes as she screamed, "My name is Alexis! Don't call me Lexi! I'm not a child. I'm a grown woman you were supposed to care about. I trusted you, and you tortured me with those letters! You made me afraid to even leave my house. How could you do that to me? How could you do that, Paul?"

"It wasn't real, Lexi. It was all an act, and you performed beautifully, just like I knew you would."

He smiled as he said that, like manipulating her was okay. She wanted to kill him for that, but her hands shook so much she couldn't aim.

Out of the corner of her eye, she saw Hunter move and turned to see him rush Paul. The two men crashed through an end table and fell to the ground. Alexis kept the gun pointed at her mark, but now she might shoot Hunter if she pulled the trigger. Frozen in fear, she didn't know what to do.

And then the sound of a gunshot exploded all around her, and she watched in horror as both the man she loved and the man who had betrayed her lay in a motionless heap in front of her.

"Hunter! Hunter!" she screamed so loud her throat burned.

She dropped the gun to the floor and backed away from it in horror. Had she shot it? She didn't know. It had all happened so fast that she couldn't tell.

And who had been shot?

Both men lay still, so she couldn't tell who had been hurt, or worse, who lay there dead. The door burst open, and two of Hunter's friends rushed in to see what had happened. They didn't say a word to her, but she wouldn't have been able to answer if they had. She didn't know what to say. All she knew was a feeling of sadness she'd never experienced before began to settle into her chest as the reality that at least one person she cared about may very well be dead just a few feet away from her.

And she may have been the one to blame for their death.

"Hunter, man, are you okay? Talk to me," one of the men said frantically as the other one moved him off Paul.

And then she saw the blood and knew the truth. A large red stain on the front of Paul's shirt told her he'd been the one shot.

Finally, she heard Hunter's voice as he spoke for the first time. "I'm okay. Where's Alexis?"

Unable to hold back the tears of happiness and sadness, she began to sob. Hunter ran over and took her into his arms, holding her tightly to him as she cried.

"It's okay. You're going to be okay, Alexis."

"I thought you were dead. You weren't moving."

He tilted her head back and kissed her tenderly on the lips. "I'm okay. The gun went off when we hit the ground and I tried to get it away from him. I'm sorry, honey. He's gone."

Alexis looked over toward where the two men stood near the body and sobbed harder. "I thought I killed one of you, Hunter. I thought I was the one who shot the gun."

He pulled her to him again and held her close. "No, it was an accident. You didn't hurt anyone. You couldn't."

"Why did he do all of this? Why would he torment me like that for months and then come here with a gun to hurt us?"

One of the men turned toward her and Hunter as the other man walked out the front door. "I can help with those answers. Your manager was up to his neck in debt, even worse than your assistant Carla, who was helping him. I'm guessing he needed to be able to say he had the biggest star in the world so he could milk that claim for all sorts of projects."

Hunter looked over at the man and asked, "I never gave you Paul's name, though. What made you check into him, Gideon?"

"If you ever paid attention to anything, you'd know that her manager announced at the end of last year that he was creating his own production company. No way you can run that kind of company with just one star, so he'd need more than just Alexis. I remembered hearing about it on some TV show once, so when you gave me the list of names, I added his to it. Turns out, he was behind this whole thing, but I didn't get the proof I wanted until I ran the prints."

"I thought I figured it out this morning. That's why I wanted to get Alexis away from New York for a while to see if I was right." Hunter looked down at Alexis and frowned. "I wish I wasn't right about him."

"What's going to happen now?" she asked, afraid for Hunter for the first time.

He kissed her on the forehead and hugged her to him. "Don't worry. Everything's going to be fine."

"I'm sorry Xavier and I didn't get here in time to stop this, Alexis. When Persephone came back to the house, she ordered us to get those prints ASAP, and as soon as we found out what we had, we started coming here. She didn't know he had a gun. She thought he was a good guy."

Alexis forced a smile and nodded. "So did I."

CHAPTER TWENTY-FOUR

SOME GAME ON the TV distracted Hunter for only a minute, but it didn't take long for Xavier and Gideon to start arguing about some statistic or some claim one of them made about one of the teams. Nothing had changed at the estate.

But he'd changed. Not that it mattered much.

Two weeks before, he'd kissed Alexis goodbye and he'd felt like an empty shell ever since. They'd promised to call one another, but he knew how that went. Two people dedicated to their work equaled a very slim chance that they could make a life together work.

Even if he wanted to believe that even the slimmest of chances could amount to something great.

"Hunter, tell this moron that there is no way the Jets have gone to more than one Super Bowl," Xavier barked in his direction as he sat lost in thought.

"What?" he asked, irritated either of them had

ruined his daydreaming.

Gideon defended himself as he tossed a football at Xavier's head. "That's not what I said. Man, you're a fucking asshole. I said I thought the Jets would have gone to the big game more than once."

When Hunter didn't respond to mediate their feud, Gideon leaned over and clapped his hands. "Earth to Hunter. Man, what are you doing over there? You look a million miles away."

"I'd say about three hundred miles away is more like it," Xavier said with a chuckle. "I think we have a new addition to the Alexis Marchand fan club here at the estate."

Hunter simply rolled his eyes. He didn't have any interest in sparring with these two tonight.

"Seriously, man. Why are you still here? Didn't Persephone give you like a month off for vacation?" Gideon asked. "If I knew she wouldn't be calling me up at any moment, I'd be lying on the beach somewhere with a drink in one hand and a beautiful woman in the other. Instead of that, you're sitting here with us like some zombie over there."

"I don't feel like going anywhere. I'm fine right where I am," Hunter answered, lying through his teeth.

He only wanted to go to one place in the world, and that was where Alexis was. As for being fine, he hadn't been anything close to fine since she walked out of his life nearly fourteen days before.

Thirteen days and eight hours, to be more exact. He couldn't bring himself to count the minutes. That just felt too fucking sad, even for him right now.

"You know, you could call her and go see her," Gideon said.

He knew his friend thought that suggestion would be helpful, but he wasn't fooling himself. They couldn't be together as long as they both had the careers they'd chosen.

"No, I can't, and I don't want to discuss this anymore," he said as he got up to leave.

"Yes, you can!" Gideon yelled as he walked out of the game room.

But he was wrong, and there was no way to get around that.

HUNTER'S PHONE VIBRATED in his pocket as he headed up to his room. Taking it out, he wondered why he'd be getting a call from the boss.

"I'd like to see you in the office right now, please," Persephone said into the phone before he even got the word hello out.

"On my way."

Like in a dream, he walked down the hall to

the other side of the house without even thinking about where he was going. He'd worked for Project Artemis for long enough that he'd made this trek to Nick and Persephone's office more times than he wanted to count.

He'd done a lot of good in those years. From the first time Nick told him about the idea, he wanted to be a part of it. He'd watched far too many women get hurt by the law to be able to ignore how much the world needed what Nick and Persephone wanted to do with Project Artemis.

But now as he stepped one foot in front of the other without even thinking, he had a feeling he wanted something else.

Tess didn't sit at her desk tonight, so he pushed open the office door and peeked his head in. Nick still hadn't returned from his trip, so Persephone sat alone at her desk working.

"You wanted me for something?" Hunter asked as he stepped into the office.

She looked up from her work and smiled that rare sweet smile Persephone so infrequently offered to anyone but Nick. "Please come in, Hunter. I wanted to talk to you."

"Any news from the cops?"

Persephone nodded. "That's all taken care of. Their investigation is complete. Accidental shooting. Case closed."

Hunter didn't respond, but he couldn't help think that she'd had to grease a few palms to get the investigation over so quickly. Money talked, though, even out in the sticks.

He sat down in front of her desk and watched her hold up a letter in front of her. Confused as to why, he shook his head.

"What's that?"

"This is from Alexis Marchand. She wrote me a lovely letter thanking me and everyone here for helping her. She also wrote to tell me she's donating a million dollars to what we do here."

Hearing Alexis had cared enough to contribute to what they did there didn't surprise him. He'd seen the good person behind the movie star. He knew who she really was.

"That's good. She's good people, Persephone. She deserved better than what Paul did to her."

Nodding, Persephone said, "Yes, she did. I'm sorry he turned out to be someone like that. He clearly didn't respect Alexis or what we're doing here. I thought he was a good person, but I was wrong."

Hunter sat back and stared across the desk at the woman in front of him. Persephone had never admitted she was wrong to any of them. It wasn't her style. He had a feeling she felt if she did show anything but pure strength that she'd be seen as less in the eyes of the men who worked for her.

Not to him, though. To Hunter, it made her an even more incredible woman, and that was saying something.

"I'm sorry your friend turned out to be the villain of this piece."

His comment made her laugh. "That's remarkably clever of you, Hunter. I never took you for a man who knew anything about theater."

He shrugged. "I lived in LA for years. No way to escape actors and actresses. They were everywhere."

"And yet it took moving to Virginia for you to meet one you could see as more than just a star."

At that moment, something clicked in his head. He had met someone who made him happy, and for the first time in his adult life, he didn't find as much happiness in his job.

"It did, so I think it's time for me to move on, Persephone."

He didn't know what he'd expected her reaction to be, but as the words left his mouth, he watched her listen, nod, and then simply smile.

"I figured as much. It's been two weeks, so I have to give you credit. You probably knew somewhere deep down inside ten minutes after she left that you didn't want to live without her. I called you in here tonight to tell you I had an assignment for you. I didn't know if it would merely take your mind off your heartbreak or make you quit and go to her, but I figured it would move you to do something. Now I don't have to do that."

Hunter threw his head back and laughed. "So much for that month vacation, huh?"

"Actually, it was Nick's suggestion. I spoke to him about how worried I was about you, and he thought this might help. I guess he was right."

"Worried about me? Really?"

Persephone twisted her face into a grimace. "Not everyone in the world has to show every emotion they have, Hunter. It doesn't mean I don't have feelings for the people I work with. It just means I don't show them all the time. You've been here with us since the beginning. I may not have always liked your methods, but we relied on you more than anyone else because you were as committed to this cause as we are. But you aren't anymore, and even though we'll miss you, there are no hard feelings. We never assumed you men would be willing to give up your lives forever."

In all the time he'd worked for Project Artemis, he'd never heard anything like what she'd just said to him. It made him proud to know his commitment to their shared cause had been seen and appreciated.

"Thank you, Persephone. We did good together. I won't forget any of you I've worked with here."

Standing up, she extended her hand for him to shake. "Good luck, Hunter. Keep in touch and I hope if we ever need your help on a case, you'll give us a little of your time again in the future."

He shook her hand and nodded. "You know my number. Tell Nick I said I'll see him soon, okay?"

"I will. I hope you and Alexis will be very happy."

Hunter took a deep breath in and let it out slowly. He hoped so too.

A FEW HOURS later, he approached Alexis's building and saw a few photographers milling around the front entrance. Good. If those vultures were there, that meant Alexis was there too.

He walked toward the glass front doors and smiled at the grey-haired man waiting just inside them. Chambers returned the smile as he welcomed him into the lobby. "Gorgeous morning, isn't it, Mr. McKary? Good to see you again, sir."

"Good to be back, Chambers."

As cool as he'd sounded talking to the doorman, as soon as the elevator doors closed, Hunter's heart began beating like a jackhammer. It felt like there wasn't enough air in that small space. Checking his look in the mirrored doors, he took a deep breath to calm himself.

Going to see the woman you loved shouldn't be so hard, except he hadn't called her before he decided to drive the five hours to see her and they hadn't spoken since she left.

Fourteen days and three hours ago.

That was longer than some Hollywood stars' marriages lasted. That thought made his stomach twist into a tight knot. Even worse, he began to wonder if she'd moved on. The life of a movie star happened fast. Maybe she'd met someone already. Maybe she turned for solace to one of her bodyguards.

Maybe he should just turn around and go back to Virginia. He reached out to push the down button, but he didn't catch it in time and the doors opened to the penthouse. Hunter looked out and saw no one. Had she left to make a film? Was that why the apartment sounded so silent?

The doors began to close, and along with them his chance to be with Alexis again, so he quickly stepped out and looked around for any sign of her. In all the time he spent there, he'd never heard it so quiet.

As disappointment set in that he may have missed her before she left to go on location, he walked down the hallway that felt so familiar now that he was back. He pushed open the door to the room that had been his bedroom and saw she still hadn't changed it back to her office. Looking in, he saw it just as he'd left it that morning when they drove away to go to the estate.

Somehow, the fact that she hadn't changed it made him feel good. True, she may have been too busy with everything else in her life, but that didn't matter to him. That she'd kept that reminder of him around gave him hope.

He continued down the hall to her room as his heart began slamming into his chest again. Holding his breath, he knocked lightly on her door and listened for her to reply.

And then she did.

"Come in and I hope you were able to find that cherry soda at the store! I'm dying for a taste of home."

Hunter slowly pushed the door open and saw her sitting on her bed with a script in her lap and a half dozen others spread out around her. She looked as beautiful as always. Her blond hair hung past her shoulders and framed her face perfectly. She wore a pair of jean shorts and a pink t-shirt, and her long, tanned legs were crossed in front of her as casually as usual.

This was the Alexis he fell in love with.

She looked up expecting Lauren, and for a moment, he didn't know if he saw surprise or hurt on her face. She stared across the room at him, as if she didn't believe her eyes, and then she tossed the script aside and jumped up off the bed to run to him.

"Oh, my God! It's you! I didn't think I'd ever get to see you again," she said as she began to cry.

Pulling her to him, Hunter held her tightly. Nothing else in his life had felt as right as when he stood there holding her in his arms.

"I couldn't keep going on just doing what I always did, so I left Project Artemis. I know I should have talked to you about it, but I guess I just let my heart do all the thinking for me."

She stepped back from him and shook her head. With tears in her dark eyes, she said, "That's crazy! Did you do that for me, Hunter?"

He nodded. "For us. I want us to be together. One of us had to give up our job, so I did it. I guess if you tell me you're not that crazy about me anymore, I'm going to look pretty stupid right now. And if I have to go back to the estate, I'll never hear the end of it from Gideon and Xavier either."

Throwing her arms around his neck, she squeezed him to her. "Not crazy about you? I love you, Hunter. I just can't believe you'd give up all that for me."

"Of course I did."

He leaned back and smiled. "I love you, Alexis. The last two weeks have been hell, and then last night, I just realized I didn't want to keep living without you, so I did it. I quit and I drove directly here hoping you wanted me as much as I wanted you."

Alexis cradled his face and smiled as tears rolled down her cheeks. "No man has ever cared as much about me as you do, Hunter. I've missed you so much. I can't believe you gave up everything for me."

"I would have died for you, so giving up my job isn't anything compared to that."

"So now you're going to be thrust into the limelight since being with me means press and paparazzi all the time. Can you handle that?"

Hunter nodded, never more sure of an answer to a question in his life. "Yeah, I can handle it. Just promise me one thing?"

"Anything."

Taking her hands in his, he brought them to his lips and kissed them. "Promise me every so often we can go to a cottage like the one on the estate and be alone away from the world and everyone in it."

She didn't answer him but ran over to the bed to get her phone. Holding it up in front of him to show him a picture of a house much like the cottage on the estate, she said, "I'm about two days ahead of you on that. I found this place that I love in this little town in Idaho, so I bought it.

But one thing, Hunter. Now that the stalker thing is over, I don't have to stay in New York anymore. I want to move back to LA. Are you okay with that?"

He'd lived there for more than half his life and had never planned on going back again. Then again, he hadn't planned on falling in love with a movie star either.

Life was funny like that. Sometimes the place you started your journey was where you belonged all along.

He nodded and pulled her into his arms. Kissing her, he whispered against her lips, "When do we leave?"

Alexis ran her hand down the front of his shirt and smiled in that sexy way he loved. "We can leave whenever we want, but I think I'd like to do something else first. We need to make up for lost time."

Closing the door behind him, he carried her to the bed to start their happily ever after. They could get back to real life and moving to LA later.

K.M. Scott writes contemporary romance stories of sexy, intense, and unforgettable love. A New York Times and USA Today bestselling author, she's been in love with romance since reading her first romance novel in junior high (she was a very curious girl!). Under her Gabrielle Bisset name, she write erotic paranormal and historical romance. She lives in Pennsylvania with a herd of animals and when she's not writing can be found reading or feeding her TV addiction.

Anina Collins has always loved a good mystery. From Agatha Christie's Hercule Poirot to Sir Arthur Conan Doyle's famous detective Sherlock Holmes to Dan Brown's intrepid Professor Robert Langdon, she's spent some of her favorite reading times with mystery novels. When she's not writing her favorite mystery couple, she can be found watching entirely too much Supernatural and dreaming about the beach.

Be sure to visit K.M.'s Facebook page at **facebook.com/kmscottauthor** for all the latest on her books, along with giveaways and other goodies! And to hear all the news on K.M. Scott books first, sign up for her newsletter today and be sure to visit her website at **www. kmscottbooks.com**

Visit Anina's Facebook page at **facebook.com/ Anina-Collins-429334270597293** for news about her books, along with giveaways and other fun stuff! Sign up for her newsletter today for exclusive news first! Visit her website at **aninacollins.com** for more details.

Books by K.M. Scott:

In The Darkness (Project Artemis #1)
After The Storm (Project Artemis #2)
Behind The Scenes (Project Artemis #3)

If I Dream (Corrupted Love #1)
If You Fight (Corrupted Love #2)
If We Fall (Corrupted Love #3)

Crash Into Me (Heart of Stone #1)
Fall Into Me (Heart of Stone #2)
Give In To Me (Heart of Stone #3)
Heart of Stone Volume One Box Set
Ever After (Heart of Stone #4)
A Heart of Stone Christmas (Heart of Stone #5)
Return To Me (Heart of Stone #6)
Forever With Me (Heart of Stone #7)
Heart of Stone Volume Two Box Set

Temptation (Club X #1)
Surrender (Club X #2)
Possession (Club X #3)
Satisfaction (Club X #4)
Acceptance (Club X #5)
The Complete Club X Series Box Set

Crave (Addicted To You #1)
Adore (Addicted To You #2)
Shatter (Addicted To You #3)
Claim (Addicted To You #4)
The Addicted To You Box Set

Hard Work (Standalone)

K.M.'S BOOKS ARE IN AUDIOBOOK TOO!

BOOKS BY K.M. SCOTT WRITING AS GABRIELLE BISSET:

Vampire Dreams Revamped (A Sons of Navarus Prequel)
Blood Avenged (Sons of Navarus #1)
Blood Betrayed (Sons of Navarus #2)
Longing (A Sons of Navarus Short Story)
Blood Spirit (Sons of Navarus #3)
The Deepest Cut (A Sons of Navarus Short Story)
Blood Prophecy (Sons of Navarus #4)
Blood Craving (Sons of Navarus #5)
Blood Eclipse (Sons of Navarus #6)
The Sons of Navarus Box Set #1
The Sons of Navarus Box Set #2

Stolen Destiny (Destined Ones Duology #1)
Destiny Redeemed (Destined Ones Duology #2)

Love's Master
Masquerade
The Victorian Erotic Romance Trilogy

BOOKS BY ANINA COLLINS:

The Eleventh Hour (Poppy McGuire Mysteries #1)
After Hours (Poppy McGuire Mysteries #2)
Top of the Hour (Poppy McGuire Mysteries #3)
The Darkest Hour (Poppy McGuire Mysteries #4)
Happy Hour (Poppy McGuire Mysteries #5)
The Witching Hour (Poppy McGuire Mysteries #6)
The Finest Hour (Poppy McGuire Mysteries #7)

www.ingramcontent.com/pod-product-compliance
Lightning Source LLC
Chambersburg PA
CBHW051633180726
48284CB00006B/1708